EARTHSIDE

EARTHSIDE

DENNIS E. TAYLOR

Earthside

ISBN: 978-1-68068-337-0

This book is published on behalf of the author by the Ethan Ellenberg Literary Agency.

This book was initially an Audible Original production.
    Performed by Ray Porter
    Editorial Producer: Steve Feldberg
    Sound recording copyright 2023 by Audible Originals, LLC

You can reach the author at:
Author Blog: http://www.dennisetaylor.org
Twitter: @Dennis_E_Taylor
Facebook: @DennisETaylor2
Instagram: dennis_e_taylor

DEDICATION

I would like to dedicate this book to my wife, Blaihin, who understands me yet doesn't run screaming from the room, and to my daughter, Tina, who completed our family.

TABLE OF CONTENTS

1. Dinosaur Hunt

August 18

As dinosaur hunts went, it lacked that movie-level grandeur. No dune buggies, no hardened mercenaries carrying big guns. Just a garden cart, loaded to overflowing with a PC, UPS, and extender battery. A cable bundle ran from the PC, up the pole Bill was holding, to a camera mounted in front of an eight-inch metal hoop, which contained an interface to an alternate Earth. The miniature gate, a smaller version of the gates used to move between the alternate Earths, allowed the group to observe without danger. Just ahead of Bill, Monica concentrated on the video image being displayed on her tablet, while he slowly rotated the pole-cam to scan for anything interesting on the Dino Planet side of the interface.

"Nothing. Let's try that way." Monica pointed in a seemingly random direction and strode off without waiting for confirmation. Charlie glanced at Kevin and Bill, then rolled his eyes in an exaggerated manner—out of Monica's sight, of course. No one would dare disrespect Gunzilla to her face. Bending into it, he pulled the cart around to follow her.

The recent failed revolution here in Outland had accomplished a few things, although not anything beneficial to the conspirators, of course. The most obvious outcome was a new nickname for Monica. *Gunzilla* had stuck, and she professed to like it. Or at least not hate it. Another item was a general respect and perhaps fear of Rivendell's police chief.

The group came to a slight rise in the terrain, and Charlie had to adjust his vector. He managed to more or less keep up with Monica's determined march, while Kevin kept a hand on the components to ensure everything stayed on board.

Bill paused for a moment to look around. The Pleistocene landscape in this version of Earth included a lot of animals long since extinct on Earthside. It was almost comical how fast the population of Rivendell had gotten used to Mastodons, giant sloths, and Smilodons. He wondered how relaxed they'd have been one world over with T-Rexes as neighbors. And speaking of which...

He broke into a jog to catch up with their leader. "You promised me a T-Rex, dammit. Still waiting."

"Did not," Monica replied. "That's a Jurassic animal. You've seen the movie, right? They were extinct by the time the Chicxulub asteroid hit. Or maybe didn't hit, in this case. So you'll get Albertosaurus or Gorgosaurus, and you'll like it." She thought for a moment. "Or whatever they've evolved into after sixty-five million years."

"Assuming your assumptions are correct," Kevin added, catching up to the pair. "We don't know for certain if the absence of a Yucatán impact is the reason for dinosaurs not having gone extinct on this particular alternate Earth."

Monica responded with a shrug. "So we collect data and observations, like good little scientists. Which brings us to this." She gestured at the cart, with Charlie still gamely pulling. "C'mon, Charlie, we're burning daylight."

Charlie didn't respond directly, but Bill was certain he'd heard a low growl.

"Another thing that's interesting is the climate on Dino Planet," Monica said to Kevin over her shoulder. "It's definitely warmer than here or Earthside. One of the results of the closing of the Panama isthmus was a significant drop in worldwide temps—"

Kevin interrupted. "That was only a couple million years ago."

Monica shook her head. "The latest research says as much as twenty-three million years ago. And with the complexity of the plate tectonics in that area—"

"It's still a significant stretch—"

Bill smiled as Monica and Kevin settled into the debate. It wasn't the first time the subject had come up, and wouldn't be the last. He was still waiting for Erin, their geology expert, to weigh in on the subject.

"Wait!" Monica held up a hand, cutting off the argument, then pointed slightly to the left. Bill rotated the pole-cam to match. He craned his neck to get a look at the image on the tablet, and Monica tilted it toward him. "Looks like a juvenile triceratops. Except..." She shook her head. "Head's different, less crest. I'm really going to have to start classifying these things, and I'm not sure I have the expertise. I didn't specialize in paleontology, especially not Cretaceous taxonomies."

"Guys," Charlie interrupted, "the UPS is down to twenty percent. We're going to have pack it in before the equipment makes the decision for us."

Bill glanced at the front of the power supply, where the warning light was strobing red. "Yup. We're done for the day. Maybe tomorrow we should try searching farther away from the forested area. I still think T-Rex—"

"Albertosaurus," Monica interrupted.

"—is too big to hunt in a forest," Bill finished, not missing a beat.

Charlie shook his head. "Can't do it tomorrow. Matt needs all the gates to clear out that CVS pharmacy we found."

Bill sighed. "Right. Forgot." He gave Monica an apologetic glance. "Too many things to do, not enough gates. We'll get back to it, though."

"Sure we will," she replied, "because you want to see a T-Rex."

"Albertosaurus." Bill grinned as she laughed, then turned to Charlie. "Can you pack up?"

"Will do, boss."

Kevin flipped his notebook closed, gave them a nod, then headed off toward the main longhouse. Monica took Bill's hand and smiled. "Pretty good day anyway."

Bill nodded, and looked at their clasped hands. Yeah, just like every single day, for him anyway.

2. Good Morning

August 19

Richard woke up slowly, letting the fog of sleep dissipate at its own pace. After almost a month on Outland, the morning cacophony of wildlife was no longer noticeable unless he consciously listened. The sleeping bag was warm, especially now that everyone had air mattresses to separate them from the cold ground.

As he turned slightly, a bare leg rubbed against his. He smiled and said, "Good morning."

Suzie stretched languorously and replied, "Hi there." She took a few seconds to greet him properly, then looked around the tent and reached out to grab her clothes. "Duty calls. People get cranky without their breakfast."

Richard laughed and gave her a quick hug and final kiss. "Speaking as one of those cranky people, I'd have to say I agree." They exchanged a smile and he reached for his clothes as well. "Ready?" At her nod, he quickly unzipped the double sleeping bag and they dressed as quickly as possible, their skin developing goose bumps in the cold morning air.

It took less than a minute to finish. Practice, plus the reinforcement provided by the chilly air, had honed their routines. Richard unzipped the front of the tent. He gave Suzie's hand a quick squeeze. Then, grabbing their toiletry supplies, they headed off for the communal facilities, which still consisted of outhouses and large trough-like sinks, kept out of the weather by blue canvas awnings scavenged from an Earthside Home Depot. It felt sometimes like being back in high school, except for the lack of any solid walls.

Life in Rivendell had quickly settled into a routine over the summer. The two original metal sheds still stood in the center of the colony, but were increasingly hard to pick out in the chaotic mass of tents, pergolas, and awnings that had grown around them. Tents ran the gamut from single-person pup tents right up to larger multiple-occupant units for family groups or simply groups of friends.

Technically, everything was the property of the Gate Owners—Richard, Bill, Monica, Erin, Matt, and Kevin—since they had purchased and transported virtually everything to Rivendell in the first place. This made allocating assets fairly at least possible, if not necessarily without a certain level of argument. But that wasn't a stable state of affairs, which was turning out to be a common topic of discussion at the committee meetings.

Speaking of which, Richard glanced at his watch. He needed to put on a little hustle if he didn't want to miss out on the coffee. Quickly finishing his ablutions, he gathered his kit and made way for the next person waiting for a spot.

Richard continued to smile as he headed for the wooden longhouse that housed the committee meetings. *Getting to be a perma-grin*, he thought to himself with satisfaction. For all that the end of modern civilization had to be considered a bad thing, for Richard it had turned out to have considerable upside. He now had Suzie, a set of friends he could trust, and a sense of purpose and belonging that he'd always felt was lacking in his life. Of course, he'd never come out and say this. Even in his internal monologue, the self-centeredness of the thought made him cringe a bit.

He had to detour around a game of pickup basketball. The ground had been stripped, flattened, and tamped down to form a more-or-less uniform play area, although dribbling seemed to be a bit of an adventure. A single portable net completed the court. There had been some talk of forming a baseball league, but there simply wasn't enough room inside the fenced area, and playing outside the fence had some obvious risks.

The front doors of the longhouse were wedged open to let the warming late-summer air circulate, and to let as much light as possible into the interior. The longhouse had been slapped up with some haste, and little details like windows had been kept to a minimum. Future efforts would doubtless be much improved.

The other committee members were already gathered at the large, sturdy table at the back of the cavernous open interior. Several carafes sat in the center, but there was no guarantee they'd still have anything in them. Coffee, as an increasingly limited resource, was strictly rationed, even for committee meetings.

Richard grabbed a mug, then shook the carafes until he found one with liquid still sloshing around inside. He carefully poured himself a cup, then sat at his usual spot at the head of the table to savor the caffeine jolt.

Officially, committee meetings started at 9:00 a.m. However, a general feeling of *mañana* had developed in Rivendell, and the meeting started when everyone felt ready. Seated around the table were himself as chair; Bill Rustad for SciTech; Lieutenant Tom Collins for Security and Scouting (Ed Tigersen having resigned); Monica Albertelli as police chief; Krista Tollefson for Medical; Matt Siemens for Scavenging; Erin Savard as the geology expert; Sam Benton for Animal Sciences; Anita Neumann for Agro; and Nick McCormack for Infrastructure. These people formed the de facto government of Outland, to the extent that it even *had* a government.

Bill put down his cup and pointed a finger at Richard. "Y'know, I remember a time when you were always the first one here in the morning. You're slipping."

Richard chuckled, waggled his eyebrows, and said, "Busy. Sorry."

Bill laughed. "I bet!"

The conversation, the first words spoken in almost ten minutes, marked the unofficial start of the meeting. Everyone sat forward, adjusted themselves, and prepared to get down to business. Richard picked up his notes. "Okay, stuff for today... Scavenging." He glanced over at Matt and waved *go ahead* with one hand.

Matt smiled and replied, "Actually, we're kind of leaning toward 'Acquisitions.' Sounds way more dignified." He gave a shrug, then turned in his chair and hitched his arm over the back. Matt never seemed willing to simply sit straight in a chair; there was always some aspect of *cat draping itself.* "The pickings are getting mighty slim in Lincoln," he continued. "We've taken everything useful that we can find—everything that's still in one piece, anyway. What's outstanding on our wish list is either stuff we can't find, or stuff we can't fit through the gate. We found a full-sized fuel truck filled with diesel, for instance, but it's too big for even the truck gate. Right now, we're bringing fuel across in gas cans, but you can imagine how long that'll take. What we really need is a locomotive-sized gate." He looked at Bill significantly.

"Don't I know it," Bill said. "And I have the plans for it, and some of the parts and materials. We did some work on it just before the eruption. Just never got everything together in time. I only need the raw steel channel and a couple of components. But they're not to be had in Lincoln. As it is, I'm juggling parts to keep everything working."

Richard nodded and chimed in, "In addition to spare parts for gates, it would be nice to make a few more portal boxes. We're something like four components short, mostly thanks to the thugs shooting up one of the PCs. Plus, when I was buying parts way back in another life, it never occurred to me to stock a couple of extra backplanes. Or cases, for that matter." He smiled sheepishly. "We may end up organizing some kind of expedition farther afield at some point, but I just don't see it happening right now." Everyone nodded in understanding, if not agreement.

Since no one seemed inclined to add anything, Richard gestured with his chin to Krista, who'd just been refilling her cup. She took the time for a sip before starting. "We now have eight pregnancies. That number's going to get bigger as birth control supplies dwindle. And that's going to be our biggest headache in half a year, give or take. I know I keep harping on this, but deaths in childbirth—either mother or child or both—are the biggest risk factor we will face—"

"Other than maybe getting eaten by a Smilodon," Bill interjected.

"So far, encounters with wildlife have not gone well for the wildlife," Krista replied. "Although I suppose it's just a matter of time. I'm just waiting for someone to lose an argument with a mammoth or something. You won't stop one of them with a shotgun. *That* will test our capabilities."

"Would we be able to handle that kind of injury?" Matt asked.

"Not really, no," Krista answered. "It's like with the gates. We've got ninety percent of what we need. Just missing this or that, but it's an *important* this or that. Like anesthetics. Or blood. Or a good stock of bandages, for that matter." She sighed. "We haven't really been tested yet. There've been any number of minor injuries and a few broken bones, but nothing E.R.-level yet. It does worry me."

Krista pushed her notes away and leaned back in her chair. Richard turned and nodded to Collins.

The lieutenant made a dismissive gesture with one hand. "I don't really have much for you. We've been acting as transport for the scavenging people mostly. Excuse me, *acquisitions* people. A lot of my troops are now discharged into the civilian population, subject to recall, of course. The local animal population has learned to avoid us, and those that didn't have been Darwined out. It's all very routine. Which is fine by me." He finished with a broad smile.

Next, Richard looked at Anita, the woman in charge of agriculture and food-gathering, who said, "We've got a large area fenced off now, thanks to Nick and company"—she nodded to him, and he smiled back—"and as Lieutenant Collins mentioned, the wildlife is giving us a wide berth these days. The few cats that have decided to scale the fences to get an easy meal will no longer be contributing to the species' gene pool. The rest seem to have developed some smarts. Meanwhile, we've been able to start some test plantings, all fall crops for obvious reasons. The soil's pretty good once you bust through the extensive root systems of the plains grass. The sun's good too, although it seems to be cooling off faster here than back home, which worries me a little. And we'll need to work out some kind of irrigation if we want to do this on any kind of scale. We're going to be plowing one entire field for winter wheat. Don't know how bad the winters will be here, so that's a bit of a crap shoot.

"Also, the aggies have found lots of locations for herbs, wild tubers, fruits, and such. So we're getting some variety into our diets now, although those are the pre-agriculture versions of the plants, so they're tough and miserly. As well, we've taken a lot of seeds from Earthside and scattered some of them randomly. They won't all take, but if enough do, in a few years we should be able to start finding naturalized versions of our food crops to supplement what we grow ourselves."

The group nodded in appreciation. By this point, even Bill was complaining about constant Chili-Something stew.

Nick gave his infrastructure report next. "We learned a few things from building the first longhouse. We've got four more under construction for winter residences, and we should be able to put them up quicker and with a few less quirks. Also, those pellet stoves you guys found"—he looked at Matt and nodded—"are amazingly efficient. We'll be building them in, and that should take care of heating. However"—Nick held up a finger—"if you can find a pellet press, we can make our own pellets from local wood supplies. Otherwise we have to keep scavenging from Lincoln, and once we run out, the stoves are pretty much useless."

Nick stopped for a moment and perused his notes. "We now have dependable water and electricity thanks to Bill, and we're seriously looking at adding flush toilets. I get a *lot* of requests for that, mostly from the ladies."

Krista cut in, deadpan. "Yeah, what's your point?"

Nick laughed, and signaled Bill to take over.

"Well, since Nick has stolen most of my thunder, I don't have much to say. You guys know there's been a lot of talk of trying to find another Earth that has a civilization that hasn't been obliterated. That means either going through Dino Planet or Greenhouse Earth. We've tried bypassing them to latch onto something, but no luck so far. So we'll probably have to establish a beachhead on those timelines, and neither will be easy without protection of some kind. To build that protection, we'd need the locomotive gate. So we're back to that." Bill sat back and shrugged, plainly irritated at the universe for being so difficult. Then he sat forward before Richard could take back the floor. "One other thing. I really need to stress this. We have electricity, yes, but the total wattage is strictly limited. Windmills, solar cells, and carefully rationed diesel generators can only do so much. I've noticed people putting up electric lights here and there—and *incandescents,* for chrissake. Those are the biggest power hogs of all. Seriously, Matt, if you find a cache of L.E.D. bulbs, please make them a priority to bring back. And I think we should just smash every filament bulb we find, on principle."

"Deliberately breaking anything, even that, makes me cringe," Richard said. "But I get your point. Matt?"

"I don't disagree. I'll add L.E.D.s to my list. Which brings it up to … " Matt made a show of examining some invisible notes. "Pretty much every item in existence. As a priority."

"And when everything's a priority," Bill said, "nothing is."

Richard looked around the table. "So it's basically business as usual, is it?" Rueful chuckles around the table acknowledged that he'd articulated a general attitude. "Any other items we should talk about?"

Krista raised her hand. "Besides the talk of going and looking for another Earth, there's also been talk of going back to Earthside. I think some people still have this idea that as soon as the dust clears it'll be back to normal. Bill, are you still getting satellite TV?"

"A couple of stations are still transmitting. It's potluck, though."

"So maybe we need a TV night or something," Krista replied. "You could DVR some good juicy sections of news and play them back for everyone."

"I don't think we need or want to show that to the whole colony," Richard cautioned. "A lot of people took it poorly the first time. There are those who want and need to know, and those who are happier without all the details. Let's just offer it for those who are interested. Maybe have it set up in one of the sheds. People who don't want to go can sit in the longhouse and sample Crazy Al's and Charlie's beer. Speaking of which..."

Krista laughed. "Still not poisonous. Believe me, I'm watching for methanol. In fact, the last batch—I tried a little—isn't totally heinous. There's hope."

Richard nodded, then looked around the table. "Anything else?"

"We've got a bit of a problem with slackers," Collins said. "There are some people who just don't want to pull their weight. We've got several identified. Bea wants to just shoot them, but Monica has an idea that might send a clear message to the other ones. She wanted to verify with you guys that you'd be okay with repatriating someone, even if it might mean a death sentence for them." He glanced at Monica as he said this, and received a beaming smile in reply.

"I've got a pretty good idea what you have in mind," Richard said to Monica. "How about if you give the miscreant a chance to come back if and when they grow a brain? That way there's not so much of an ethical issue."

Monica nodded. "I can do that. Expect fireworks soon."

3. EARTHSIDE: KOREAN AFTERMATH

The Yellowstone eruption a month prior was a disaster for more than just the continental U.S. Ash and gases from the volcano ascended to the stratosphere and were carried around the globe, even crossing the equator to affect southern hemisphere populations.

On the Korean peninsula, the last of the city fires were finally out, and there was no longer a detectable night glow. Three weeks after the conflict between North and South, there was still no sign of life near any of the nuclear strikes.

North Korea had been attempting to acquire resources, so was motivated to destroy as little as possible. The South was not so limited, and was fighting for its very existence. Once the North realized it wouldn't prevail, it abandoned any thoughts of conquest in favor of vengeance. In the end, China, fearing a spread of the conflagration, had nuked the military installations of both Koreas indiscriminately.

The resulting nuclear firefight left only the cities in the southern tip and the northern edge of the Koreas unaffected. It would likely be decades before the irradiated areas would be even remotely habitable.

However, most of North Korea outside the cities was anything but a military target. The majority of the population had always lived in near–Stone Age conditions, with dirt roads, no electricity, no malls, no factories—none of the trappings of the modern consumer economy. Other than the bright flashes, many North Koreans had no idea anything untoward was afoot. The skies had only recently begun to fill with ash, and plant life had yet to begin any kind of mass die-off. For most of the feudal population, life went on, but perhaps suddenly with a little less oversight from the central government.

4. Early Results

August 20

It was dinnertime, and Bill and his friends were seated in their usual place on the lawn. Several of them were still mopping up their Something Stew with the bun that was part of today's meal. Bread was still enough of a rarity to be considered a special treat, and Bill made a point of savoring it.

He settled back on his elbows, enjoying the post-meal lethargy, and brought up the subject of their portal hunts in Dino Planet. "So, yeah, it just keeps getting more and more interesting. We finally did some measurements. The atmospheric pressure and oxygen content are higher than here, but Monica says they're not as high as they would have had to be back in the Cretaceous."

"That's right," Monica said. "We're not looking at the same level of global jungle as during the dinosaurs' reign. I don't know if the really big species will have died out or adapted. Pretty sure the really big pterodactyls won't still be flying around." She thought for a few moments, then continued. "We've seen a lot of small stuff, including velociraptors—which, by the way, are not as big as the things in *Jurassic Park*. We've also seen a couple of the bigger herbivores, which leads me to believe that adaptation is the more likely scenario."

Erin, having finally been brought up to date on Monica's theories, weighed in. "The closing off of the Central American seaway between the Pacific and Atlantic still would have had a major impact on climate. I like it as a theory, but I'm not sure how we'd go about checking." She looked at Kevin, who gave her a lopsided smile.

"I, uh, think you're overestimating my expertise in this area," he commented. "Just because I thought up the math doesn't mean I'm suddenly an expert on all alternate Earths. But if Monica is right that the Yucatán asteroid didn't hit Dino Planet, then that could very well have affected crustal movements. I wouldn't rule it out."

Bill took a moment to be impressed with the new Kevin. Somehow everything that had happened in the last several months had brought him out of his shell, and he was actually able to participate in conversations now. Bill said, "Given that we don't know for sure, we're doing most of our investigation using the small gate, which we've sealed to prevent a cross-breeze. And insect contamination. The last thing we need is something getting loose on this side."

"We need to get over there in order to check for other timelines further out, though, right?" Matt said. "How are we going to handle that part of it?"

Bill smiled. "We've been discussing this in the Mad Science Lab. We're going to try to put together an airlock of sorts. Over the longer term, the safest thing is to go underground if we want to have a permanent structure. But to make it workable, we need more portals, and we especially need a bigger gate. So again, it's back to that." He looked pointedly at Matt, who rolled his eyes.

"Same goes for going through Greenhouse Earth," Bill continued. "We've scavenged some of those firefighting suits from a couple of firehouses back home. They'll protect against the atmosphere and the temp, and give the wearer breathable air, so we could do limited amounts of work there. But we need the infrastructure and more of a plan."

"What's the point, exactly?" Matt asked.

Richard spoke up. "A lot of people aren't happy with the idea of just spending the rest of our lives here. There's been agitation to go looking Earthside for surviving communities, and there's been agitation to go looking across timelines for another Earth that still has civilization. Each idea has its problems, but there's still a lot of pressure. When we finally get around to elections, I'm betting those will be major campaign issues."

Erin nodded. "I keep thinking things are going to get simpler at some point, but it never seems to go in that direction."

Richard sighed. "You ain't wrong…"

"Since when are we taking direction from special interest groups?" Monica asked.

"It's not like they're being unreasonable, Mon," Richard replied. "But a lot of different people means a lot of different opinions on what we should be working on, or at least aiming for. We won't be able to run this place as a kind of feudalistic technocracy for much longer. And I don't want to live in an armed camp. So, elections, government, then decisions that we might not necessarily like."

"And more time for me to work on my crap," Bill said. "And this time, let's try not to screw up the planet."

5. FIRE

August 21

Matt sat on the edge of the pickup bed, watching his group prepare for the day's scheduled duties. The truck, a diesel F-350, was now the official lead vehicle. He felt a moment of regret. His trusty old F-150 had done stalwart duty, but it was gasoline powered, and gas was beginning to go bad. Only diesel engines could be depended on now. And at some point, even diesel would start to develop sludge. According to both Bill and Lieutenant Collins, though, that could be filtered out without too much trouble.

Meanwhile, motorcycles were becoming a rare sight on Earthside. Fortunately, they'd managed to liberate a couple of diesel ATVs from a local dealer.

"All set," Charlie said, interrupting Matt's reverie. He gestured to the truck gate, which was set up on the Nebraska plain on the Outland side, but not yet activated.

"Okay, thanks, Charlie." Matt raised his voice. "Everyone got your priority lists?" Every member of the crew raised a handwritten note in the air. "Good. I know I've said this the last couple of times, but it bears repeating. If you see anything that's of moderate value but may not last much longer—because of weather, structural issues, or whatever—make a note of it and make sure you get the info to me. Our priority nowadays is *rescue it now and sort it out later.* Questions?"

There were none. This crew was all experienced personnel, with many scavenging outings under their collective belts. Matt gave a nod to Charlie, who raised the tablet and poked at the UI. With a shimmer, the interface opened to a view of downtown Lincoln, Nebraska.

There was still a little bit of loose ash on every horizontal surface, but by now most of it had been washed off by rains, leaving only a stubborn gummy coating. The loose stuff would have run into sewer and drainage systems, and because of the characteristics of volcanic ash, many of those systems had clogged up. Lincoln now featured many new, shallow lakes with street names. Paradoxically, this created an increased risk of fire, as the water corroded metal storage containers and support structures.

"Okay, guys," Matt said. "Four hours maximum. Radio if you get in trouble."

With that, the crew began filing through the interface, some on bicycles, some on foot, and some on ATVs. When they were all through, Charlie carried a radio mast through the interface and stood it up on the other side, while Matt set up a folding table and spread a map of Lincoln.

"The collection crews are more than a week behind," Charlie said as he walked up to the table.

Matt looked down at the plastic-covered map, where erasable marker notes indicated valuable stashes needing to be picked up. "Yeah, I know. But the new policy has just widened the criteria for marking a location as important. So, more locations, but still the same number of gates."

"And Bill can't build any more?"

"Not without parts, Charlie. And while most of the parts are stock items, like tower PCs and sheet metal, the parts that *aren't* stock items are show-stoppers. Nobody, but *nobody* sells programmable controller cards off the shelf. Or lasers. Or waveguides or beam-splitters."

"I thought Bill had some ideas ... "

"Bill has *lots* of ideas. About *lots* of things. The problem is he can't spend enough time on any one thing to make any progress. Plus, he has the attention span of a gnat." Matt chuckled. "It wouldn't surprise me if he took off after a squirrel sometimes."

At that moment, the radio squawked, and a woman's voice said, "We have a problem, guys."

Charlie grabbed the mike. "What's up?"

"Fire. I think. There's a dense plume of smoke coming from the northeast. We did a rough parallax, and we think it's somewhere around the Gateway Mall."

Matt and Charlie traded alarmed glances. "That's got some of the biggest stashes of inventory we've identified," Charlie said.

"It's also in a heavily suburban area," Matt replied. "Lots of buildings that could catch. Even if we had a fire department, we probably couldn't do anything. We'll just have to hope it burns itself out without taking out the whole city."

Charlie turned back to the radio and pressed the "transmit" button. "Send everyone with ATVs to try to get a read on location and extent, and whether or not it's spreading. Don't take chances, though. Report back when done. Normal operations are cancelled." He put the mike down. "Fuck. We had stacked up a ton of clothing for winter wear, to be brought across. Probably all gone."

The scavenging crew popped back through the gate in ones and twos, expressions uniformly morose. Matt did a head count, then motioned Charlie to shut down the interface. As the view of Lincoln shimmered out to be replaced by the Outland plains through the gate frame, Matt paused and considered his next words. Then he turned to the group. "We can't do anything about this. That's the first thing to understand. This isn't anyone's failure, so let's not get bent out of shape about that. And we always knew we were racing against time and chance. Well, we lost this one. We'll come back tomorrow and try to ascertain the extent of the damage."

"It probably won't spread very far," said Cleo, the woman who had reported the fire. "The layer of ash isn't much, but it provides some insulation so that the embers can't automatically start up a fire wherever they touch down. I saw a lot of them land on roofs and just go out."

Matt frowned. "How close did you get, Cleo?"

She grinned back at him. "What you don't know, you can't give me shit for."

Matt rolled his eyes. "Mutiny now. Okay, fine. And that is good news, I guess. First good thing that's come out of the ashfall." He looked around the temporary camp. "All right, folks. Let's pack up and head back to Rivendell. I'll talk to the committee. We may have to alter priorities."

6. The New Reality

Every day, the same people did the same things at the same time. They were all so predictable. It was like a dance, rehearsed day after day, until the steps had been worn right into the nervous system. Oh, there would be the occasional variation, but nothing out of character. It was a constant source of amusement, and if he was being honest, contempt.

But if he was being honest, that contempt was two-way. He knew in principle that his behavior was off-putting, but numerous attempts to analyze and correct it had ended in failure. Doctors and psychologists had attempted to explain the details, but it was all just words. Acronym after acronym, really nothing more than an attempt to name things that they didn't understand. The bottom line was that he simply couldn't perceive, let alone replicate the fine interactions that acted as social lubricant for most people.

But he wished he could just talk to people sometimes. He felt the occasional pang as he watched groups and couples, laughing and walking together. He had to wonder, though. Did it matter so much, anymore? Earth was toast, whatever the drones might loudly hope for. In this new, dare one say *frontier* society, the rules were different. To the extent there were rules. And to the extent there were people to enforce them.

Resentment from a lifetime of exclusion bubbled up—of rejection, of being made the *other*. He gritted his teeth. Did he really owe them anything? Then he took a deep breath and shook his head as if to clear the fog. That way lay madness. He had long ago decided that he would not listen to those aspects of himself. It would be an admission of failure, and it was a path that couldn't be abandoned once selected. He might be a pariah, but he refused to be a psychopath.

The scavenging groups were happy for his strong back when collecting salvage, but they were not any more tolerant of his quirks than anyone else. He was happy to help out just to have something to do, as well as to have a chance to look for items that he needed.

Some, like Sean and his posse, went out of their way to be cruel, to prove how big they were by making him feel small. He wanted to smash those smug faces, to make them scream. But that kind of confrontational bravura was beyond him. He'd simply lock up, be unable to speak, then end up running away with his tail tucked between his legs, to laughter and yells of derision.

But it wasn't all bad. There was Suzie, walking toward her morning job. Right on time. She'd have said goodbye to her boyfriend about thirty seconds ago, and he'd be right... there. He smiled to himself, the correct prediction yet another small victory.

He smiled at Suzie as he walked past her, and she smiled back. One of the few kind ones. One of the few who didn't make him dream of vengeance of the most violent form.

7. Dinosaur Sighting

August 23

Between Bill's schedule and Matt's need to use the gate for scavenging, it had taken almost a week before Monica and Bill were able to try again at looking for carnosaurs on Dino Planet.

They used the same setup as on the previous outing, including Charlie acting as wagon-jockey. Kevin tagged along again as well, having expressed a desire to see whatever passed for a T-Rex these days.

"I still want to start in the forest, though," Monica said. "I think you're probably right about large carnosaurs being plains creatures, but there's a lot of interesting smaller stuff in the trees."

Bill shrugged, willing to go along with Monica's plan. As far as he was concerned, there was simply no downside to this activity. Unless something tried to climb through the pole-cam into Outland, of course. They habitually covered the aperture to prevent insect contamination in either direction, but plastic wrap certainly wouldn't stop something larger and more determined.

"So listen," Charlie said, breaking Bill's train of thought, "what species would we still see on Dino Planet? I mean, what's likely to be common to both there and here? And Earthside, of course."

Monica stopped and glanced at him, frowning. "Fuck-all, Charlie. If there are still dinos there, then the temporal split had to have happened at least sixty-five million years ago. There are a few species that might be relatively unchanged, like turtles or alligators, but everything warm-blooded that we're familiar with on Earth evolved after the dinosaurs bit it."

"So no wolves, horses, large cats ...?"

She shook her head. "Possible but unlikely. It's the butterfly effect writ large. Without the ecosystems being purged by the Chicxulub impact, leaving every niche open to evolve into, you simply wouldn't have gotten the explosion of adaptation that we're familiar with."

"Assuming the impact is the crucial event," Kevin retorted.

"Sure, assuming." Monica glanced at him and shrugged. "Doesn't matter, though. Whether it's that or something else, the logic still holds. Presence of dinos means absence of kitty cats."

Bill and Charlie looked at each other. Neither was willing to dispute the point, and Bill really didn't think she was wrong. Seeing no argument, Monica went back to examining the image on the tablet.

"Found a game path, I think," she said after a minute or so. She pointed, and Bill began moving in the indicated direction until she said, "Stop."

"Recording?" Bill asked, and Monica nodded, now totally focused on the tablet. Over the next hour, they saw numerous small raptors and a surprisingly large number of mammal-like animals, including one particularly ugly specimen about the size of a small lion.

"What the hell is that?" Bill asked, spotting the animal.

"No analogue in our fossil record," Monica replied. "It's either never been discovered or it's an alternate evolutionary path. I can't even positively identify the genus. It looks a little like an Andrewsarchus."

"Andrew who?" Charlie quipped, looking over their shoulders. Monica shot him a brief eye roll.

"Definitely carnivorous," Bill replied. The animal, looking something like a cross between a wolf and an alligator, seemed to be all teeth and claws. The jaw was a significant fraction of the beast's total length.

After another half hour of scanning, Monica spoke up. "This is not as busy as I expected. Weird. The biota density should be comparable to here in Outland, but it's more like the Earthside level. Let's try the plains."

Charlie had a very good memory for that kind of thing, and he pointed out the location on the Outland side that would place them outside of the trees on the Dino Planet side. This, however, would put them outside the Rivendell fence on the Outland side, which was plenty dangerous in its own right. There was a short break while they obtained weapons and a couple of volunteer guards.

Finally ready to continue, Bill reactivated the pole-cam, and the entire group moved out to the proper location to view the Dino Planet clearing.

This time, it took less than ten minutes before they saw something—actually several somethings—through the camera, moving in the distance. Quickly heading in that direction, with Charlie valiantly pulling the cart for all he was worth, the group soon found themselves looking at a couple of large carnosaurs on the Dino Planet side, feeding on a carcass. Everyone spoke at once:

"Holy shit."

"Sonofabitch!"

"Wow!"

"To be honest, I'm not sure if they're Albertosauruses or Gorgosauruses," Monica said, staring at the image on the tablet, "or something else that evolved from them."

The two T-Rex lookalikes were each more than twenty feet from tip to tail. They were feathered, but in a brown-and-green pattern that looked almost like army camouflage clothing. Like vultures, their faces were bare.

The two behemoths were standing on either side of their kill, something elephant-like or at least elephant-sized, and were alternately dipping their heads and taking bites out of their meal. Each time a head would dip, the tail would rise into the air. Bill chuckled and said, "Dipping Birds. Large economy size."

Monica turned to look at Bill, looked at the image on the tablet, then looked back at Bill, her jaw hanging open. She moved her lips a few times, trying to say something, then started to laugh. Within seconds, she was doubled over. The men looked at each other in perplexity, then back at Monica, who was now sitting on the ground whooping and trying to get her breath.

"Hey, babe, I'm glad I'm so entertaining, but I sure wish I knew what I'd said." Bill tried to keep a smile on his face to mask his confusion.

Finally, Monica wiped the tears from her eyes and got up. It took her a few seconds to completely get control of the giggles, but eventually she was able to talk.

"Bill, you know that T-Rex had very short arms, right?"

"Sure, the short-arms jokes were all over the place back on old Earth. Although come to think of it, it was always the same three jokes."

"Uh huh." Monica gave him a look of impatience. "It wasn't just T-Rex, though. So did a lot of the larger carnosaurs. And no one ever had a really convincing expla- nation for that. There've been a lot of theories, of course, but none that seemed definitive."

Bill cocked his head and said, "And you've just figured it out?"

Monica nodded, smiling. "It's so stupidly simple. After all the really complex theories people have come up with over the years, turns out it could be the head. The carno- saurs evolved bigger heads, bigger teeth, bigger jaw muscles over time, in order to be a more effective predator. That was directed evolution of a desirable trait, and no one argues the usefulness of that big bite. But there are always trade- offs. In order to balance the increased weight from all that weaponry, they would have either had to increase the coun- terweight back of the hips, or decrease some other weight, forward of the hips. Increasing the weight back of the hips would have increased their total weight and slowed them down, which would be counterproductive ... "

Bill's eyes widened. "So the front arms atrophied—"

Monica laughed. "Reducing the weight up front, and balance was maintained. Yup. Now if only I could figure out how to publish!"

8. FALL PLANTING

August 25

The event had drawn a large crowd, possibly the biggest since the first ultralight flight. People stood outside the lawn fence, watching as the tractor slowly pulled the plow back and forth across the field.

"Anita says we're starting a bit early," Matt commented to Richard, "but depending on the winters here, it might be necessary."

"Yeah, which means we're taking a chance with the wheat seed we use up," Richard replied. "Still, I think everyone agrees it's worth it. Mmmm ... Bread ... "

Richard looked over at Bill and grinned. Bill did his best to look offended, but couldn't stop a return grin.

Matt laughed. "Did he just steal your schtick?"

Bill rolled his eyes. "Everyone's a comedian today."

They made their way toward the main longhouse, passing the four almost-completed residences. The buildings had the same general footprint as the first longhouse, but had been set up specifically as residences for the general population. Which meant more windows, plus some significant extra features.

"Real, actual bathroom fixtures ... " Matt commented as they walked past. He was giving voice to the thought at the front of most people's minds. After what felt like months of using outhouses and washing in communal sinks and basins, people were very excited about the idea of modern plumbing. Nick and his crew were almost done building the structures, and would be turning on the water as soon as they'd finished setting up the new septic fields downslope.

"I'll have to skip the meeting today," Matt said. "Too much happening right now with the scavenging crews." He waved goodbye as they got to the main longhouse, and continued on his way. Richard and Bill entered the house and walked to the back where the committee meetings were always held.

The others were already gathered and enjoying their morning coffee. The new arrivals grabbed cups and set about getting their own fix.

Finally, Richard looked around the table. "Today's discussion, if you didn't already know, is about future directions for the colony. The plowing out in the field has made it clear to people that we might be here permanently. There's been a significant uproar, with loud voices on both sides of the debate."

"It's not a debate," Bill interjected. "We're staying long-term. Anyone who wants to go back Earthside is welcome to do so."

"I know, Bill, but it's a controversial topic."

Bill shook his head. "No, it's controversial in the same way that the Flat Earth debate is controversial. If people argue, they think that makes it a controversy."

Richard sighed and looked around the table before continuing. "I know, Bill. But we work with what we have, and we seem to have at least some residents who think they can change the facts by throwing a fit." He paused. "So we've got people who are fine with the idea of staying long-term, but they want to create a formal government and have elections.

We've got people who don't want us to do that because they don't want us to get comfortable. That group consists of people who want to work on getting back to Earth, and people who want to go through the gates and find an alternate Earth that's still in one piece."

"Leaving aside the question of what they'll do when they meet their alternate selves who are already comfortably ensconced in their lives," Bill replied. "Ask them to step away, maybe?"

"Add to that," Krista cut in, "the people who are okay with a permanent Outland colony but want to set up expeditions to rescue more Earthside people."

"And then there are the people who want a specific society built around their particular dogma," Collins added. "Far left, far right, libertarian, communistic, radical green, free-market capitalism, some other stuff I can't even understand, let alone categorize. You'd think we had a bunch of ivory-tower intellectuals living here." He grinned to answering laughs around the table.

"If it isn't one thing, it's a dozen other things," Bill said. "Meanwhile, I'm trying to achieve practical goals, like increasing our electrical supply, winterproofing our water and sewage systems, work out a large-scale sawmill system, establish controlled-environment storage for perishable goods, develop the basis of industry for things like manufacturing clothing and furniture, and on and on and on."

"Some of those projects aren't mutually exclusive," Krista pointed out.

"No," Bill replied, "not in theory. But as usual, we're up against resource constraints. In this case, warm bodies to actually do all this stuff."

Richard spoke into the silence that followed. "And we have the failed revolutionaries to deal with, still. Lieutenant

Collins has them doing grunt work at gunpoint, but that's obviously inefficient. We'd be better off having the people on guard duty doing the work."

"Shooting them is beginning to look not so bad," Bill said.

"Tempting, but a really bad idea," Collins said. "I guess I'm one of the people in the form-a-government camp, for just this reason."

Richard leaned back and looked up at the ceiling. It never ended. "Are we getting any really serious grumbling about the current state of affairs?"

Collins shook his head. "No, not so far. It was established fairly early that you guys own everything except what other people brought with them. Although there's a feeling that anything brought over from Lincoln since then is community property. And people recognize that we need a system of administration of some kind rather than just chaos, so they're willing to accept the dictates of the committee." He looked around the table. "For now. But if a feeling develops that you aren't really interested in changing, things could get tense."

"I couldn't care less," Bill said. "Less time in committee means more time doing engineering. No downside for me."

Richard nodded in his direction. "I think that's generally true for everyone here. We're not really career politicians, which actually might be why people are more willing to accept us in this position. But Tom is right; eventually, we have to become a nation of sorts."

"Someone got the crap beat out of them yesterday," Krista said, changing the subject abruptly.

All heads turned to her. "Why?" Richard asked.

"Not sure about the why, but I know who did it. Someone named Jimmy. Some kind of local tough."

"I think I know who you mean," Monica said. "Big dumb guy, got picked up in one of our scavenging expeditions. Not a student. He's willing to work, unlike some other people I can think of, and he's fond of showing off his strength, but he seems to have a problem with his social coping skills."

"Huh. That could turn into a real problem if he makes a habit of this particular conflict-resolution tactic." Collins thought for a moment. "We might need that justice system sooner rather than later."

"Or I'll just shoot him," Monica said. Collins rolled his eyes but didn't reply.

"Hey, has anyone noticed a lot of mountain bikes lately?" Nick said into the silence.

"My idea," Bill replied. "We're trying to conserve gas, although it's already starting to go bad anyway. There aren't a lot of diesel motorcycles or ATVs, so we're trying to convert to muscle power for the long term. It's quieter and less stinky as well."

"We have a couple of diesel ATVs, actually," Matt interjected. "But yeah, they weren't really mainstream before the eruption, so there aren't a lot."

"Interesting." Richard stroked his chin. "There's going to be a lot more of that kind of change as we gear down to a lower level of technology. Horse power, for instance."

Sam perked up. "Already a going concern. Every mare in our inventory is preggers. We had a large supply of, uh, donor sperm that had to be used up before the freezers gave out. Let's hope we get some males out of the new batch, or horses will be going extinct."

"Wow." Richard looked around. "Any other items? If not, let's call this. I need lunch."

❧ ❧ ❧

Bill and Monica walked slowly around the perimeter of the Rivendell fenced area. They weren't holding hands since Monica was on duty and had one hand on her AR-15. Her head swiveled constantly as she tracked movements and watched groups of people.

"We're not done," he said into the silence.

"With?"

"Revolutions. Tom's comments today really freaked me out. A lot of people are demanding that things be run their way, and most of those ways conflict. I can't think of a single movie where that kind of thing is settled by a civilized debate."

Monica chuckled. "You ain't wrong. Our failed revolutionaries were probably just the first act. And the most impatient."

"And dumbest."

"Yeah, that too. That means we have to up our game for the next set of assholes. They'll have seen how we prepped, they'll know we're trying to be ready for them, and they'll plan accordingly. Rocks in the gun safes won't work this time."

"That's just what they'll want us to think," Bill said.

"See, that's the thing. We'll be trying to outguess and outmaneuver each other. But they have the advantage in that we don't know who they are until they make a move."

Bill sighed. "So we have to figure out a double-double reverse to fool people who are expecting a double-reverse. Fun times."

"Sure is," Monica said with a smile. "Let's see what we can do."

9. Nightmares

The cat lay on its back, intestines laid out for examination. It opened its eyes and looked at him; opened its mouth, showing a very human tongue and teeth; and said clearly, "Killer."

He woke with a jolt. He didn't cry out; he never cried out. But he hadn't had those nightmares in years. They always terrified him, and could leave him jittery for the entire morning. He sat for a few seconds, waiting for his breathing and heart rate to come down, then checked his watch. Five minutes early. Oh, well. Might as well get on with it…

He looked at the pills in his hand. He was now at half-dose on two of his meds. He was slightly surprised that this didn't concern him more, then shrugged off that thought. He was coping. The *normals* would stay out of his way, as they always did, so he didn't see a potential problem. He would try to go Earthside with a crew today and check out a drugstore, more because he needed to finish things than from any real perceived need.

He waited the extra five minutes until his schedule had re-synchronized, then left his tent and started his walk.

There was Amy, saying goodbye to that dolt of a boyfriend. And here came Suzie, with her usual affectionate smile. Poor girl, having to put up with Richard, day after day.

Ah well, places to go, things to get done.

He stood with the crowd while Matt Siemens discussed notes and lists with his assistants. He spotted Matt's girlfriend, Erin, in the group. How he hated her. The few times he'd approached her, she had rebuffed him—and not gently. Her arrogance galled him, but it was well-known that Matt was an accomplished martial artist. And he probably would defend his girlfriend. So hands off. For now.

It was a new world, though. Things might change.

The discussion ended and Matt turned to address the crowd. "All right, everyone. It will come as a total surprise to absolutely no one that our priorities have changed. Again." He paused for the inevitable groans. "With the fire the other day, we've decided we're on a deadline for acquiring all the stuff we've already earmarked. So for the next few sessions, we won't even bother to look for new stashes. We've got six groups today, but we're going to have to share gates, so our coverage of the city will be limited. Check the lists for what group you're assigned to. If you're not on a list, see me. There's plenty to do in the warehouses."

He shuffled forward as individuals checked the lists and moved off to their assignments. *Please, not with Sean and his friends. Please.* He wasn't sure who his supplications were addressed to, since he didn't believe in any kind of deity. It was heartfelt, though. Sean Fulton and his two buddies were merciless in their mockery and insults. A life-time of such treatment had taught him that complaining would do no good, and would only make them redouble their efforts. If there were any alternative tasks that he could stomach, he'd have long since moved to another work-group.

His hopes were dashed, though. There in black and white was his name under the Home Depot group, below Sean, Ivan, and Merv.

"Hiya, buddy!" Sean draped his arm in fake camaraderie across his shoulders. "Guess we're workmates again. Ain't it great?"

He wanted to smash the exaggerated, mocking smile off Sean's face. He could feel himself tense up, start to shake, the urge to kill the smarmy, smug son of a bitch right there in front of everyone almost overpowering.

But no. As usual, his terror at the idea of confrontation paralyzed him. Sean gave him a knowing smirk and a shove, and his friends snickered. His face burned with humiliation and shame.

10. Repatriation

August 26

Monica sat in the shade, watching the medical tent. She was due for a meeting with Lieutenant Collins in a while, to discuss the malingering problem. She smiled to herself at the thought: *That's how we schedule meetings now—"in a while" and "later."* But meanwhile, she was on stakeout, watching for any one of several women.

After a few minutes, she saw who she was looking for. A woman had left the tent and was standing there with that goofy expression people get after good news, while repeatedly touching her stomach. Satisfied, Monica got up and headed for her meeting.

Monica dropped into the chair in front of Lieutenant Collins's desk. "Josh McAllen," she said. "He's our sacrificial lamb."

Collins looked up at her and nodded. "Okay, I don't even care why. What about what Richard suggested?"

Monica smiled. "If we play this right, we shouldn't actually have to gate him at all. I'll need four of your men, same size as Josh. And he's not a little guy. A couple more for driving and such. We'll need to work a few things out. And I need to arrange a bit of theater."

"You're enjoying this, aren't you?"

Monica just grinned.

Monica walked up to the man lying in the deck chair. She looked down at him silently for a few seconds. He glanced up, smiled a leering smile, and said, "Something I can do for you, sweetness?"

"As a matter of fact, Josh, yes." Monica made sure her high-volume voice was engaged. "You can stop being such a lazy selfish fucktard and start pulling your weight, you useless jackass."

Josh reacted exactly as expected. "Hey, bitch, when I want your opinion, I'll give it to you. Now beat it." He deliberately closed his eyes and made himself comfortable.

Monica took the glass of water she'd been holding and poured it on his chest. With a roar and a curse, he jumped up from his chair and turned on her. However, a lifetime of dealing with older brothers had taught Monica just how far away she had to be to avoid contact. In a few moments he had stopped his reflexive swings and locked eyes with her. As soon as he started to step forward, hands balled in fists, Monica unholstered her sidearm and stuck it into his groin.

"Planning on being mean to me, Chucky?" She looked up at him with a nasty smile. "Make a move, and I'll make you sing soprano."

Josh glared at her, probably trying to decide if he should call her bluff. However, Monica was one of very few people in Rivendell—even counting the Guard—who had actually killed someone, so after a few seconds Josh obviously decided to go with some kind of Plan B.

"Yeah, you're mighty tough when you have a weapon in your hand, bitch. I wonder how tough you'd be if you didn't have that."

Monica drew out the silence and her stare, then replied, "Yeah, you're mighty tough when you're facing off against someone that you outweigh by a hundred pounds. I wonder how tough you'd be if I shot out your knees first."

She gave him another two-count to think about that, then stepped back. "Anyway, Josh, this isn't about a fair fight. There is no fight. There is no ring and no referee. We're having this conversation … "

At this point, Josh gave her the silent finger, a nasty grin, and started to turn back to his chair. Without missing a beat, Monica aimed the Glock and put three quick shots into the ground by his feet. Josh did a quick dance, then looked at her in shock.

"Disrespect me just one more time, motherfucker. I dare you." Now everyone in the area was watching, and Monica was no longer smiling. She waited a moment to see if he'd react, then continued, "As I was saying, we're having this conversation because you've worked exactly two shifts as far as anyone can remember, and you did a shitty job on those. The rest of the time, you sit around, eat, and generally act obnoxious. Explain to me why you're still here."

Josh appeared to be getting some of his bravado back. "I'm here because I want to be. What are you going to do about it, bitch?"

"What I'm going to do, Josh, is repatriate you. Today's your lucky day. You're going home!" With that, she put her hand in the air and made a summoning motion. Two National Guardsmen appeared on either side of Josh. Two more positioned themselves just behind and outside his vision. The first two took Josh's arms and one said, "This way, buddy. You're going on a trip."

As expected, Josh reacted violently. He yanked his arm out of one soldier's grip and swung at the other. However, the intended target had stepped back immediately, and the three others stepped in. There was a short, sharp exchange of pleasantries, which ended with Josh on the ground yelling in pain. The soldier on top of him backed off on the armlock slightly and said in a conversational voice, "There are four of us and one of you. We're armed, you aren't. We're trained, you aren't. Don't be stupider than you can absolutely help. If necessary, we'll hog-tie you. You won't like that."

The soldiers lifted Josh to his feet. One picked up the pile of belongings beside the chair. Another soldier chose that moment to appear with the rest of Josh's belongings, collected from his tent.

Josh's expression was angry and sullen, but he wasn't ready to give up the bravado. "Fuck you, bitch. You can't keep me tied up or locked up forever, and believe me, there's gonna be payback."

"So you know how to build a gate?" Monica asked innocently. "Maybe I wasn't clear enough. These guys are going to take you and the stuff you brought with you—and not one item more, since you've eaten far more than you've earned—back to the university location, and they're going to push you through a gate. And then you can see how well you survive in Lincoln when you don't have a bunch of people to leech off of."

Finally, reality dawned. Josh's eyes got wider, and he exclaimed, "You can't *do* that! You have no right!"

"*Bzzzzt.* Wrong, but thanks for playing." Monica motioned to the soldiers, and they frog-marched Josh off toward a military vehicle that just happened to be waiting nearby.

Monica watched them go, then turned to the crowd of onlookers. There was dead silence. Then someone yelled, "Fascist!"

Monica yelled to the soldiers, "Wait! Hold up!" The soldiers stopped immediately, almost as if they'd been expecting it, and brought Josh back.

"This is your lucky day, Josh!" she said to him. "This guy"—she motioned to the man who had yelled the imprecation—"has volunteered to do your work for you, as well as his own." She turned to the now very uncomfortable-looking man. "What's your name, Chucky?"

His mouth moved a few times, then he squeaked out, "Billy."

Monica smiled at him. "See, Billy, someone needs to do the work that Josh isn't doing, in order to create the resources that Josh is using up. That isn't fascism, it's simple economics. Since you don't like my solution, we'll go with yours. That *was* your solution, wasn't it?" She looked at him with one raised eyebrow.

Billy, looking increasingly uncomfortable, shook his head.

"Oh, my mistake," Monica replied, her grin getting wider. And meaner. "You meant for *someone else* to do the work that Josh doesn't want to do. Okay, how about you turn around and point out five people that you've selected to do the work for Josh."

Monica waited for a moment. Billy seemed to have been struck mute.

"Okay," she continued. "Billy's having a problem making a decision. Can I get volunteers? Five people to do Josh's work so he can sit around all day on a sun chair like a stupid useless piece of shit. Anyone? Anyone? Oh, by the way, we have at least three other lazy assholes that we know of, and we'll need volunteers for them, too. Otherwise we'll be repatriating them as well."

At this point, Monica saw what she'd been waiting for, and why she'd been deliberately drawing things out. Bea had taken a bit of time to find Josh's girlfriend, Nina, and was leading her to the confrontation.

Monica turned to Josh and spoke in a calmer voice, but still clearly enough that the crowd could hear. "See, Josh, you have three choices. You can refuse to pull your weight, and get sent back Earthside. Or you can refuse to pull your weight, and get tossed over the fence. Or you can grow up, be a man, pull your weight, and give your child a father it can look up to and a world it can grow up in."

Josh, who had been looking petulant, did a double-take and said, "What??"

Monica turned to Nina, who was starting to tear up, and said, "Tell him."

Nina looked at Josh with tears running down her face and nodded. Josh staggered with surprise. After a moment he moved toward Nina, the soldiers' grip having magically disappeared. Josh wrapped his arms around her and put his face down on the top of her head. The crowd was already starting to move away, sensing the need for some privacy. Monica walked up to the two, and said to Josh in a low voice, "You can't build a world for your child while sitting in a chair, Josh. And it'll be your baby's food you're eating. You let us know what you decide."

Monica could see Josh's head nodding. She motioned to the soldiers, and they started wrapping up.

❧   ❧   ❧

"Okay, that was impressive," Collins said. "How'd you pull that off? The timing was just too good."

Monica laughed and replied, "A little bird told me that Nina had a doctor's appointment today. I had instructed that little bird to inform me if certain women made appointments, specifically women with lazy assholes for boyfriends. Nina came out with the *I'm-pregnant* look on her face and rubbing her tummy. Mrs. Albertelli didn't raise her no dummies—well, except for my brothers." Monica grinned, and Bea snickered. "Anyway, a guy with a child on the way is either going to grow up real fast or he's going to show himself to be a waste of skin. If Josh had shrugged off the news, I'd have put him through myself without a second thought."

Bea nodded. "And good riddance."

The pair laughed and did a knuckle-bump. Collins shook his head. "You two are really scary, you know that?"

Monica replied, "And Billy needs a big attaboy. He gave a great performance."

11. Earthside: Russian Provinces

Oleksander Fedir watched as his squad worked the equipment. The distant sounds of war were a constant reminder that the Russian army was gradually wearing down and driving back the defenders.

Olek's expression hardened. He yelled at the workers, urging them to greater speed.

Russian troops had been steadily advancing through his homeland, taking territory and resources. But Olek and his compatriots would leave them a little gift. Every field, every load of stored grain, every animal was being laced with a surprise for the invaders. The defenders had to make do with whatever they could get their hands on, but they had the blessing and the cooperation of what was left of their government and military. Radioactive isotopes, nerve gas components, chemical warfare stocks, even pesticides—it all went onto the crops and into the fields. The Russians would conquer a poisoned, unusable land. Olek smiled. It was not ideal, but it was good enough.

12. Hardware Problems

August 27

Another dinosaur hunt was coming to an end. With several hours of video saved on the tablet, the group decided to pack it in. Bill took the handle to the wagon to give Charlie a break, and they began the trek back to the shed they'd dubbed the Mad Science Lab. Partway there, Bill spotted one of his assistant engineers double-timing it out to meet them. That probably wasn't good.

Peter arrived out of breath, but managed to recover in a few seconds. "Matt's looking for you guys. One of their portal boxes quit on them partway through an operation. He needs the spare."

"Which means it's no longer a spare. Dammit." Bill glanced back at the wagon, then at Peter. "Okay, take it. But I think this has just jumped to number one priority."

"Along with all the other number ones?" Monica chided him. "Things will improve once the scavenging runs tail off."

Charlie pulled the cart past the group. "I should go with Peter. Sounds like they need all hands. See you guys later." The two men hurried toward Rivendell, both pulling on the wagon.

"The problem," Bill said to Monica after a pause, "is that the fewer working systems we have, the longer it'll take to get everything across from Earthside. Even the stuff we *can* get across. And every building that collapses before we can clear it, every fire that consumes a few city blocks, is a loss of valuable resources."

"But what can you do?"

"I've been kind of hinting that we should send an expedition to Omaha to visit our erstwhile parts supplier. Maybe I should graduate from subtle hints."

"Subtle? You? Since when?"

Bill replied with a grin and a shrug. "Next meeting. I'll bring it up again."

13. Radio Reception

August 28

Lieutenant Collins looked up as Corporal Timminson entered his office and came to attention. The "office" was really nothing more than a desk, chair, and cot in a large tent. Collins saw no reason to take up space in the long-house—compared to a lot of the residents of Rivendell, he was rattling around in this size tent anyway.

"Report." Collins kept his face neutral, but he had a hard time not breaking into a smile every time he dealt with Timminson. The corporal was newly promoted since Chavez had been discharged, and he took his new position very seriously. Hopefully he'd loosen up a little soon. But for now, it was *yes sir* and *no sir* and salutes on everything.

"Sir, the radio scanning you ordered set up on Earthside has come up with something potentially interesting. Reception's lousy, but we've made out 'Omaha' several times. Whoever is on the other end is terrified and begging for help."

"Any other details, Corporal?"

"No sir. It took several hours of listening to get even that much. Then they went silent, and haven't transmitted again."

"This may finally force the issue," Collins muttered. "Thanks, Timminson. Find me if anything else comes through."

❧ ❧ ❧

Collins found Richard Earthside, working in one of the warehouses in Lincoln. Despite Richard being on the committee and one of the Gate Owners, Collins knew that he made a point of participating in the never-ending manual labor required to prepare the colony for the long term. In this case, they appeared to be moving large quantities of merchandise from *here* to *there*.

"Hey, Tom," Richard said, straightening up and stretching. "Looking for me?"

"Yes. Something I want to discuss with you when you have a moment."

"Now's good." Richard gestured to one of the other workers, who gave a thumbs-up in reply. "Bill's got a bug up his butt about proper storage of our inventory. Something about lack of climate control."

"Uh huh. He's worried about things being stored in cold, damp conditions all winter and being rendered useless. I've gotten the lecture too."

"The guy's going to have a stroke, worrying about so many things at the same time." Richard motioned toward a table in the corner with jugs and cups scattered on it.

Collins picked up a jug and tried to glance inside. "Water," Richard said. "A couple of hours of hauling stuff around, and you really start to appreciate the simple things."

Collins snorted, then told Richard about the radio message.

When he was done, Richard said, "I take it you'd like to go investigate?"

"I think we're obligated to. But Bill has been talking about a trip to Omaha anyway. Something about gate parts. And I understand one just died."

"Not a gate, just the associated portal box." Collins frowned, and Richard hastened to explain. "The gate is the thing we step through. The portal is the box that looks like a tower PC. It actually *is* a tower PC, but with an additional controller board that Matt programmed to Kevin's specs. Either one is useless without the other."

"And the tablets? You guys always seem to be using a tablet to control it."

Richard grinned. "The original portal control system was literally a breadboard rig with rocker switches and analog meters. Straight out of a RadioShack fever dream. But Matt redesigned the U.I. as a web page, which we run on iPads, connected via Bluetooth. It's still kind of a kludge, but—"

"Okay, you've lost me, so there's no point in continuing to shovel more manure. Bottom line—does Bill have a reasonable chance of picking up some parts in Omaha?"

"Actually, yes. The parts supplier we were using—Omega Scientific—is based in Omaha. We had several outstanding orders when Yellowstone blew, so Bill thinks it's possible they might have received at least one order, which could still be in their warehouse or shop or whatever they used for their business." Richard shrugged. "For all we know, it was some guy running a company out of his basement."

"Wow, I am filled with confidence." Collins gave Richard an eye roll. "Nevertheless, it's the best offer we have."

"Agreed. Let's go talk to Bill."

Collins sat down across from Bill at the long table. Bill had been writing in a notebook, and only the look of intense concentration on his face gave any indication that he was doing anything other than doodling.

"What are you working on, Bill?"

Bill looked up. It appeared to take a moment for him to switch mental gears. Then he smiled. "Hey, Tom. I'm working on ideas for building way stations on Greenhouse Earth and Dino Planet. The requirements are obviously very different for each; on one you want to avoid being parboiled, on the other you want to avoid being lunch." Bill chuckled, then continued. "I've actually got an idea I'm working on, but it's so cheap, easy, and obvious that I'm second-guessing myself."

"Well, you can run it past any of us when you're ready," Collins replied. "Meanwhile..." The lieutenant looked up to see Richard entering the longhouse. He gave a small wave, and Richard walked over.

Bill looked from one to the other. "This has the look of a setup. Are you guys about to kidnap me? Say, you aren't aliens disguised as my friends, are you?"

Richard laughed out loud. Collins shook his head and said, "God, I hope that isn't contagious." After a moment, he continued. "Nothing dramatic, Bill. We just wanted to talk to you about an idea I've been playing with. We've been discussing the various factions in the colony that are pushing for different actions. Well, I wanted to have an informal meeting to push my own idea. I'd like to mount an expedition to Omaha, with part of the Guard."

Bill raised an eyebrow. "Okay, I have reasons for being in favor of that. What are your reasons?"

The lieutenant sat back and relaxed in his chair. "For one thing, we've gotten several garbled shortwave messages from Omaha. Not a lot of detail, but the senders appear to be in some kind of danger. It sounds like something that the Guard should be investigating." He hesitated for a moment and shifted slightly. "And in the longer term, you can think of it as a test run. I believe we will have to try for other centers of civilization on Earthside, and soon. The longer we wait, the more death from violence and starvation. I don't really know how bad the roads will be between here and California, for instance. An expedition to Omaha will allow us to test the process. And worst case, we could get back to Lincoln on foot, although that would be a bit of a hike."

Bill nodded. "Honestly, Tom, it feels like a no-brainer. The university there has a full medical track, which will make Krista happy, and a significant engineering department, which might mean more portal parts—which means you can convince some of the other committee members into supporting you if you sell it as a way to build more gates."

Collins nodded thoughtfully. "And there's the radio transmission we received, which means there's still a chance of survivors in Omaha, at least a better chance than there will be come spring. I think we've pretty much found everyone in Lincoln by this point."

"Which would make me happy," Bill replied. "I'll spare you my rant about needing more warm bodies—"

"Appreciate that," Collins interjected.

"And," Richard added, "if you can get the raw materials to build a truly large gate, you'll make Anita happy. And Matt."

"Right." Collins gave Bill a hard stare. "So the next question is, will you come along?"

Bill's face fell. "Sure, because I'm not busy enough already." He sighed. "Sorry, I didn't need to be snarky. But I didn't really think it through until you asked just now, and I don't think I can take the time off."

"Can someone else go in your place?" Collins asked.

"Sure, Matt could go. He knows the gate tech almost as well as me, and the portal side better than me. He's obviously our most experienced scavenger, which seems to me would be a lot more useful than an ability to spend money like water. And he can shoot a gun."

"That last item's not an asset," Collins replied. "I've got enough people who can shoot. And after Monica, I'm even more reluctant to let a civilian get involved."

Bill looked at Collins askance. "She did a great job, I thought."

"Yes, I admit, she did. That time. But she's a bit of a cowboy. Girl. Whatever."

Richard laughed. "Gunzilla. Not for nothing."

"Okay, let's reel this in," Bill said. "Matt can handle it as well as I could. Frankly, he's being underutilized running the salvage ops. Charlie can take that over without a problem. Matt was just running it because he had the only truck for a while."

Collins nodded. "Sounds good. I'll talk to Matt, then bring it up at the next committee meeting." He looked at his watch. "Speaking of which, today's meeting should have already started."

Bill grinned. "Monica says we're developing an attitude of *mañana*, but I think we're just all so busy we can't keep up. It'll start when it starts."

"Twelve pregnancies. Twelve. And counting." Krista rolled her eyes and looked around the table at the other committee members. "I'm beginning to think we'll end up *doubling* our population in a year. Can't you people stop having sex?"

Looks of amused disbelief were enough answer.

"Yeah, well, doesn't work for me either," Krista said with a wry smile.

"I could give it up for Lent, I guess…," Richard said, smiling back at her.

"Too late for you, dummy!" Krista replied, then clapped her hands over her mouth.

A frozen silence descended upon the room. Everyone looked at Richard, then at Krista, then back at Richard, who hadn't moved.

Finally, Krista spoke. "Oh God, I'm sorry. I'm sure Suzie wanted to tell you! She'll kill me!"

"I think you just killed Richard," Bill pointed out.

Richard took a visible breath and his eyes regained focus. "Could, um, we take a recess?"

"Yeah, pretty sure you won't be good for much," Bill said, reaching for the coffee carafe. Everyone else leaned back in their chairs and grinned at Richard's rapidly disappearing backside.

An hour later, they were back in session. Bill pointed to Richard and said, "You know, that starts to hurt after a while." Richard looked confused, and Bill pantomimed a large grin.

"I'll live," Richard answered, still beaming. "So, what've we got for today?"

"Well, other than the obvious good news, we've also had some more fights," Krista began. "A couple were over personal issues, one was an attempted theft. No weapons used yet, but I think it's a matter of time. On the attempted theft, bystanders got in on it. The miscreant is pretty beat up, which of course uses up *my* team's resources."

Collins cut in. "This place is getting wilder than the Wild West. We've been okay so far because our citizens are basically intelligent, educated people who've been raised in a civilized society and are in the habit of acting in a law-abiding way. Most of them, anyway. But that wears off. Plus, they're still mostly twenty-somethings, so inclined to hot-headedness. I'd say we're probably a month or less away from a fatal shooting."

"So what do we do?" Nick asked.

"We need a formal government, as I've been carping about at every meeting," the lieutenant answered. "Laws, justice system policies, and so on. Eventually we'll even need a monetary system of some kind."

Richard sighed. "Yeah, I get it. We've got the basic survival stuff mostly nailed—" Bill snorted derisively, and Richard glared at him. "I guess it's time to start thinking about the social stuff. We should probably put together a committee to look into it. I'll talk to one of the Poli-Sci guys." He made a note, then pointed to Nick.

"The longhouses are way ahead of schedule. I'm not used to having workers who have so much personal invest-ment in the outcome, I guess." Nick smiled at the group. "The indoor plumbing seems to be a huge incentive. We decided since we have the time, we'd put in sinks and show-ers too."

"I can hardly wait," Krista said. "How many people per house?"

"We're designing them to handle up to two hundred in a pinch, but fifty is optimal if people are going to have some privacy. Initially, everyone will be sleeping on the floor, until we build enough for the entire population. If we find the need, we'll build or import bunk beds."

"There's something I need to bring up," Bill cut in. "Not something we necessarily need to take action on right away, but we need to think about it. Right now, most of our material and supplies are still coming overside, courtesy of the scavenging group. But that's been drying up. Roofs will continue to collapse, stuff will get damaged as the elements get into buildings, there will be more fires, and so on. Sooner or later we have to start making our own, and that goes for everything from penicillin to bunk beds. I know it'll be great if we can build a bigger gate and bring across farming equipment and fuel trucks, but eventually we have to consider horse-powered alternatives. And so on."

Richard rubbed his chin in thought for a moment. "That's something else we're going to have to go into in more depth at some point. Bill, maybe you and Nick can agree on the top three items that are going to be our biggest issues. We'll have another look at it next meeting." Richard looked around the table. "Good?"

Everyone nodded, but no one was in a hurry to leave as long as the carafe still held coffee.

14. IN COMMITTEE

August 29

Everyone was seated, holding steaming mugs. Technically the committee meeting was in session, but so far not much was getting done. The silence stretched longer than usual, as no one seemed to want to break it.

Finally, Bill put down his mug with a *thump* and gestured to Krista with his chin. "So, any bombs you'd like to drop on us this morning?"

Krista laughed, gave Bill the finger, then said to Richard, "I am still embarrassed about that. You guys are okay?"

Richard chuckled. "S'okay. Suzie says the sight of me looking like a deer in the headlights more than made up for the blown surprise."

He took another sip of his coffee, then put it down and activated his tablet. "Okay, meeting of the committee, yadda, yadda, come to order, blah blah. Krista, you first."

Krista nodded. "I had another patient in last night who was pretty beat up. There's some guy who's apparently got an anger control issue—"

"That'd be Jimmy," Monica cut in. "Again. The guy seems to fancy himself an underworld heavy or something now. He's actually tried to shake a lot of people down."

Krista continued, "Yes, and he's a big guy, so there was some significant damage. I'm actually going to bump up the

tenor of my whining about lack of equipment because of it."
She smiled at Matt, who started looking at the ceiling, out
the window, at his notes, while whistling tunelessly.

"Monica, anything you can do about this guy?" Richard
said.

"Sure," she replied, "but most of my options involve
shooting him." A few people started to chuckle then cut it
off when Monica showed no trace of amusement. "Seriously,
Richard, this isn't the type of guy who can be reasoned with.
Back on Earth, he'd be destined to die in a shootout or in
prison. He's just going to keep pushing until we have to deal
with him like we would a dangerous animal."

Richard sighed. "Okay, let's table that for now. I think
it's going to be a part of our discussion about formal government." After a moment, he continued. "Bill?"

Bill put his coffee cup down. "Water and electricity
services, nothing noteworthy. I'm sure you've all heard
about our adventures with spying on Dino Planet. If anyone wants to see the video, I just finally got it transferred
to my phone."

Several people put up their hands, and Bill passed his
phone along. There were exclamations of amazement and
delight, along with comments about "dipping birds" and
some laughter.

"Yeah, Monica wants to return to Earth so she can
publish a paper on Forelimb Atrophy as an Evolutionary
Adaptation for Weight Distribution."

Monica grinned and gave a *What's your point?* shrug.

When Bill had his phone back, he continued. "I've got
an idea for building way stations on alternate Earths, *including* Greenhouse Earth. But the truck gate isn't quite big
enough, so I'm going to be upping my whining about getting more materials to build a bigger one."

He looked at Matt with a grin. Matt looked up at the ceiling and started repeating, "Blue room. Blue room..."

Richard turned to Collins. "Tom, I think that segues nicely into what you wanted to bring up."

Collins nodded, leaned forward and placed his elbows on the table. "I've been speaking to people individually on this, but I guess this will be my official request now that I have all my ducks in a row. I want to mount an expedition to Omaha, using part of the Guard. This would accomplish several goals: looking for medical supplies, engineering parts, refugees, any other military units, and providing a dry run and training exercise for an expedition further afield. Which we all know is both inevitable and morally necessary."

"You'd need a gate," Matt said.

"We'd need *two* gates," Collins replied. "I'm expecting that to be one of the sticking points..."

"And you'd win that bet!" Matt replied, a crazed expression on his face. "Head exploding in 3...2...1..."

Tom laughed, and then added, "...which includes the truck gate."

Matt sighed and closed his eyes for a few seconds. "It means essentially no scavenging operations while the Omaha expedition is gone. And it means no backup here." He glared at Bill.

Bill looked at Richard. "Help me out here. We had most of the items we needed for a fourth portal and the locomotive gate. What were we missing? I know for the gate hardware, it was some wave guides and two lasers."

Richard thought for a second. "Actually, for the portal box, it was just a PC power supply and backplane. We could rip the innards out of any old tower PC and use that, as long as it didn't have a bargain-basement power supply." He looked at Matt. "If you can find a name-brand PC over the next couple of days, we'll have solved half the problem."

Bill added, "And although I don't have enough to make the truly huge gate I was trying for, I *may* have enough for a somewhat smaller one. Maybe even big enough for a ten-foot culvert section."

"Say what?"

Bill smiled. "For the interdimensional way stations. You take a section of ten-foot culvert—you know, the corrugated pipe they put under roads to let creeks and rivers through—you place it on end, you dig out the ground in the middle and under the edges. The culvert gradually settles into the ground, giving you your reinforced walls at the same time. When you have it completely in the ground, you cap it, cut an entrance of some kind, and then cover it with a foot or two of soil."

Everyone thought about this for a few seconds, then Collins said, "So…about Omaha. We were talking about Omaha…"

"Um, yeah," Richard said. "Bill and Matt, see if you can set us up with a fourth gate and portal. If you're successful, then I don't see anything in the way of the expedition."

15. Playing with Gates

August 30

"Ready?" Kevin had the tablet, and his finger was poised over the "OK."

Bill nodded. They were just connecting to Earthside, so this wasn't a particularly dangerous move, but they had established protocols for the gates. As such, Bill was standing in front of it with a shotgun, and Kevin was standing off to the side so that he would be out of the line of fire if there was trouble.

They were using the new portal and gate, which Bill had managed to make big enough for a mid-sized car. For testing, they had shoved it up against one of the sheds so that they would only have to worry about one side.

Kevin hesitated for one more second, then pressed the button. The interface shimmered into existence, then showed the warehouse parking lot, still burdened with a significant amount of ash. In the middle distance, a group of crows was picking away at a couple of food sources. Bill and Kevin looked at each other and made disgusted faces; neither wanted to get a close-up of what several weeks would have done to two corpses.

"Well, the new system works," Bill said. "Might as well shut it down, and I'll disassemble it."

Kevin poked at the tablet a few times and the interface closed.

As he started to disassemble the gate, Bill said, "Hey, Kevin, there's something that's been bugging me. Remember the night we brought Monica on board and the Smilodon tried to climb through the interface?" At Kevin's nod, he continued, "Well, I understood the whole *go where it most likely is* thing, but what if the subject didn't have the freedom to do so?"

Kevin perked up as he was presented with a scientific problem. "What do you mean?"

"Well, at the simplest, what about throwing a rope through the gate and staking it to the ground on both sides? Or better yet, put a bale of hay on the west side of the Outland gate and one on the east side of the Earthside gate, then poke a stick halfway through the interface and turn the gate off. The stick can't end up on the Outland side because it would be embedded in the Outland hay, and it can't end up on the Earth side because it'll be embedded in the Earthside hay."

Kevin looked at Bill in surprise for a few seconds, then his face went slack.

"Buddy, you've got to stop doing that. Really," Bill said to him. There was no response, so Bill shrugged and continued to disassemble and load the gate.

A few minutes later, Kevin sat up straight and his face reanimated. "Just from some cursory calculations, the minimum-energy solution would be for the object to continue to stick through the interface."

"Even without power?"

"Yep. It'd be more work to do anything else, including slicing or ejecting the stick. Also, I think at that point it's a non-collapsible hypervolume, so it can't close anyway."

Bill thought about this for a few seconds. "What if the stick was a pipe? Could something go through the pipe and cross over?"

"I, uh, I don't see why not. I'd like to try, though."

"You and me both."

"So what we have here, Kevin, is a length of ABS sewer pipe." Bill held up a six-foot length of four-inch drain pipe, originally scavenged from Home Depot. "I now direct your attention to these seemingly ordinary rebar rods." Bill held up a pair of three-foot lengths of rebar.

"They *are* ordinary, Bill," Kevin said.

Bill smirked. "There's a heckler in every crowd. Just turn on the gate."

Kevin complied, and Bill stepped through.

They'd had to move the gate around until they could find a patch of unpaved soil on Earthside. Now Bill drove a rod into the ground on Earthside, then stepped through and did the same in Outland. Finally, he placed the piece of pipe on the end of each rod, through the holes that he'd drilled, and placed a small clamp so that it held the pipe tightly to the bar. The end result was a pipe sticking through the interface, half on Earthside and half on Outland, secured to the ground at each end.

Bill stepped back to Outland, then indicated to Kevin to turn off the gate. Kevin operated the tablet, and the interface faded out, leaving just a large empty metal hoop through which the Outland scenery was framed.

Except for the pipe, which ended in midair, right at the plane of the gate.

The two walked up to it and walked slowly around it. Bill then leaned over and looked through one end, while Kevin looked through the other.

"I see Earthside," Bill said. "Looking at the street."

"Me too, except I see the building," Kevin said.

Bill unclipped the clamp holding the Outland end to the rebar, and pushed the pipe slowly up off the bar. There was a bang, a flash of light that didn't illuminate anything, and the pipe disappeared.

Bill and Kevin looked at each other, smiles slowly growing on both faces. "That is *so* cool!" they both said simultaneously.

"We don't need the portal equipment anymore?" Richard had a disbelieving look on his face.

"No, no." Bill waved his hands in the air in negation. "We need the gate and portal to open a connection, but if you stick a pipe through it and secure it, the connection can't collapse. You end up with a path through the pipe that's persistent, as long as you don't free the pipe from its restraint on either end." He grinned. "It means we can create interfaces from world to world without having to have umpty-ump gates and portal boxes. You create a gate opening for people, disassemble the gate from around the pipe, and walk away."

Richard's jaw dropped. "Okay, that's huge … "

Bill nodded. "It also makes checking for alternate human civilizations suddenly a lot more practical. But now I *really* need that big gate so I can push those culverts through. I sure hope Matt has good luck with the supplier."

16. Confrontation

August 31

Monica and Bea were taking a rare break in the long-house when a woman burst in. "Jimmy's beating on someone again," she forced out between gasps.

Bea dropped a baseball bat that she'd been casually balancing on one finger and checked that her weapon was in place. Monica made sure of her sidearm and grabbed a little something special that the scavengers had come back with a few days ago. That something was a Taser, and Monica had immediately set it aside for Jimmy.

Bea called to a couple of Guard troops as she and Monica followed the woman. It wasn't hard to find the altercation; a sizeable crowd had gathered. People were yelling insults at Jimmy, but no one was willing to step in and intervene, given his size.

Monica pushed her way through the crowd and found Jimmy Korniski holding some guy by the collar with one hand and slapping him open-handed with the other. He was yelling something, punctuated by each blow, but Monica didn't bother trying to figure out what the issue was. The fight—if it could be called that—wasn't even remotely an even contest. You could have made two of the other guy out of one Jimmy. Without breaking stride, Monica ran right up and stuck the Taser into his side. There was a crackling

66

sound and Jimmy went rigid. Bea grabbed the other guy and pulled him away as Jimmy hit the ground like a felled tree.

Monica turned to one of the onlookers. "What was it about this time?"

The man shrugged. "Nothing, really. Ted there was trying to explain something about volcanoes to Jimmy, and Jimmy wasn't having it. So Ted made some crack, asking how many geology courses Jimmy had taken. Of course, asshole there decided some 'shrimp' wasn't going to talk to him that way…"

Monica sighed and looked up to heaven. "Right. The usual bullshit. Thinks people should tiptoe around him." She turned back to Jimmy, who had regained partial control and was slowly heaving himself around to a sitting position. Someone had already taken Ted over to Medical.

Monica looked down at Jimmy, and he glared back defiantly. "That was your last free life, Jimmy. Next infraction, you're going back Earthside. There's nothing about you that's useful enough to put up with this crap."

She glared at him, waiting for his backtalk. Unusually for Jimmy, he said nothing, just glared back at her. Monica shrugged at Bea, glanced at the soldiers, and motioned back to the longhouse. Leaving Jimmy still sitting on the ground, they walked away.

"He's going to be trouble," Monica said.

"He's *already* being trouble," Bea replied, again balancing the baseball bat on one finger.

Monica sighed, leaned forward and put her elbows on the table. "The Committee is talking about formalizing a lot of things, like structure and rules and such. Right now, I'm thinking that's a pretty good idea. I'll give you better than even odds that the next time we have a confrontation with Jimmy, we'll have to shoot him."

Bea nodded. "The fact that he doesn't fit in with a crowd composed mostly of academics doesn't really help. I doubt he's even got his high school diploma. He's trying to be a local tough guy and form his own gang, and no one is really interested. So people try to ignore him, and it just spirals."

Monica smiled, a little bleakly. "I think I'm going to suggest to the Guards that are still on duty that they start carrying zip ties. We should probably do so as well."

"And the Tasers," Bea added. "Maybe Matt can find some more of them."

"Sure, go ahead and suggest it. If you can take the eye-rolls."

"And the overacting."

17. EARTHSIDE: FOOD RIOTS

The angry mob surged forward against the police line. It was a futile gesture, as the line was bolstered by military personnel, but the crowd was long past rational decisions.

It was the sixth straight day of food riots in France. Other European countries were also experiencing recurring riots, but none with the dependability or enthusiasm of the French citizenry.

The first day of unrest had started out as another demonstration by the labor unions against cutbacks and layoffs. The unions had miscalculated, however. Citizens facing the prospect of no food on the table had run out of sympathy for workers protesting cutbacks in sick days or vacation pay. The result had been dozens dead, and scores more injured. Since then, the streets had been held by people looking for the government to provide simply the basic necessities.

The police and military responded with tear gas and water cannons. Just enough force was applied to keep the mob from overrunning the line. The police were well aware that the people they faced were rapidly running out of strength.

In a few more days, the streets would be empty, regardless of government response.

Etienne flipped through the channels, trying to find some news. As his thumb pressed the *up* button in a steady rhythm, he admitted to a certain surprise that the TV was working at all. According to any post-apocalypse movie he'd ever seen, by now people should be running around in S&M garb and eating each other.

Instead, he still had working channels, although not nearly as many as before; electricity most of the time; and, most important, a roof over his head. The landlord wasn't attempting to collect rent anymore, concluding quite correctly that tenants who weren't paying were still better than squatters.

Etienne had always been a loner and an inveterate bookworm. Now, with no job and no real responsibilities, he had all the time in the world to indulge himself. As long as the internet stayed up, anyway.

Etienne glanced at the door to his apartment, where a metal security pole was wedged under the door handle. He had cut a notch in the hardwood floor for the butt end of the pole, an act that would have gotten him evicted in another time. Now it would hold against almost anything; an invader would have to break the door itself to get through.

A large supply of canned and packaged foods and drums of water completed his fortress of solitude. He'd been rotating a stockpile for years, thanks to those same end-of-the-world movies and books. As long as the utilities held out, life was pretty good.

18. Omaha Preparation

September 1

Lieutenant Collins walked into the Mad Science Lab and looked around. Spotting Bill, he waved and walked over. "Hey, Bill. How goes it?"

Bill smiled back. "Hey, Tom. Well, mostly good news, and the rest is not really bad. We got a couple of PCs back from Matt's last expedition—and some medical supplies, which Krista was really happy about, but that's another story. With the PCs, we've been able to build a fourth portal box. It doesn't leave us with a lot of spare parts, so nothing had better break.

"As for the gate, I was able to make a car gate. Which means it's not as big as the truck gate. You can get your average car through, but that's about it. Still modular, though, so it can be disassembled and passed through the six-footers."

"So you're still in business while we're gone," Collins said.

"Right. But the trucks will have to stay on this side while they scavenge on Earthside. Oh, and Matt's okay with going to Omaha. I talked to him. Charlie will take over the Asset Reclamation Group, and cover for Matt in committee while he's gone."

"Asset Reclamation Group?"

Bill smiled at him. "Charlie's new name. I think he's just marking his territory, now that he's in charge. They call it ARG. Usually with feeling. Everyone approves."

Collins chuckled. "Seems appropriate, actually. So we'll be taking four trucks and all three Humvees. We debated taking the fifth truck but decided to leave it here for emergencies. But I want lots of firepower in case we run into something on the way."

"Oh, hey, you'll never get an argument from me about being overprepared!" Bill grinned, and Collins laughed. Bill's knowledge of plot twists and ironic movie endings was legendary, as was his paranoia about the unexpected.

"Corporal Timminson will be coming with us. Chavez is still officially discharged, but she's agreed to be a consultant for the duration if and when necessary. I've put Private Hardwick in charge here."

"Sounds good. You mean Sarah, right? She seems not especially crazy. Hopefully she'll be bored stiff the whole time."

"Here's hoping."

The two gave each other very sloppy parting salutes, and Collins headed out to work on his preparations.

19. EARTHSIDE:
ILLEGAL EMIGRANTS

After the Yellowstone eruption, there were massive migrations of American populations, fleeing unlivable locations for what they hoped would be better conditions. Those who were able joined the populations of other states. However, migrations were always along the path of least resistance, and many states closed their borders once their populations reached saturation, which inevitably altered the flow of refugees. Many people soon found themselves on the Mexican border.

The irony of refuges from America trying to cross over southward wasn't lost on the government of Mexico. In fact, in an example of overwhelming celebratory payback, the Mexican administration closed its borders to all entry from America and enacted border controls even more draconian than those formerly used by the U.S. government. Several hundred American citizens died before the point was made.

But there was one major difference between the current and previous situations. These refugees included some of the most gun-crazy, highly armed people on the planet, from a culture that virtually *invented* the concept of Manifest Destiny.

The first sign the Mexican border guard had that there was a problem was a series of simultaneous explosions spaced out over several miles along the border. This was immediately followed by a concerted rush of heavily if somewhat miscellaneously armed invaders. As the Mexican guard moved to head them off, they were pelted by a series of rocket-propelled grenades. The guard moved back into defensive positions, only to find themselves now subjected to mortar fire and a steady strafing from machine gun emplacements.

The last straw came when the artillery shelling started. Within minutes, the Mexican military was in full retreat, and the colonization of Mexico began in earnest.

Ned Feller grinned as he crouched and aimed. This was the way it should be. No rules, no laws, just the application of power by those who had it. The betas would just have to accept their place in the new order. He grunted in disappointment as the Mexican soldier disappeared behind a building. Well, no matter. He'd get that one or another one sooner or later. There was certainly no lack of targets. These uneducated peasants had no balls. As soon as they'd lost the advantage, they ran.

Ned grunted as he stood, his belly pushing against a bulletproof vest that was still too tight, even after weeks of skimpy rations. Well, it was one way to stay on a diet, he supposed. But there would be more to eat once they'd cleared this town of the former owners. He glanced left and right, but his flankers were out of sight. That wasn't really a good—

Pain lanced up his leg and he fell heavily on his side. He looked down at his thigh, where blood was fountaining out of a wound. Trying to regain some control, Ned reached for his AR, which had slid a few feet away when he fell. Before he could drag it to him, a booted foot stomped down on the strap.

Ned looked up at a Mexican soldier. The soldier grinned down at him and pointed his weapon at Ned's head.

The last thing Ned heard was "Hasta la vista, baby," done in a truly atrocious Austrian accent.

20. OMAHA EXPEDITION

September 3

The Guard was lined up, three Hummers and four trucks ready to move out. They had decided to take a minimal number of personnel in order to leave as much carrying capacity as possible for refugees and salvage. One of the trucks was pulling a fuel trailer. And two dirt bikes, driven by Crazy Al and Joaquin, would be assisting the convoy in getting out of Lincoln.

Near the front of the line, a small crowd of people stood, comparing notes and making last-minute suggestions.

"We'll be radioing every evening," Lieutenant Collins said, "but we don't really know how well the pole-cam will work for shortwave reception. We have to accept that we may be out of communication for the duration."

Richard nodded. "Not sure what we could do anyway. I'm just hoping there's nothing out there big enough to take out your whole unit."

"You and me both," Collins replied, smiling. "And if we run into people, we'll be sending them back here. Charlie and his crew will monitor the warehouse area on a daily basis. You'll be prepared for an influx, right?"

Richard nodded. "Bill will be happy, anyway. More people means more workers."

Charlie glanced at Matt, then gestured to a man standing beside him. "Norm will be tasked with checking the warehouse area every day for new arrivals."

Matt grinned at Norm. "So you're the new assistant gatekeeper? Don't let Charlie B.S. you. I absolutely have not had him going 24/7."

Norm smiled back and shrugged. "The hours may suck, but at least the pay is lousy."

The lieutenant looked at his watch. "Time to go. We'll try to keep this to three weeks maximum. If you haven't heard from us by the end of that time, *then* start worrying."

He gave a minimal salute to Richard and turned to the lead Hummer. Giving the *Go* sign, he climbed in. The sound of multiple large vehicles starting up broke the morning calm.

Kevin, meanwhile, had opened the truck gate. Monica and Bea stood on either side of it, watching for trouble from Earthside.

The trucks started forward. As soon as they had all gone through, the truck gate was shut down, disassembled, and passed through the smaller gate to the waiting soldiers on the other side.

"Sure hope we don't end up regretting that," Richard said.

The convoy waited until the truck gate had been stowed, then started moving again.

In the lead vehicle, Matt and Collins sat in the back, while a soldier with an assault rifle sat in the shotgun seat, and Corporal Timminson drove.

"We're going to try going straight up the highway," Collins said. "This will give us a good indication about how bad the major routes might be."

Matt nodded. "Assuming we can get out of Lincoln ... "

The lieutenant grinned. "Well, there is that."

An hour later, Collins was forced to concede that Matt had been right on the money. Several attempted routes out of town had each put the convoy at the back end of a virtual parking lot of abandoned and broken-down vehicles.

"We'd be all day pulling vehicles out of the way, sir," Timminson said.

"Off-road?" Matt asked.

"We should try, I suppose," Collins replied. Getting out of the vehicle, he signaled to the dirt bikes. The two riders, Al and Joaquin, had been assigned to give the convoy any required assistance getting out of Lincoln, and this situation was exactly what had been anticipated.

"Al and Joaquin will see if they can find us a route," Collins said to Matt as he climbed back into the cab. Then, to Timminson, "Shut it down. No point in wasting fuel while we're waiting."

Timminson shut off the engine then radioed the other vehicles to do the same.

In less than ten minutes, the bikes were back. Al leaned into the window and said, "We've found a pretty direct route, as long as you're okay with knocking over a few fences."

"If someone complains, we'll apologize profusely," Collins replied. "And offer them a ride. Let's do this."

In just over an hour, leaving a trail of destruction behind them, the convoy finally drove up onto the freeway.

The ash didn't look like it would be a problem. Most of it had been washed off the raised roadway by the unusually heavy rainfall over the last couple of weeks. What ash remained had been packed down to the consistency of clay. For the large military tires, it would not be an issue.

However, while the freeway wasn't a total parking lot as the city streets had been, it was obvious that the convoy was not going to be hitting the speed limit, or even coming close. Many, perhaps most vehicles had attempted to pull over to the shoulders when they died. But this had evidently happened in waves, so there were several rows of dead vehicles on each side of the highway, leaving limited space in the middle for navigation. Any accidents or stalls in the remaining roadway would have to be cleared.

Collins sighed. "This is going to be a slog. I don't think we'll be getting to Omaha today."

Matt shrugged. "That's no kind of surprise. I guess Bill's pessimism has been rubbing off on me. Only now I call it *realism*."

21. RETRIBUTION

September 4

Monica left the longhouse, rubbing her eyes. Another long day. She'd never in her life had trouble getting to sleep at night, but since coming to Rivendell, she was often unconscious before she'd finished climbing into bed.

They'd just finished a late-evening discussion of "gearing down," Bill's term for developing lower-technology alternatives for things they depended on. She was sure she'd heard the term before, but couldn't remember where.

Kevin had been surprisingly helpful. While his interests tended to be narrow, his memory was truly astounding, even concerning things that he'd only heard in passing. For instance, he knew the exact process for creating penicillin, having once read a biography of Fleming. Monica smiled to herself. Life in Outland had affected different people in different ways. In Kevin's case, it had been all to the good. He was still quiet, and would never be a sparkling conversationalist, but he could talk to people now without lecturing, and had developed actual friendships.

Lost in her thoughts, Monica failed to react quickly enough to movement at the corner of her eye. There was a powerful blow to the side of her head, and she went down hard. As the stars started to clear, she felt a hand grab her by the hair and haul her up.

"Fucking bitch!" she heard. "I'm going to teach you some *respect*! Before you die, you'll be begging me for mercy!" There was another blow, and Monica went down again. This time she managed to retain enough awareness to turn her head and see Jimmy in the dim light, rage on his face.

Monica reached for her sidearm, but she was too groggy to handle the movement quickly. Jimmy laughed, a short ugly grunt, and grabbed her arm. He bent it back, hard. She managed to bite back a scream, but couldn't stop a moan from escaping.

Jimmy smiled—a nasty, evil smile—and said, "Oh, that's just the beginning." He pulled back his fist to deliver a straight punch...

And suddenly someone was on him, arms and legs wrapped around his upper body and head. She could hear yelling. It was Kevin, calling for help. Jimmy roared with rage and tried to pull Kevin off, but it was like trying to remove a cat that has latched on in panic.

Monica was still trying to get her sidearm out, but couldn't seem to make her limbs work properly. She gritted her teeth and attempted to focus all her attention on getting her hand onto her gun.

Meanwhile Jimmy had managed to land a couple of awkward punches that knocked the wind out of Kevin. Shouting from nearby indicated that someone had seen what was happening.

Jimmy finally ripped Kevin off of him. Holding Kevin in the air with one hand—Monica was impressed at the sheer strength of the guy—Jimmy started to punch him as he dangled. Kevin was managing to mostly deflect the blows, but he was getting visibly weaker.

Suddenly there was a wet *smack*, and Jimmy screamed and went down on one knee. It took Monica a moment to focus. Then she realized it was Bea, and she was waving her bat like a katana. As Jimmy dropped Kevin, Bea wound up and brought the bat down on his arm. Jimmy screamed again and hugged his arm to his body. Now Bea turned the bat and thrust the end of it into Jimmy's forehead. It sounded like a coconut being broken open. Jimmy went over on his back. He wasn't out cold, but he was definitely out of fight.

At this point, one of the Guards arrived and pulled out a couple of zip ties. It took only a few seconds to truss Jimmy up. Several bystanders came over to help Monica and Kevin up. Both were bleeding from the mouth and nose. Monica went over to Kevin and gently put her arms around him. She could feel him go rigid for a moment, then he relaxed and hugged back.

The committee had been called to emergency session. In the room were Richard, Monica, Kevin, Bill, Bea, and the Guard who had arrived at the end, Private Hardwick.

Bea was in a rage and waving her bat to punctuate each statement. She had created a one-bat-radius exclusion zone around herself. "Just *shoot* the motherfucker," she snarled. "Treat him like a rabid dog!"

"Bea, I can't begin to tell you how much I'd like to do that," Richard said. "In fact, I'd be okay with you beating him to death with that bat, and I'd cheer you on." Bea looked down at the bat as if just realizing it was there. With a slightly sheepish expression, she put it down on the table. Other people edged over to fill the now non-lethal space.

"We've been talking about formalizing things," Monica said. The medical team had done what they could, but her face was bruised and swollen, and she was having a little trouble speaking clearly. "As usual, too little, too late. We can't wait for a constitutional convention to create laws. We're going to have to decide *now* what to do with this cretin. And then *do* it."

Richard thought for a few seconds, rubbing his chin. "Actually, I'm thinking maybe a full vote by everyone would be a good idea. It'll force people to think about the problem, and make them feel like they're part of the decision-making process. Maybe they'll be less inclined to just let some committee make decisions after that. It'll be a good dry run for the constitutional convention, too."

Bill leaned forward in his chair, nodding. "Yeah, give them a list of options. Simple paper ballot, choose one through five. Majority rules. Choices might be everything from incarceration to hard labor, repatriation, or firing squad."

"Good thoughts, Bill," Richard replied. "But let's add *do nothing* to one end of that list."

"What? Why?" Monica said angrily, then flinched in pain from sore flesh.

"There will be people who will complain about any list we give them. So we give them that option so they can't complain that we forced them into anything. And if they complain that they didn't like any of the options, we'll tell them they should have suggested an alternative. Not that it matters. We'll get a half-dozen people who will vote that way anyway. And another dozen who will complain anyway."

"I'd like to add something to the other end," Kevin added. "Exile to Dino Planet." The others looked at him in surprise. "I'm not being vindictive," he explained. "I'm being logical. Punishment implies some hope of rehabilitation, and I don't see that happening in this case. Repatriation just hands the problem off to someone else. And a lot of people don't like capital punishment. Exile is like sending a mean dog to the pound. And I think that describes Jimmy about perfectly."

Kevin stopped, visibly embarrassed. This was probably the longest non-math-related speech he had ever made.

He needn't have worried. The response consisted entirely of thoughtful nods. Monica spoke up—carefully. "I like it. It covers everything that's possible, and gives people a range of choices. Let's do that."

Sam cleared his throat. Everyone looked at him. "Planning on having a trial?"

"What for?" Monica asked incredulously. "Is there any doubt that he did it?"

Sam shook his head sadly. "Not the least bit, Monica. But trials aren't just about guilt or innocence. First, they're a statement that we aren't a mob; we have laws, and we follow them. It would be a very bad thing if we started this new society by forgetting that. And they're also about mental state, extenuating circumstances, intent, accomplices, and level of crime. For instance, I'd have no problem pegging Jimmy for first-degree attempted murder for his attack on you. He planned it, he hid and waited, and he stated his intention to kill you. For Kevin, not so much. Kevin just got in the way. Sorry, Kevin, I know it hurts just as much. So for Kevin, second-degree battery or something like that. Now, I'm not a lawyer, so that's a layman's understanding of how these things work. But you get the idea."

Richard nodded and sat back. "Sam's right. We don't want to start this off by acting like a mob. We'll have a trial. We'll make it fair. And *if* we find him guilty"—several people snorted—"then we'll let the citizenry decide on the sentence. Sound good?"

One by one, each person around the table indicated their agreement.

22. In the Kitchen

September 5

Suzie made her way slowly to the large cooking area that people laughingly referred to as a kitchen. Originally constructed under tents and tarps, the kitchen had recently been moved into one of the partially constructed longhouses. It was a significant improvement over the previous open-air setup, but would be even better when the plumbing system started delivering hot and cold running water.

She was surprised to find she was a little excited. It had taken a while, but the Animal Sciences team had finally built up their chicken population to the point where the birds could produce a significant supply of eggs. Suzie's group had been saving them up for a week, and now they had a fridge full of eggs and all the other ingredients for a half-decent omelet. Of course, it wouldn't be much per person, so breakfast would still include a large portion of bison, but it was a milestone, and exciting for the colony. She expected a large, early turnout this morning.

As she walked along, lost in her planning, she suddenly realized Creepy Guy was approaching. *Every frigging morning!* she thought to herself. Suzie felt a little sorry for him. She understood why everyone called him Creepy Guy, but it sure couldn't be fun for him. She smiled at him as he went past, and he made that face that he always did, which she *thought* might be his version of a smile.

Well, never hurts to be nice to people, she thought, and continued on.

Arriving at the kitchen, she found that several of her coworkers were already busy. They'd done some planning the day before, as this was going to be a big deal and no one wanted to blow it. Suzie quickly washed up and then dove into the familiar comfortable routine of meal prep.

Maddie nudged her with an elbow as they were working and said, "So how's things going with the new beau? Any gossip worth sharing?"

"You're insatiable, Maddie! But then, so is Richard..." Suzie's smile turned into a grin, and she blushed slightly, and Maddie laughed loud enough to turn heads.

"Now *that's* what I like to hear!" she said. After a moment she asked, "Have you seen Trish lately? She's starting to show."

Suzie took a moment to hand off a full bowl to the next worker, then nodded. "And Alex wants her to stop riding horses. You can imagine how *that's* going over." Trish's love of riding, and her skill at it, had become legendary. She was effectively the lead horse wrangler for the colony, and everyone deferred to her judgment. Everyone except Alex.

"Will it be a problem for them?" Maddie asked. "They make such a cute couple."

"Not a chance. They adore each other. They'll argue for a while, then Alex will give in. It's the natural order."

Maddie chuckled. "Well, looks like we're ready." She looked at the large crowd waiting for the serving line to open. "And so are they!"

23. FLYING LESSONS

Bill flew carefully into the updraft. The dark terrain below was creating a steady upflow of air that had attracted several birds of prey. The birds were slowly circling and gaining altitude. Bill eased the ultralight into the air current and began to do the same. He looked back at Goro Yoshida, who nodded in approval.

Bill turned to stare at the birds that he was sharing the air with. He was, as usual, amazed and delighted at the complete lack of fear they displayed.

Of course, they had never learned a reason to fear anything in the air. One of them, a falcon of some kind, floated just off his left wing, studying him just as intently in return. Bill smiled and gestured wordlessly to the bird. Goro nodded and spoke, his voice only slightly raised over the engine noise. "Just make sure he doesn't get in front of us, or he might get pulled in."

After a few more minutes, Goro tapped Bill on the shoulder and indicated that he should cut the engine. Bill complied, and the resultant silence was almost a transcendental experience. The ultralight immediately started to sink, and Bill quickly adjusted his glide path to pick up the updraft again.

"You'd get better lift, of course, if there weren't two of us," Goro noted.

Bill nodded without comment, concentrating on finding the sweet spot. The falcon, still fascinated and now emboldened by the lack of noise, moved in closer.

For this, I'd almost give up engineering.

Goro pointed, his hand just poking into Bill's peripheral vision. "Looks like a migration. Going south for the winter, you think?"

Bill looked in the indicated direction, and saw a massive herd of something—it was too far away to make out the species—moving more or less as a unit. He glanced at his compass. Sure enough, they were heading south. And in early September. That seemed ominous.

Bill turned in his seat to face Goro. "Seeing migrations this early concerns me. It's not even officially autumn yet. Are we in for it this winter?"

"Only one way to find out, unfortunately. We'd better be ready for the worst, though. We'll have to lay in some extra firewood."

"No," Bill replied, "we've got the pellet stoves, and Matt found a pellet press. I'm going to suggest we try to harvest all the dead trees in Lincoln instead. I don't want to raze this entire environment in our first year."

Bill could hear the smile in Goro's voice as he replied. "Are you turning into a closet greenie, Bill?"

"Not that over the top, no. But it's not all or nothing. There's a whole spectrum of possible responses between tree-hugger and rabid capitalist."

"True. I don't want to die for the environment, but if we can do the same thing two different ways..."

"Pick the less damaging. Yeah." Bill pointed to his eight o'clock, where they could clearly see Rivendell and the immediate environs. "It already looks like a scar on the land. I guess there's no help for that, with more than four hundred people now, but… Aw, I dunno, Goro. I guess I'm getting sucked into all the arguing, despite my best efforts."

"Y'know—watch it, Bill, you're falling out of the updraft—we really do have a chance to rethink everything. No one has made a big point out of it yet, but there are relatively few old people in Rivendell. There's the two retired cops, Sam, couple of profs from the university, Lieutenant Collins, and maybe half the people the Guard brought with them. And Collins is on the youngish side, so I'm not sure where I'd put him. The thing is, none of them are trying to take over. Even the refugees that came with the Guard seem to be content to go along with whatever you guys want, at least mostly. So it's beginning to feel like it's all on us."

Bill chuckled. "Sam's in his late forties, Goro. I wouldn't call him an *old person* either."

"Close enough. Who was it said, 'Never trust anyone over thirty'?"

"Uh, beats me," Bill replied. "And Roger Daltry sang 'I hope I die before I get old.' Of course, he's a senior citizen now, so he may have softened his stance a little."

Goro laughed. "Yeah, okay, but the point is that there's a disconnect of some kind between the way people above a certain age and below that age look at the world. It's always been that way, of course, but since the turn of the century it's been accelerated and amplified. And the old people have always been in control. Essentially, we've always had gerontocracies, no matter what other labels were used to muddy the waters. Here and now, things are different. The geriatrics don't have the numbers, the authority, or control of the resources necessary to enforce their will on us."

"Uh… is this just you blowing off steam?"

"Not by a long shot, Bill. It wasn't new even before Yellowstone. But we can actually do something about it now."

Bill was silent for a moment. "Shit. The whole election thing is going to be even messier than I thought, and that's saying something. I need to have another talk with Monica. Time to head back." The ultralight banked, then surged as Bill brought the engine back online. "Please place seat backs and tray tables in their full upright position," he quipped. "And thank you for flying Outland Airlines."

24. TEST DIG

September 6

"Here's good." Kevin waved at the general area. He winced a little as the effort awoke abused nerves. Two days after the incident with Jimmy, he was still visibly bruised and still moving carefully.

Jackson and Miguel, the two men who had agreed to help him with his experiment, let go of the cart handle and proceeded to unload and set up the portal equipment. Kevin had packed the six-foot gate. He had also packed a couple of shovels.

Once the equipment was set up, Kevin placed the gate flat on the ground. He activated the interface, to no effect.

At the perplexed looks from the two men, Kevin said, "I didn't really expect it to activate. There's probably grass sticking up on the other side. I need you guys to grab either end of the gate and lift until it activates."

Jackson and Miguel complied, and when the gate was a little more than a foot off the ground, the interface activated. The vegetation on the other side was different enough to make it obvious.

At Kevin's hand motion, the two men lowered the gate to the ground. They then grabbed the shovels, and began digging.

"How deep do you need?" Jackson asked.

"Couple of feet," Kevin responded. "But it doesn't have to be really wide."

After a few minutes of effort, the men had finished. At Kevin's direction, one of them lifted one end of the gate while the other stood guard with a shotgun.

Kevin looked through the inclined gate at the hole in the ground of Dino Planet, then looked under the gate at the undisturbed soil of Outland. Nodding with satisfaction, he deactivated the gate and gave instructions to pack everything up.

"What was the point of that?" Miguel asked.

Kevin answered, "If we're going to be exploring strange new worlds"—he attempted a smile, which earned him another twinge of pain—"then we're going to want some kind of way station on each one. And something pretty safe, would be my vote. We're thinking underground. With this system, we can basically do the excavation from this side, with minimal fuss and danger. Bill was talking about ten-foot-diameter culvert pipes, buried on end and capped at the top. Under a couple of feet of soil, they'd be safe even on Greenhouse Earth."

The two men nodded. Then Jackson said, "By the way, nice job with Jimmy. I don't know if I'd have had the guts to jump on his face like that."

Kevin blushed. "Well, what I lack in skill I guess I make up for with poor planning." The two men laughed, and he continued, "Monica is my friend. And I had a pretty good idea what Jimmy's capable of. I also knew Bea was close by." He finished with an awkward wave of dismissal.

"Yeah, okay," Miguel said. "Still…" He looked at his watch. "We'd better get moving. The general meeting is in a half-hour. I don't want to miss this."

Jackson glanced reflexively at his own watch. Then, without further discussion, they quickly packed everything up.

"Can I have your attention, please!" Richard stepped back from the microphone for a moment to survey the crowd.

Thank God for P.A.s, he thought. After his first attempt at public speaking, he'd asked Matt to watch for anything that could be a public address system. Matt had accommodated, and Richard's vocal cords were thankful.

"The purpose of this general meeting is to decide what to do about James Korniski—"

"Shoot the fucker!"

"String him up!"

There were several more suggestions from the throng, each trying to outdo the previous one.

"Okay, okay." Richard made calming motions with his hands. "Not that I disagree, but if we're going to be a functioning society, we can't start out acting like a lynch mob. I've asked around, and purely by chance we don't have any lawyers or law students ... "

A spontaneous cheer went up, and Richard had to stop speaking for a moment to get his face under control. " ... so we'll have to play it by ear a bit. The trial will be public, and *if* the defendant is found guilty"—there were derisive laughs from the crowd—"then there will be a vote on the sentence."

Richard looked around at the mass of people in front of him. "Trial starts tomorrow, if we can find someone willing to act as defense."

He nodded to Kevin, who responded by turning off the P.A. Richard gave a wave to the crowd, which was still making loud suggestions about Jimmy's potential fate.

❀   ❀   ❀

"Well, that went well …," Richard said.

Monica laughed. "What did you expect? It's not like Jimmy is everyone's fave. He's probably threatened or intimidated half the population at one point or another."

"And on that subject," Sam cut in, "I went and asked Jimmy who he would like to act as his defense. He told me to, um, well, *go away*, let's say. He also suggested that he would make us pay for the way we're treating him. That boy is just not right." Sam shook his head in sorrow.

"So, we'll either ask for volunteers or we'll assign someone," Richard said. "I have a feeling this is going to be an uphill battle, even without Jimmy's help."

25. Spare Parts

September 7

Bill looked up as the soldier walked into the Mad Science Lab. He blanked out for a second before he remembered the woman's name, then it clicked. "Hey there, Ashanda. Aren't you on radio duty?"

"Yeah, but shortwave's crap until sundown, so it's not like I'm being worked to death. However, I've been getting sporadic transmissions from a military satellite, and I wanted your help."

"Hmm, that stuff's heavily encrypted. Hardware *and* software keys. I doubt I could—"

"I'm not looking for tech support, Bill," Ashanda interrupted. "I *am* tech support. But you have inventory…" She waved a hand to take in the contents of the shed. "I'm hoping you have a spare satellite dish."

"What, consumer grade?"

"Quantity has a certain quality all its own, civvie. All I have is that shitty little twelve-inch dish. If you can beat that, I can adapt it."

"Hell, I can beat that in my sleep. Hold on." Bill began rummaging around the chaos that was his spare parts inventory. Within a minute there was an *"aha!"* and Bill emerged with a box under his arm.

"Still in the box?" Ashanda said. "I'm impressed. Sure you don't want to enlist? We could use you."

Bill grinned and handed her the box. "You can never be too rich, too thin, or have too many spares. Especially the last one. So what are you picking up? Anything useful?"

Ashanda turned the box and began reading the small print, answering in a distracted fashion. "We have satellite WAN capability, at least in theory. The ash knocked reception to hell, of course, but I think it's coming back. The satellites themselves will stay locked for years, even without ground control. Unlike civilian GPS, which isn't going to be useful for much longer..."

"Yeah, tell me about it. We're already getting drift. Charlie's compensating, but at some point, we'll register as being in Russia. Or Hawaii."

Ashanda laughed and tipped the box in his direction. "Thanks, Bill. I owe you one. Come by when you have a chance, and I'll show you whatever we get. And I won't even kill you afterward."

Bill smiled and gave her a wave. A wide-area network connection. Now that was interesting. He sat slowly on whatever was behind him, his eyes already staring unfocused into the distance.

26. Clearing the Road

Matt sat in the Hummer and watched the activity with the satisfied feeling of someone who doesn't have to be involved. Truthfully, he'd have been happy to help, if only to get some exercise, but the Guard troops seemed to have a system for assigning tasks, and he felt like he threw them off when he tried to volunteer.

The convoy had run into its third roadblock of the day, and the soldiers were clearing it. Some vehicles could be simply rolled off the road, either by putting them in neutral and giving them a push, or by literally rolling them over sideways. However, the bigger vehicles, and especially those that couldn't be taken out of "park" without a key, took a bit more work.

The crew had settled on a set of routines based on specific circumstances. In this particular case, they were simply pushing the vehicles off the road with the Hummer, while loudly making bets about how many times they'd roll.

Finally, they had the road cleared enough, and everyone piled back into their vehicles.

"Aw, you have got to be kidding me!" Matt exclaimed, giving his frustration free rein. They'd just come to an overpass that had completely collapsed onto the highway. There was no simple way to get past this roadblock without the aid of heavy equipment.

"I think we're done for the day," Lieutenant Collins said. "Timminson, pass along instructions. We'll go back about a quarter mile so we have some line-of-sight around us, then set up camp on the roadway. We'll deal with this situation tomorrow."

"Yes, sir," Timminson replied, then picked up the radio and began to relay the orders.

Collins turned to Matt. "You *did* bring coffee, right?"

Matt laughed. "Of course. Bill's best stuff. Enough for everyone. Plus some for bribes, if it comes to that."

The lieutenant nodded. "Good coffee and all the steak you can eat. I've been on worse operations."

"Maybe someone brought some of Crazy Al's beer," Matt said, with as straight a face as he could manage.

"Not if there's any mercy in the universe," the lieutenant responded with the same deadpan delivery.

While some soldiers set up camp, a few others went through the personnel gate and came back a short while later with a small deer tied upside down on a pole. Within a half hour, camp had been set up, fires were going, meat was cooking, and guards with night-vision goggles had set up a perimeter.

Collins took a deep breath. "It occurs to me that if there's anyone still alive downwind of us, the smell of coffee and steaks should bring them running."

Matt gave him a side-eye. "Let's just hope it's only people. Bill told me a story a while back about some dire wolves that may or may not have gotten loose on this side. Not that he knows how or why, mind you."

"Wonderful," Collins replied. "Timminson, put up a few more guards, will you?"

Matt was silent for a few moments. "Tom, I've been thinking…"

"That usually means more work. What's up?"

"We were watching for heavy equipment in Lincoln, and we tagged a few items, but of course we never got a big enough gate to bring them through. But for what we're doing right now, a wheel loader would be ideal."

"One of those big shovel-equipped jobs with tires, right?"

"Yes. I bet one of those babies could clear the road ahead of us without even slowing down."

"We'd need to worry about fuel, though," Collins replied. "Our fuel trailer would be massively inadequate."

"Well, that's the other thing. Omaha's a bigger city. That's both good and bad, of course, because it means more area to search. But I was thinking maybe we could find a fuel delivery truck and fill it up. The big semi-trailers can hold something like fifteen thousand gallons."

"That seems like overkill, Matt. You have something else in mind?"

"You've mentioned expeditions to the coasts. The easiest way would be by the freeways, and the easiest way to do that would be with some heavy equipment for clearing the way."

Collins nodded slowly. "Not to mention that we'd only have to do it once per highway, and it would re-open the road for everyone. Two birds with one stone. I like it."

"Actually, if we could find multiples of that kind of equipment, we could send crews in multiple directions." Matt frowned in thought before continuing. "They'd need protection, I guess, although I'm not sure how many actual *Mad Max*–style gangs are roaming the wilderness these days, looking for a fight."

Collins grinned. "That's a Bill-worthy reference, Matt."

"Well, I've been hanging around with him a lot of years. A certain amount of cross-contamination is inevitable."

"Okay, Matt, good idea." Collins nodded. "We'll send off a crew to look for those items when we get to Omaha. And we'll keep an eye open along the way as well."

27. TRIAL

September 8

The logistics, as it turned out, were far more of a problem than the trial itself. Eventually they decided to simply bring tables, chairs, and equipment outside and have the whole thing on the lawn.

"Can I have your attention, please!" Richard waited for the crowd noise to subside.

"The trial is about to begin. For the record, this is the trial of James Korniski. The charges are first-degree attempted murder and second-degree assault. We asked Jimmy if he wanted a trial by judge or by jury and he told us to fuck off, so we've made our own decision. Trial will be by jury." Richard paused to gesture at twelve people sitting in a group to the side of the podium. "As I mentioned last time, we have no actual lawyers or law students"—he was interrupted as a cheer went up from the entire population, followed by laughter as everyone reacted to that—"which means we are going to be a lot more informal in this trial. The idea is to get the content of justice right, even if we skimp on some of the paperwork." That also got some appreciative laughs and catcalls from the audience.

Richard motioned to Kevin to turn the P.A. down a bit, then continued. "Sam Benton will be presiding as judge, because as one of the most recent arrivals, he's more likely to be able to remain objective. Beatrice Chavez will act as prosecution, and Fred Mack will act as defense. I'll give the mike to Bea now, and she'll present her case."

Bea took the mike to loud cheers and whoops, and started in immediately. "I have no idea what the proper process is, so I'm going to just present my case, and if the defense has issues with any of my statements, then we'll get into witnesses and stuff. I'm sure a lawyer would burst into tears at the way we're doing this, but tough."

Bea spent a few minutes recounting the actual events of the night in question, including Kevin's intervention and her use of the bat, then concluded her opening argument.

"The defendant has demonstrated pretty convincingly that he either can't or isn't interested in controlling his temper, and that he sees beating people up as a perfectly valid tactic for conflict resolution. There's no reason to think this is going to change. The defendant himself is very clear on that point. Between telling everyone and anyone to fuck off, he repeatedly promises that he will beat the crap out of anyone who disrespects him, that they deserve it, and that he'll get back at each and every one of us for what we're doing now. Every single person in this town is in danger as long as he's free to walk around. I don't see that we owe him enough to let him keep doing so. To be honest, the next time he does something like this, Monica is just going to shoot him anyway."

Bea handed the mike back to Richard and sat down, to applause and calls of approval.

Richard stood up and said into the mike, "And now, the statement from the defense." Richard handed the mike to Fred Mack, one of the two security guards who had come over with the original wave of refugees from UNL. As he took it, the crowd booed him mightily.

Fred just grinned and waited for them to run down. "Yeah, I know, I know. But if we're going to do this at all, we need a defense of some kind. I don't know why they picked me; I used to put guys like this in jail."

This statement produced a good bit of laughter. Although they were both retired cops, Fred and Anson had been popular with the students at UNL because of their relaxed attitude and complete absence of authoritarian arrogance.

"And honestly," he continued, "I don't have much. Jimmy there told me to fuck off when I went to talk to him, so I guess you can add *stupid* to his list of sins. About the only thing I can come up with is the question of premeditation. I don't think we can really be sure that he was intending to kill anyone. Maybe he'd have just beat them up until he felt he'd made his point."

At this point, Jimmy—who had been sitting quietly watching all this—yelled out, "I sure as fuck *was* going to kill the bitch! No more than she deserved. And I'm going to do the same to the rest of you fucks…"

Jimmy was winding up to a good conniption. Sam motioned to the soldiers who were guarding Jimmy and made a zip motion across his mouth. Using some duct tape that they'd been supplied with, the guards put an end to the ranting.

Fred sighed and hung his head. "Like I said," he said into the mike. "*Stupid.*" He turned to Sam. "I'm sorry, Judge. I got nothing."

"And with that note," Bea interjected, "the prosecution rests."

Sam motioned for the mike. When he had it, he began to speak. "A trial is really for two things. One, to determine if a defendant is guilty. And two, to ensure justice is impartial and appropriate. In this case, the defendant freely and glee-fully admits to his guilt, makes it very clear that he'll do it again, shows nothing even vaguely resembling remorse, and expresses the opinion that no one has the right to tell him what to do. Although I really played with the idea of investigating an insanity angle, the fact of the matter is the defendant knows what he's doing. He just doesn't care."

Sam then turned to the jury. "Your job is to determine if he's guilty or not. Simple as that. As was explained before we started, if you come back with a guilty verdict, the citizenry at large will vote on the appropriate sentence."

He pointed to the longhouse. "It's all yours for as long as you need. Send someone to let me know when you've made a decision, and we'll reconvene."

It took less than five minutes for the jury to come to a ver-dict, to no one's surprise. Nor was the actual verdict any kind of shock.

Sam looked at Jimmy. "You've been found guilty on all counts." There was a roar of approval from the crowd, which lasted almost a minute before Sam could continue. "The citizens of Rivendell will have to decide the sentence. You've all heard the case. The committee put together a list of pos-sible sentences. You will all have a day to think about it, and tomorrow after dinner there'll be a vote. Richard is going to put up a list on a board.

"Remember this when making a decision. Sentences are handed out with three things in mind: deterrence, rehabili-tation, and preventing re-offending. You try to deter people from committing crimes in the first place by providing penalties that they don't want to pay. You try to rehabilitate convicts so that they won't feel the *need* to re-offend. And if rehabilitation doesn't work, you try to prevent re-offending by either warehousing the convict until they die or are too old to re-offend, or you deport them to get rid of the problem, or you execute them. There are a few other options, like chemical castration, exile to Australia, or cutting off the right hand, but you get the idea."

Sam got up from his seat and handed the mike to Kevin. Meanwhile, Richard set out a large whiteboard. On it was a list:

1- DO NOTHING
2- INCARCERATION
3- FORCED LABOR
4- REPATRIATION
5- EXILE TO DINO PLANET
6- FIRING SQUAD

Richard took the mike. "Here are your choices. Let's make this count."

28. TUNNELS

September 9

Richard was puzzled by the strange sight. A fifteen-to-twenty-foot length of corrugated metal culvert, perhaps ten feet in diameter, stood on end, partially embedded in the ground. Muffled shouts and sounds of digging could be heard from inside. A scaffolding had been set up, which was being used to haul dirt up out of the center.

"This is for Dino Planet, right?" Richard asked Bill.

"Yep. We want the culvert to be deep enough so that a T-Rex can't just push it over. We'll anchor it as well, of course." Bill motioned with his hands. "Say a third below grade, anchors driven horizontally through the bottom edge into the Dino Planet soil. We'll cut some small slits and cover them with plexi or something similar, for looking around."

"But you're building it on this side ... "

"Look closely, and you can see the gate lying on the ground encircling the construction area. We're actually digging into Dino Planet soil. When we're done, we'll lift the gate up over top of the installed culvert and it'll disappear completely from this side."

"Huh. That's brilliant." Richard frowned. "Uh, I'm sure I'm not the first person to ask this, but how do you get in and out?"

"Oh my God!" Bill's face registered exaggerated shock. "We forgot..." He couldn't hold the expression and burst into laughter. "Relax, Richard. Technically, we don't really need an entrance. We just gate through from this side. And if we decide to throw caution to the wind and go outside—you've seen the *Jurassic Park* movies, right?—we can just gate through from this side *outside* the enclosure."

"Huh. That doesn't sound like it'll work for Greenhouse Earth, though."

"Um, no chance. For that, we were trying to design a double-hulled system of some kind. A person with a pole-cam inside a container, which is placed inside another container, then the inner container would be—"

"Nope." Richard grinned. "Even I can tell that would fall over under the weight of its own kludgieness."

"Hah. Yeah, we've kind of settled on an airtight chamber, and a couple of people with firefighting gear inside, running a pole-cam."

"That'll work?"

"Some testing needed. But remember, all we want to do is lock onto any timelines past Greenhouse Earth. After that, we can bypass Greenhouse Earth and connect directly to them."

Richard shook his head. "Good luck getting volunteers."

Bill snorted. "One way or the other, we'll end up doing it. Even if we do find more timelines beyond Dino Planet, there'll still be the question of what's beyond Greenhouse Earth."

Richard crossed his arms and stared at the construction in silence for a while. "Seems like a lot of work. But less than the way-stations idea."

"Yeah, but we've discussed options—*we* being Kevin, Matt, and me—and the general feeling is that we don't want to take any chances with Dino Planet. Even Matt was making *Jurassic Park* references right and left, and you know how sarcastic he can be when *I* get referencey. And if we find something beyond either timeline, we might have to use the same process there."

"Plus, you're having a lot of fun and get to play secret agent."

"The two goals are not incompatible." Bill grinned. "And the downside of failure is significant. I always thought the T-Rex-loose-in-L.A. sequence was a bit over the top, but y'know, I'd just as soon not test it here."

"With you all the way, Bill." Richard nodded and marched off to his next daily check-in, whistling the *Andy Griffith* theme, which always seemed to pop into his head as he did his rounds.

29. ASHLAND

September 9

L ieutenant Collins lowered the binoculars and let the neck strap take their weight. "Yep. That's completely fucked."

Matt couldn't help a brief smile. Collins cursed so rarely that it was always an event when he let one out. In this case, Matt had to agree.

Interstate 80 crossed the Platte River at the Platte River Bridge. The eponymous and unimaginatively named bridge was not, however, currently navigable. Both spans were intact; that was the good news. But the line of cars stretched a good mile to the west—and on both sides of the highway. It appeared people fleeing Lincoln had decided traffic laws were merely suggestions.

"Looks like some kind of massive fire near the east end of the bridge," Collins commented.

"Across both sides of a divided highway? What, someone nuked it?"

Collins put the binocs to his eyes again and played with the zoom. "I think I see the remains of a tanker truck. Maybe. A fuel explosion could spread to the opposite lanes. Probably ignited some of the vehicles there."

"It would take weeks to clear that jam," Matt observed.

"And it's probably pointless. If these cars couldn't get clear, the blockage must be total on the other side." Collins sighed and stared into space for a moment. "We can go up to Ashland and try the bridge there, or head over to another bridge in Louisville. Ashland is closer, but there's a risk either or both of them will have suffered some similar fate. Other people would have had the same idea."

"So..." Matt cocked his head but didn't look directly at the lieutenant.

"Well, it's a coin flip, so let's try the closer one first."

A lot of refugees had apparently had the same idea, and dead vehicles lined the side of Highway 66. But not, Matt was pleased to note, to the point of blocking the road. Traffic must have been able to get across.

The convoy proceeded cautiously, not expecting an attack necessarily, but being off the interstate induced a claustrophobic feeling, as if they were being led down a chute to the slaughter.

The drive was uneventful, as it turned out, needing only three stops to clear the road of accidents and other blockages.

They received a surprise, however, as they approached the intersection with Highway 6. A barricade had been placed across the road, which seemed to consist of semi-crushed vehicles. Piled fifteen to twenty feet high in a running bond pattern like giant metal brickwork, the impromptu junkyard formed a most effective wall.

Collins ordered a halt several hundred yards from the barricade. He put his binoculars to his eyes and scanned the scene for several minutes, not saying a word. Matt was almost to the point of yelling "What?" when Collins finally dropped the binoculars to his chest.

"There are armed guards on the top of that wall," he reported. "And they've seen us, obviously. The good news is they aren't shooting, or even aiming their weapons yet. But they aren't coming out with cries of joy and open arms either." He turned to Corporal Timminson. "Park the convoy. We'll drive up in the unarmed Humvee and see if they'll talk to us."

The drive was short but tense. The figures on top of the barricade visibly went to high alert as the Humvee approached, although never quite to the point of aiming weapons. The driver stopped the vehicle just outside conversational distance, and Collins and Matt stepped out. Matt could see a slight relaxation on the part of the barricade guards at this obvious sign of peaceful intent.

Collins strode up to the barricade and looked up. "Residents of Ashland?"

"That's right," came an answering voice from above. "I'm Chief Cummins."

Collins waited, but no more information was forthcoming. "I'm Lieutenant Tom Collins of the National Guard. We're trying to get to Omaha, and the interstate bridge is blocked."

"Try the 50."

Collins glanced at Matt, the slightest sign of an eye-roll betraying his irritation.

"Is the 6 down?"

"For your purposes, it is. We're not allowing passage."

Collins stepped back and scanned the barricade from end to end. It was showmanship, Matt knew. He'd studied the wall and discussed it with his demolitions expert before ever leaving the convoy.

"We're National Guard, on lawful business, Chief."

"I appreciate that, Lieutenant, and I don't want to get into a pissing match with the Guard. If you were just the usual travelling band, we'd have placed a couple of bullets at your feet the moment your convoy stopped."

Collins smiled briefly. "Likewise, I'd just as soon not get into an argument with residents who appear to be doing no more than defending their patch of earth. But we do have to get to Omaha, and we're on a schedule. Can you assure me that the bridge on 50 is navigable?"

"Sorry, sir, can't do that. No one that we've sent on their way has come back to report, so far."

Collins turned to Matt and spoke in a low voice, "We could go around via Outland, of course, but we'd have to come back to Earthside somewhere in town in order to be able to access the bridge. It would probably end up as a running battle, with people I don't actually have a quarrel with."

"Take your time, Lieutenant," came the voice from above. "We've got all day."

It was sarcasm, of course, but Collins deliberately ignored it. "Thanks, Chief. Won't be long." Then to Matt, "I wonder if we can do a deal. I bet they could use some fresh meat."

"A couple of antelope or deer would do it."

Collins raised his voice and spoke to Cummins. "How about if we pay for passage? Say, a couple of fresh deer? Food must be getting scarce in Ashland by now."

"That sounds real fine, Lieutenant. Except for a couple of small problems. For one, no game around here. Hasn't been for most of a century. And maybe more of an immediate problem, we didn't build a door into this barricade. Weren't really intending to invite anyone in."

"Chief, we can resolve both of those issues to everyone's satisfaction. All I need to know right now is whether this is *in principle* an acceptable offer."

"For passage through to the bridge? Nothing else from us? Yeah, we'd go for that. So you pull out your magic wand and get started. Like I said, we've got all day."

Two hours later, one of the transports drove up to the barricade. Collins and Matt stepped out of the cab, and four soldiers piled out of the back, with two deer carcasses suspended on poles. Matt could clearly hear gasps and exclamations from the top of the barricade.

Cummins's voice drifted down from above. "We can probably winch those up pretty quick."

"No need, Chief," Collins replied. "Give us ten minutes, and we'll have our convoy on the other side of your barricade. Then we can all have a barbeque. We've brought our own cooker, but I'm betting you can rustle some up as well."

"What makes you think there's room over here?"

"We already checked. Trust me, I'll explain that. You have a couple hundred yards of clear road from the barrier, and a small parking lot on the north side. I just want to make sure we have a deal first."

More muttering and some angry, raised voices followed. About two minutes later, Cummins called down, "Okay, I don't know where you're going with this, but if you can get to this side with that meat in tow, we've got a deal. So let's see that magic."

Matt grinned, turned, and made a twirling gesture in the air with his hand. In response, several soldiers hurried to the front of the convoy with equipment and a battery pack in tow. They had performed this sequence so many times already on the drive out from Lincoln that it was as habitual as putting up a tent.

First, the truck gate went up, and the vehicles drove through one at a time. Gasps and cries of consternation were clearly audible from up on the barricade as each vehicle disappeared into thin air. Then the smaller gate was opened from the other side and the disassembled truck gate was carried through. Finally, all that was left were Matt and Lieutenant Collins grinning up at the boggled, staring barricade guards. "We'll start coming through on the other side in about two minutes," Collins called up. Then he and Matt stepped through the personnel gate, and it closed.

It wasn't anywhere near the entire original population of Ashland, Collins thought to himself. For that matter, it probably wasn't the entire *current* population. Of course, most of them had probably left town in the first hours of the eruption. And of those who remained, some probably had obligations or essential duties elsewhere. But if it was less than about eighty percent of the current population, he'd be amazed.

About a hundred and twenty people, by quick head-count, crowded the street, walking around or circling the numerous barbeques and smokers that had magically appeared once word got around. The Ashlanders had brought a significant quantity of beer to the party as well. The aroma of roasting meat wafted around the neighbor-hood, very probably attracting more citizenry. Not that it was an issue. They'd eventually killed two more of the large, Pleistocene deer, and they would leave them with the townspeople.

Collins sat with Cummins and members of the town council, who had showed up for the food and the story. The way Cummins was digging into his venison steak, he had obviously been missing protein in his diet for a while.

"So another version of Earth?" Cummins said around a mouthful. He paused to swallow. "I'd say you were shitting me if I hadn't seen your vehicles disappear over there and appear over here. At this point, you could tell me you're Santa Claus and I'd sit on your knee."

"Not me," Collins replied. "Matt. He's one of the inventors of the gates. I don't think I'm exaggerating too much when I say they might just make the difference between survival and extinction for the human race. Or at least human civilization."

Cummins nodded slowly. One of the aldermen or councillors, a Mr. Brady, said, "Lincoln, you say?"

"That's right. Up to you, of course. If you choose to stay here, we can no doubt come up with some kind of trade route or something. But it would be easier if everyone were in one place. Plus"—Collins waved a hand in Matt's direction—"our other resident genius has a bug up his... uh, in his ear about minimum population needed to bootstrap civilization. Matt and I have both heard the rant often enough to be able to repeat it by rote."

Matt grinned as Cummins glanced at him. "You've been warned."

"Okay. So what's that about?" Cummins said.

Collins groaned and Matt laughed before replying. "Look, if every single person in Rivendell—"

"Rivendell? You've named your encampment *Rivendell*?" Brady turned to Collins. "And you stood still for this?"

"I wasn't there when they set up, sir. It's run by nerds. You'll need to get used to that."

"Aaaaaaanyway," Matt continued, "if every single person in Rivendell had a useful skill or knowledge set and no duplications, we *still* wouldn't have all the skills we need to reboot a civilization. On top of that, many tasks require more than one person; construction, for instance. Or farming. So that reduces the potential skills coverage even more. We simply need a certain minimum number of warm bodies just to cover all the basics."

"And you don't have them."

"Not even close. Plus, in a lot of cases, we don't even have anyone with the basic knowledge—for instance, blacksmithing skills. Someone with some metallurgy knowledge could eventually reverse-engineer the techniques, but while they're doing that, they're not doing something else. We've got three pre-meds, but without interning experience they're just book-smart."

Cummins and Brady nodded slowly, almost in sync. Cummins leaned forward and put his hands out to the fire to collect some of the warmth. The low buzz of other conversations around the fires and barbeques provided a background to the crackling of the campfire, but they'd been left alone to pursue their conversation. Collins doubted this was accidental.

"Are you effectively in charge, Mr. Brady?" he asked.

"Yes, for all intents and purposes. Mayor Hammond succumbed to the ash a few weeks ago." To Collins's and Matt's murmurs of sympathy he replied, "He had issues already. Old cancer diagnosis, ex-smoker. And he refused to shelter in place. Kept going around, visiting people, directing operations. So it's unfortunate, but not really a surprise. We had a funeral. The whole town showed up. And I'm acting mayor now. Crenshaw and Knowles"—he gestured to two men who had said very little so far—"are the two remaining councillors."

"Any other deaths?"

"Couple of suicides. Couple of other people are probably chronic now. No idea about what might have happened with the people who got out of town, of course. But we've survived pretty well, all things considered."

"Thanks to the barricade?"

"That was part of it," Cummins said. "The Platte River Bridge got messed up early in the evacuations. And everyone had the same idea as you, to take the Ashland Bridge. On the way, a lot of them stopped in town to do some stocking up, far too often at the point of a gun. There were a lot of deaths on both sides." Cummins stopped and got a haunted look. It took a few seconds for him to recover his voice. "So we set up a defensive line where the barricade is, and that worked until people started charging the line with their vehicles. More fatalities. We finally got some heavy equipment and moved some of the wrecks to form the barricade." He shrugged, but Matt could tell it was more bravado than dismissiveness. "No more deaths, at least on our side."

"How are your prospects? Long-term, I mean," Collins asked.

"Not great. We'll get through the winter, we think, but eventually we'll run out of necessities. Our only hope has been that the government would show up with some kind of relief. That's becoming less and less likely, though."

Collins replied gently, "Government isn't an option, Chief. We still have some communications with scattered military units, and the situation is uniformly bad. No operational federal infrastructure. State infrastructure is operating as independent units mostly, and strictly local. Internationally, *no one* is unaffected. Even the countries in the best shape are struggling just to hold their own. So there will be no relief efforts from elsewhere."

Matt spoke up. "The southern hemisphere might be in better shape ecologically. But politically, countries down there have never been large, rich, or particularly stable. With a few exceptions like Australia and New Zealand, and I don't see them being of any help to us anytime soon."

"We are still getting shortwave activity in North America," Collins added. "Mostly West Coast, though. The central U.S. and Canadian prairie provinces were the most affected, with the East Coast not far behind."

"Then the Atlantic weather patterns would have carried a lot of the atmospheric crap up to Northern Europe." Matt made a disgusted noise. "It's the gift that just keeps on giving."

Cummins looked from one to the other. "So you have a suggestion?"

"How's the steak?" Collins asked in an apparent non-sequitur. "Rivendell has no lack of food. Or space. We need the people and their skills; you need a long-term plan. It's less than thirty miles to Lincoln. You could *walk* that if you had to."

Brady chuckled. "Well, maybe you could, you whipper-snapper, but we've got a lot of retired folk here. But I get your point—it's doable." He thought for a moment. "We'll need to have a town hall about it. Can you stay overnight?"

"Sure, no problem. If you decide to take us up on it, we'll give you instructions and an address, and we'll let Rivendell know you're on the way."

"You'll continue on to Omaha?"

"We have to, Mr. Brady, for several reasons. We may not get another chance to do this."

Brady frowned. "Omaha isn't going anywhere."

"But the buildings are," Matt said. "If our supplier's warehouse collapses, we lose everything. And there's no alternative source."

Brady nodded. "Okay. That'll be a factor in the discussion." He looked around. "We'd all feel a lot safer with a National Guard escort."

"Hmmm..." Collins stared off in the direction of the parked vehicles for a few seconds. "We can send one transport and four soldiers back with you. That'll give you some extra cargo capacity as well for anything you want to bring with you. Does that help?"

"I think it will. Thank you." Brady glanced toward the barbecues. "Y'know, I think there's still venison left."

"We've set up some meat grinders in Rivendell," Matt said. "And we have some very limited baking going. So, venison burgers. You have to try them."

Brady grinned. "You had me at *baking.*"

30. DEATH SENTENCE

September 10

"Can I have your attention, please!" Richard stepped back from the microphone for a moment to survey the crowd.

"I'll just summarize briefly. There is a list of alternatives on the board behind me. You pick one of the choices, write the number on your ballot, fold the paper and hand it to one of the people at the desk, and give them your name. You move away so someone else can do the same.

"It's not rocket science," he muttered, after deliberately lowering the mike.

The line-ups were already fully formed for the vote. Jimmy hadn't been anyone's favorite person before; the lawyers' statements and his behavior at the trial had enraged people.

And because of what came out at the trial and eyewitness accounts, Kevin had been promoted to a kind of folk hero, and was having trouble adjusting. He still had a tendency to blush furiously when it was brought up.

Things moved quickly. People had had plenty of time to debate and argue, and now it was time to deal with the issue. Within an hour, everyone had voted, and the vote counters were working feverishly.

Voting having finished, the Booze Brothers had brought out their latest attempt for public appraisal. It was generally acknowledged after sampling that this batch probably wouldn't induce catastrophic mutations. In fact, several people expressed a need for multiple samples, just to be sure.

Eventually, the counts were done, and the results were posted:

1- DO NOTHING:	5
2- INCARCERATION:	16
3- FORCED LABOR:	39
4- REPATRIATION:	65
5- EXILE TO DINO PLANET:	173
6- FIRING SQUAD:	79

There were a few moments of silence as people closest to the board read the results. Then the lawn exploded in a roar of conversation and argument.

"Well, Richard, looks like no one is happy," Monica said. "Probably not even the people who voted for door number one."

Richard shrugged. "It's like herding cats. Honest to God." He pointed at the last item, the Firing Squad vote count. "That seems high. Should we be worried?"

Monica gazed at the board for a moment, biting her lip. "I don't think so. Jimmy beat up or intimidated or attempted to shake down a lot of people. And he made it pretty clear at the trial that he's not going to change. People want him gone, permanently. And honestly, I don't think option six is necessarily the cruelest punishment on the list."

Richard raised an eyebrow and made a show of re-examining the board. Then he nodded and said, "I can't say you're wrong."

The two turned and headed for the longhouse to discuss things with the rest of the committee.

The gate was set up and ready to be opened. Jimmy stood, under guard, hands zap-strapped behind his back. Monica and Bea stood to the side, rifles at the ready. Several more soldiers stood ready to cover the gate when it opened.

Richard glared coldly at Jimmy. "The gate will be opened. Your bonds will be cut. You will proceed straight to the gate, picking up the supplies that we've placed in front of it. You will then step through the interface. If you try anything else—ANYTHING—even some half-wit *Ah'm better un alla yaz* speech—then Monica and Bea have blanket permission to shoot you anywhere they want, as many times as they want, and alive or dead, we'll toss you through. Understand something, asshole. You are being *discarded*. If we ever see you again, for whatever reason, under whatever circumstances, you will be shot. No questions, no discussion."

Richard didn't wait for an acknowledgement. He nodded to the Guard, who stepped forward and snipped the zip tie that had been holding Jimmy. Kevin, over by the portal, turned it on. A steady breeze came from the interface, combined with unidentifiable odors.

Jimmy smiled contemptuously, stepped forward, and picked up the items in front of the gate. He turned to the watching crowd and opened his mouth—and Bea put a bullet into the ground at his feet. Then she deliberately raised the barrel to point at his groin. Monica grinned from ear to ear and raised her gun as well.

Looking less certain of himself, Jimmy turned and stepped through the interface. Immediately, Kevin closed it.

✤ ✤ ✤

"Well, that was fun." Monica had a look on her face like she'd just eaten something bitter.

"I know, I know," Richard said. "It's one thing to talk about it, another to actually do it. We've just basically sentenced him to death."

"It's not just that, it's the déjà vu. Wasn't long ago we did something similar with some mobsters. Is this going to come back to haunt us?"

Richard gave Monica a long-suffering look, and walked over to the portal box. Picking it up, he said, "Come on, let's get back home."

31. Earthside: Weather

Residents of the Pacific Northwest woke up on a September morning to a very rare sight: snow. By the time most people were up, there was almost six inches of accumulation. In an earlier time, this would have produced a disaster of a rush hour; but these days, there was very little traffic even at peak. Gas shortages had curtailed personal driving habits, electrical shortages had closed many businesses down, and rampant unemployment left most people with nowhere to go in the morning anyway.

In the absence of cash flow, most people had simply stopped paying their rent or mortgage. The banks—those that hadn't closed their doors already—had neither the time nor the resources to pursue multiple foreclosures, nor would they have been able to do anything with the seized properties in any case. And of course, houses with residents would be better cared for than abandoned ones. Rental management companies in many cases weren't paying their property managers, so no one was serving or enforcing eviction notices.

Food was less of a problem in the PNW; the relative lack of ash had left most livestock and crops largely unaffected. However, the refugee load from neighboring states had been heavy, and all remaining infrastructure was under stress.

Now an early snowfall meant farmers were forced to harvest crops prematurely, and greenhouses were forced to crank up the heat, using fuel that was becoming increasingly scarce. Homeowners who still had electrical or natural gas service turned up the thermostat. Those who didn't, used fireplaces.

There had been riots in Seattle, in Tacoma, and in some of the larger satellite communities. There would be more as the shortages mounted.

The biggest growth industry in the PNW, as in most places, was crime. Break-ins and robberies were up five thousand percent according to some local sources. Which meant that shootings were up proportionally, as owners acted to protect their families and property. Many failed criminals were now sharing mass graves, as the municipal governments struggled to keep up.

Evan darted his head quickly out, then back into the shadow of the alley. No one in sight. With his cargo carefully tucked into his shirt to look like a beer belly, he began walking toward his apartment building. Slouched, no hurry, "nothing to see here" oozed out of every pore. He couldn't depend on law enforcement if someone challenged him—there was none, not enough to matter anyway. And these days, if cops stopped him, they'd be as just as likely as not to confiscate his groceries as evidence. Might as well take his chances with the crooks and thugs. At least with those, he could shoot back. Evan caressed the pistol in his hand, hidden in the kangaroo pocket of his hoodie.

There'd been a lot of muggings early on, until it became clear that a lot more people owned guns than expected. Evan smiled to himself. With the political and social issues the last couple of years, a lot of so-called liberals had decided that in order to beat them, you had to join them.

A few hundred dead muggers later, things had tailed off a bit.

But the crooks weren't stupid either. Now they were banding together. A mugging by a half-dozen armed low-lifes wasn't something you could win. Evan eyed the front door to his building, gauging the distance. Brett from upstairs had suggested the building tenants go out in groups for mutual protection. Others had scoffed, but right now Evan could certainly use a friend or two.

"Hey, you! Stop!" The yell came from behind him. Not very far behind, either. Without looking back, Evan broke into a run, awkwardly cradling the groceries hidden under his hoody. He dodged left and right as he ran, just in case—

A shot, and a ping as a bullet struck just to his left. He was only a dozen feet from the entrance, but he'd still have to unlock the heavy door to get in. It would take valuable time he might not have, and leave him an easy target.

The door opened to reveal Mrs. McMannis from two units over. She gave him a quick *get over here* gesture while holding the door open. At the same time, shots rang out from over his head. He glanced up to see Brett aiming a rifle from a second-floor window.

Evan scooted through the open door, and Mrs. McMannis slammed and locked it behind him. He turned to her, relief causing his limbs to shake. "Thanks. I guess Brett's going to get his way."

"Damn right," she replied, patting her silver hair back into place. "Those motherfuckers want a war, we'll give them one." She gave Evan a grandmotherly smile as he stood there stunned into immobility. "What? You think you invented the word? Kids these days."

32. LEAVING ASHLAND

September 11

The trip up Highway 6 was uneventful, at least for a post-apocalyptic world. The soldiers had turned road-clearing into a competition of sorts, with leaderboards for most flips, most distance, quickest clear, and biggest vehicles.

They discovered corpses on several occasions. Scavengers had done enough of a job to make it difficult to identify cause of death. But in a few instances, expended bullet casings were found under or near the resting place.

"I'm sure it was every man for himself," Collins said. "Or woman. I'd hate to have been part of the exodus."

"I think this stretch might even have been more dangerous than average," Matt added. "A lot of people funnelling through here. At least until Ashland choked off the flow."

Collins looked down at the latest set of remains, seeming pensive. "We can't afford to take the time to bury them, either. We'd be weeks at it."

Matt nodded, silent. Without another word, they climbed back into the Hummer.

The intersection of 6 and 31, just before the on-ramp to I-80, had a pleasant surprise for the convoy.

"Nebraska Crossing." Collins snorted. "Weirdly appropriate. Shall we check it out?"

"There's a pizza place right there." Matt pointed at the sign, laughing. "Probably cold by now."

Collins grinned, then gestured to Timminson. "Let's do a survey. I want to know if there's anything valuable enough to take with us, and whatever else is useful enough to do another trip in the future."

The two most interesting shops turned out to be Under Armour and The North Face. Both outlets specialized in outdoor and cold-weather clothing and base layers. Most of the rest of the clothing stores were geared to a more-civilized world with central heating and warm vehicles.

"At minimum, we should grab all the base layers," Matt said. "And cold-weather footwear. This is all stuff that we lost in the Lincoln fire. We might not get a third shot at this."

"Agreed. There's enough here for a return trip as well, I think. Especially the winter jackets and gloves."

Matt sighed. "It's gonna take up a lot of storage space, though. I hope we don't end up regretting it."

Collins answered with a shrug, then began giving orders. It took most of the rest of the day to sort through the product and load the most valuable items.

33. MOVIE NIGHT

"Oh my God, I'm almost late!" Suzie sat down quickly in one of the few remaining open spots on the floor. Maddie, Joy, Stephanie, and Frankie were already seated. Frankie was chewing on a piece of buffalo jerky, and sipping a mug of what Suzie guessed must be beer.

Maddie smiled at Suzie. "Not quite yet. Movie starts in five. Meanwhile, we're watching to see if Frankie keels over dead."

"Ah," Suzie answered. "So that *is* beer." The women laughed, and Frankie looked slightly chagrined.

At one end of the longhouse, a humongous TV had been set up. The scavenging crew had brought back several of the largest TVs they could find. Now the TV and home theater system was the star attraction at the regular movie night.

At the front, Suzie could see someone opening a box. Tonight was Random Grab night, so the title would be a surprise.

"So where's Richard?" Stephanie asked.

Suzie decided to ignore the slightly needling tone, and just answer straight. There was no point in taking offense; Stephanie would just deny any accusation.

"Richard's going to watch with his buds. We've agreed that we shouldn't try to be together 24/7. TV nights are for friends."

❧ ❧ ❧

Richard walked hurriedly toward the longhouse. He especially liked Random Grab, as he often ended up watching movies that it would never occur to him to pick. He had yet to have a bad time. *Of course,* he thought, *watching with a bunch of friends helps a ton, too. Just another reason to not care if we never go back to Earthside.*

"Hey, Richard."

The voice startled him, lost in his thoughts as he had been. He stopped and looked around to see Monica walking up. He smiled, always glad to see her. "Hey, Rambette. Word is your reputation is even better since the Jimmy thing. Maybe you should run for president."

Monica laughed. It was always a good laugh, and guaranteed to make a guy lose track of what he was talking about. And on that subject…

"Monica, I've been meaning to talk to you. About the way things ended up with us. I know I cut off kind of abruptly—"

Monica held up a hand to stop him. "Richard, it's cool. Look, one thing I realized about you early on is that you're an all-or-nothing person. In most things, but in particular in relationships. When you commit, it's balls-to-the-wall, full-speed-ahead, damn-the-torpedoes. Which is great, when you've got a girl who is looking for that. But that's never been me. Might never be. So I kept you at arm's length, and you went looking." She shrugged. "Not really a surprise, and not a bad thing. You're happy now. Suzie's happy. Bill and I do fine. I know I'm second fiddle to his engineering projects, and that's okay with me." She smiled up at him. "It's good to see you doing well. You're not nearly as serious anymore."

Richard thought about her words for a moment and responded with a shrug. "Can't argue with that, I guess. Especially since as usual, you're right. That's really irritating, by the way." He grinned at her, and they turned to head into the longhouse for the night's entertainment.

34. Approaching Omaha

September 15

"Easier to go overside," Matt said to Collins. The two were looking at the collapsed overpass. A couple of soldiers had just come back and reported that there was no really good spot to go around it in either direction. The Hummers, of course, could climb just about anything, but the trucks weren't nearly as nimble.

"Okay," the lieutenant said. "We set up the gate, drive through, then move forward a hundred feet or so. Meanwhile the troops on this side move the gate to the other side of the overpass and set it up again. We drive through, and badda-bing badda-boom."

Matt nodded. Collins turned to Corporal Timminson. "Get the gate crew on it."

Timminson saluted and jogged off. A few moments later, he was back with a couple of soldiers. They unloaded the portal equipment from the truck.

Once everything was set up and the generator was running, Matt watched approvingly as Timminson went through the startup sequence. In a few seconds, the gate was open.

It took only minutes to drive all of the vehicles through the gate. But between disassembling the gate, hauling all the equipment very carefully to the other side of the collapsed overpass, and setting everything up again, it was a full hour before they had the gate open and were waving to the waiting convoy.

Another short wait for the convoy to drive through, and they were ready to proceed.

"I have to admit, it's kind of nerve-wracking sitting and waiting," Collins said to Matt afterward.

"Yeah, I'm a little surprised at myself," Matt answered. "I keep expecting an ambush to hit us at just that exact time. It seems Bill has gotten into my head."

The rest of the trip was uneventful, if slow. There were many blockages to clear, and one other collapsed overpass they had to bypass. It was nearly the end of the day when the convoy finally reached the outskirts of Omaha.

"We'll camp here," Collins announced. "I'd like a full day to do an initial exploration of the city, and I want a good line-of-sight for our encampment." He looked at Matt with a smile. "Paranoia is catching, I guess."

"And once we're settled in, we can discuss an itinerary for tomorrow," Matt replied.

Collins nodded to Timminson. "Extra guards tonight, Corporal. We'll be showing lights within sight of a major potential source of unknowns."

"Like zombies," Matt added.

Collins sighed. "That's what we need. Zombies on top of everything. Thanks, Matt."

35. Humiliation

He could feel his face burn with embarrassment and rage. And that little puke Sean just stood there, daring him to do anything. Backed up by his two friends, of course.

"Stop trying to think and just do what you're told, okay? That's a good boy," Sean said, and turned away. His friends chortled and followed, but not before Merv threw the bag he'd been holding directly at his head. He barely got his hands up in time to intercept it, and fumbled the catch. Some of the contents spilled out onto the floor.

"Cleanup in aisle three," Merv called over his shoulder, producing more laughter from the group.

Sean seemed to relish the opportunity to belittle him, even working to ensure they were on the same reclamation parties. He had spent most of his life enduring treatment like that, swallowing his rage, controlling his impulses. He knew what those feelings said about him. He knew that if he gave in, he wouldn't be able to stop. Wouldn't want to stop.

But then again, so what? This wasn't Earth. This wasn't America. Technically, there weren't even laws. Maybe it was time to re-evaluate his career path. He snorted with derision. Not that a college degree would be marketable in this new world. Whatever *marketable* meant when there was no money, no economy. No, everything was truly different now. His career path wasn't the only thing he should reconsider.

And if there was ever a good reason, it was Sean. He and his friends were relics of a system that didn't exist anymore. The power structure that protected them was dust. The family connections that ensured they'd always land on their feet and be shielded from consequences were on the other side of an interdimensional portal.

But Sean and his two buddies still thought they were invulnerable, protected, untouchable. He mused on this novel line of thought as he resumed moving boxes.

36. EARTHSIDE: MIGRATIONS

The loose band of refugees moved slowly down Interstate 30. All were on foot. More than a month after the eruption, there were very few working vehicles, and those were jealously guarded. Anything other than a dirt bike would have been next to useless in any case; even this far south of the volcano, the highways were still clogged with enough abandoned vehicles to make travel all but impossible for anything on four wheels.

By this point, only the relatively fit remained. Anyone unable to keep the pace had been left behind, along with any loved ones who decided to stay with them. Those that were still able to move had only one imperative: to work their way south to find food. There was no law enforcement, other than the occasional small-town department. There had been several firefights as locals attempted to keep this and other groups from scavenging. However, people without hope are also people without fear of death. With each wave of migrants, the communities had been forced to shrink their borders to maintain a defensible perimeter. Each wave also used up their stocks of ammunition. Eventually, they all fell. In many cases, the former community members were now part of the migrant group.

As the groups made their way south, they scoured the land clean of any usable salvage and anything even remotely edible. What wildlife had managed to survive the first few weeks of ashfall now inevitably fell to the hungry human scourge. In their wake the mobs left a landscape almost as barren as the surface of the moon. There would be no ecological recovery from this final insult.

37. AGITATION

September 16

"Wow," Richard said. He lay what looked like a small novel on the table and looked around at the other committee members. "Who else has read this?"

A few hands went up. "For those who haven't," Richard continued, "this is a screed from our local greenie faction, laying out in exhaustive detail all the things we should do— and not do, of course—in order to protect the environment of Outland."

"Like just all slit our own throats," Sam muttered.

"Well, they aren't quite Greenpeace," Richard replied. "Although if we stuck to this, we'd be living in caves and wearing animal hides within a generation."

"No caves around here," Bill pointed out.

Richard sighed. "Mud huts then. The point is that this is unworkable at any practical level."

"I think that's the way twenty-first-century politics works, though," Krista said. "You make extreme demands, throw a fit if anyone questions them, and hope to get maybe fifty percent of what you asked for."

"The New Conservatives held a rally today in front of the sheds," Monica added, changing the subject.

"Jesus. Anything happen?"

"There were twenty of them, Richard. They probably could have fielded a bigger crowd except for something really interesting." Monica paused and looked around, drawing out the moment. "A little bird told me that they specifically planned their rally to not include any jerries."

"What the hell are jerries?" Sam said, exasperation clear in his voice. He looked around as no one answered. No one would meet his eyes. "Okay, now I'm getting uncomfortable."

Monica finally replied, "Short for geriatrics. It means anyone over a certain age. Mostly it means anyone who was old enough to become part of the prevailing political and economic structure on Earthside."

"Well, shit, does that include me?"

"Uh." Bill looked embarrassed. "I was having a conversation about this very thing not too long ago, and your name came up. I think, to the people who are thinking in these terms, you're a jerry, Sam."

Sam gave Bill an unbelieving look. "So what's the deal?"

"It's like Greta Thunberg, right?" Krista replied. "She never explicitly called for an ageism war, but she was pretty clear that her generation was inheriting a clusterfuck of a planet, all thanks to boomers. It was a call to arms for a lot of activists." She paused, looked around the table. "Now we're in a position where most of the population of Rivendell is under thirty, *and* most of the people in a position of power are under thirty. There's a general feeling that the boomers had their shot. So we're getting all these political groups pushing their various agendas, but they're mostly run by UNL students and they're mostly intolerant of anyone who is *not* a student trying to steer the ship. Or even get involved."

Richard put his hands over his face. "Aw, fuck." He removed his hands and gave the others a wan smile. "And with that, I'm frankly out of fucks to give. In fact, I'm back-ordered. We're going to let the citizens of Rivendell go at it, we'll accept whatever they decide, and to hell with it."

The citizens of Rivendell were spread out on the lawn, await-ing today's announcements. The sound of dozens of individ-ual conversations and arguments formed a roar reminiscent of a waterfall as each group tried to make themselves heard.

Richard raised the microphone and said, "Can I have your attention, please?" His voice boomed over the loud-speaker, and the crowd quieted quickly. Richard's habit of asking bystanders to punch anyone having a side-convo had swiftly trained his audience to shut up and pay attention.

"Here's the bottom line: We need a government. We're going to be here an indefinite amount of time. We most likely can keep going with the current system, and in fact we should make the current system one of the options." Richard paused for breath. "However, we want buy-in from everyone, or at least a significant majority. So we're asking all of you to come up with options. We'll have debates, speeches, all the bullshit that seems to infest politics everywhere … " Richard waited for the laughter to die down. "Then there will be voting. It won't be simple most-votes-wins, since it's almost certain that no one will get a real majority, and I don't see us adopting a system just because sixteen percent support was the highest number. But more on that later."

Richard paused and motioned toward Monica and Bea, both of whom were standing nearby with AR-15s in their hands, surrounded by the National Guard personnel left in Rivendell. "But understand this, and understand it clearly. There will be no intimidation. There will be no violence.

This will be a civilized debate. Until a new system is in place, Monica Albertelli *is* the law, and I don't have to tell you that she gets cranky really easy."

More laughter, and Monica waved to the crowd, resulting in cheers. Richard suppressed a smile. Monica was incredibly popular with most of the residents of Rivendell, young and old.

Richard leaned forward and resumed addressing the mike. "We will decide on a government type, then we will form that government and vote as required by whatever system we decide on. That new government will decide things like a monetary system, a legal system, and the status of the Gate Owners' property. Yes..." He held up a hand as the crowd roared, arguments and imprecations swelling. "Yes, we will give up our ownership of all Rivendell assets as part of the changeover. I doubt that feudalism is going to be high on the list of preferred systems anyway."

Richard pointed to Sam. "Sam here has volunteered to act as secretary to the Rivendell congress. He will take notes, answer questions if he's able, or bring them to committee otherwise. Once the number of political parties seems to have stabilized, we'll move to the next step." Richard paused and looked around. "*Please* don't burn down the place."

He grinned at the crowd and stepped back to more laughter and a number of suggestions, mostly anatomical and scatological in nature. The crowd broke up, and groups grabbed whiteboards that had been conveniently set out.

"That was fun," Richard said to Monica.

"Thomas Jefferson, you ain't," she replied with a grin. "But hey, maybe we can get some stability and then be able to make some long-term decisions."

Richard grunted and headed off to the longhouse. Maybe it was time to sample some of that beer.

38. Experiment

In another life, it would have been a piece of a sewer or drainage line. Matt had spotted the section of five-foot-diameter HDPE corrugated pipe at the side of the road where a highways project had been interrupted by the Yellowstone event. Knowing what Bill was looking for, he'd made a point of bringing it back. Now Bill stood, drill in hand, and arched his back to stretch out the cramp. "Getting old before my time." Kevin, Charlie, and Charlie's new assistant, Norm, watched the performance.

"I'll do the other side," Kevin said, holding out his hand for the drill.

"Uh…" Bill hesitated, unsure how to phrase what he was thinking.

Kevin gave him a long-suffering look. "I promise I won't drill a hole in my foot. This isn't the same as driving a forklift, Bill. And honestly, I think you guys exaggerate how bad I was."

Bill grinned at him. "Come back without a new hole in your body, and I'll consider apologizing." He handed over the cordless drill.

Carefully planting his feet on either side of the target area, Kevin lined up the drill and pulled the trigger. The bit skittered alarmingly around the inside of the pipe for a moment before Kevin put his weight into it. Then the bit dug in, and a few seconds later popped through.

Kevin held up the drill, an unreasonably smug smile on his face. Bill gave him a slow clap in appreciation. "You'll make frontiersman yet, Kev. Okay, let's set up this experiment."

Charlie, who always managed to be around when Bill and Kevin were doing something interesting, activated the car gate. The warehouse complex's dirt overflow lot shimmered into being in the gate's aperture.

Bill checked the gate setup. They'd dug a small trench to set the gate in so that the bottom of the aperture was slightly below ground level. That way, the pipe wouldn't rest its weight on the gate frame. Bill wasn't sure how it would affect the connection otherwise, and he didn't want to take a chance on damaging anything.

"Give me a hand, Charlie," he said. The two men shuffled the corrugated pipe forward by increments, slowly inching it through the interface. When they were done, four feet of pipe sat on the Earthside side of the gate, resting in the parking lot.

"Alrighty then, let's peg her down." Bill motioned to Norm, who was standing nearby with an AR-15. The man stepped through the pipe, crouching, and in moments yelled "all okay" from the other end. Bill followed, a sledgehammer and railroad spike in hand.

He looked around as he came out of the other end of the pipe into a typical Lincoln September day. The sky was still gray, but it was just possible that at least some of that gray was good old-fashioned cloud cover. The air was definitely colder than it should be for this time of year, which was no surprise. Months of haze had allowed the air to cool more than usual. Winter in Nebraska would almost certainly be brutal this year.

There was no movement anywhere. No life. No birds, no insects, no plants. Even the crows had given up on the two corpses in the parking lot. The ash had completed its job of obliterating the local ecosystems. If there were seeds under the ash, hopefully they would come up in the spring to a somewhat better climate.

It was the work of a few seconds to spike down the pipe through the hole that Kevin had drilled. Bill gave the pipe a couple of shakes to confirm the spike was well planted, then headed back through, motioning Norm to follow him.

On the Outland side, Bill repeated the process, then attached a buckle-and-chain setup that held the pipe secure at both ends but could be released using a rope. Now the pipe was firmly anchored, one end in Outland, the other end in Lincoln. "Shall we?" he said to the others.

"Let's get some distance first," Charlie said. "The tablet's Bluetooth connection will be fine out to twenty feet or so." The group moved away from the pipe until Charlie stopped and turned. "Ready?"

Bill grinned and nodded. Charlie pushed the button on the U.I., and the interface presumably shut down. Presumably, because Bill couldn't tell from his position at a right angle to the gate. He could still only see four feet of pipe. It hadn't disappeared entirely or returned to Outland, so that part at least seemed to be confirmed.

He stepped forward at an angle and verified that he could see Outland rather than Lincoln through the part of the car gate surrounding the pipe. So the gate was definitely off. And the pipe ended right at the gate. Again, according to theory. Now, the moment of truth.

Bill leaned down slightly and looked through the pipe. And sure enough, he was looking at the dirt overflow lot in Lincoln.

"Well, I will be dipped in shit," Charlie said, staring around Bill at the sight.

"Not how I'd want to spend my Fridays, but we can arrange something." Bill grinned at Charlie and received an eye-roll in reply. "We should test this. Might be dangerous, though. You first."

"Oh, hah hah," Charlie said. "Outa my way, chicken man." With that, Charlie marched around Bill and through the pipe. He straightened up at the opposite end and grinned back at his audience. "Sonofabitch. It works."

"Let's remove the gate," Kevin said.

Charlie hustled back through the pipe. Bill directed Norm to watch the pipe for anyone or anything coming through unexpectedly. It seemed a very low probability, but it was a universal law that the best way to guarantee something bad would happen was to assume that it wouldn't.

Bill and Charlie quickly undid the latches that held the gate segments together, then pulled them apart. They stacked the pieces of gate carefully in the truck, pulled the small wagon with the portal equipment farther away from the pipe, then grinned at the rest of the group and gave a thumbs-up.

"One more check," Bill said. He disappeared into the pipe, then came out a few seconds later. "Yep. Still there."

"Final step," Charlie said. He picked up the rope attached to the buckle and chain, and before anyone could protest, he yanked on it. The setup, running through the pipe, released the restraints at both ends more or less simultaneously.

There was a bang and a sort of flash. The pipe seemed to buck then disappeared, while the buckle and chain shot away in the opposite direction, yanking the rope out of Charlie's hands.

"Ow, sonofabitch!" he yelled, looking down at his hands.

"You okay?"

"I guess. Rope burn. That was pretty violent."

"Way more than I expected, to tell the truth," Kevin said. "I'm not sure where the energy came from."

"So, notes for next time," Bill said. "Don't be in line when disconnecting."

"We should retrieve the pipe," Kevin said.

"You bet. C'mon, Charlie, let's set up." Matching actions to words, Bill grabbed some gate components.

In less than a minute, they had the gate set up again. Bill activated it, and Charlie stepped through, followed by Norm. Charlie's pleased expression turned to concern, then perplexity, as he appeared to search the parking lot on the Lincoln side.

"It's not here," he finally said.

"The pipe?"

"Yep. Gone."

Bill frowned and stepped through the interface, followed by Kevin. Sure enough, the pipe was nowhere to be seen.

"Maybe it got flung a distance?" Charlie said.

"Empty field. Don't see it," Bill replied. "It would have to fly something like three or four hundred yards to be out of sight."

"Soooooo..." Charlie turned and looked at Bill and received a baffled shrug in reply.

Kevin had been at it for hours. Alternately scribbling furiously on a tablet and going slack in math mode, he had steadfastly refused to respond to questions. Now he finally sat back and stared upward for a few moments.

Bill and Richard waited, then Bill finally broke. "Well?"

Kevin lowered his gaze to focus on his audience. "I'll have to double and triple check this, but it looks like the pipe was launched into its own timestream. A new timestream."

"So it creates a new version of what? Outland or Earthside?"

"Neither," Kevin replied. "No Earth. No nothing. Just pipe."

"Whoa," Bill said.

"That doesn't sound healthy," Richard added.

"I could be way off," Kevin replied. "I mean, I'm trying to interpret the math in terms of what it produces in the real world, and I could be totally misinterpreting this. But the math says the pipe does not produce a split, but a new universe. It's all about the way the hypervolume collapses."

"Does this tank my idea, though?" Bill said.

"No, I don't think so. I mean, it's not like it's building up pressure or anything. Just make sure when you stake it down at both ends that you *really* stake it down." Kevin smiled, one of his rare attempts at a joke.

"That seems like good advice, Kev," Bill said. "Let's do that."

Richard snorted. "And you needed a master's in engineering for that."

"Say, which of us invented the gates?" Bill made a face. "Oh, right. You and Kevin." He grinned at his friend. "Seriously, though, I think we'll have to be really careful setting up our interdimensional highway."

39 EXPLORING

He crept carefully up the stairs. The building did not look to be in great shape, but by the same token it hadn't actually collapsed.

He needed to retrieve something from his dorm room on the UNL campus. It was a special kit he'd had for years. He was no longer sure why he'd taken the risk of keeping it on campus, but he'd always felt the need to have it nearby. The kit was a fantasy prop for some of his darker, more violent urges. It had never actually been used, on human beings anyway, but that was about to change.

The room was dark and smelled moldy. Not surprising; almost two months without heat or air circulation could do that. He moved carefully around the room, picking up items and putting them in his pack. Finally, his kit. It was packed into a normal travel toiletry bag. He smiled. He'd always liked that touch.

Satisfied, he turned and left. The room no longer held anything for him. This whole Earth, in fact, could be discarded like old clothes that no longer fit. Outland was his new home, with new rules and new opportunities.

To make his plan work, he needed an alibi, that he was nowhere near Sean and company. Then, he needed his bike, so he could sneak away unseen. And just to cover himself, he'd have to pick up something useful for the drones so they wouldn't wonder where he'd been. He would return with a wheelbarrow-load of salvage, like a good little gatherer.

The great thing about cycling was that it was a solitary activity. No one to berate you, complain, deride, criticize, or just pin you with a withering gaze. He'd spent most of his life on his bike, going on rides whenever life got too hard. Although he'd never competed, he was sure he could place in the top ten percent in any amateur road race. So he could get from A to B and back quickly enough to have an apparent alibi. Which he would need, since he would probably be one of the first suspects they'd think of.

And the bodies would have to disappear. That way, they couldn't even be sure whether or not it was foul play.

He snorted. *Foul play.* What a great term. He'd be sure to play with Sean a little, first.

It was going to be a good day.

40. Refugees

September 18

Richard looked up as a messenger rode up on a mountain bike. The man jumped off, paused to catch his breath, then said, "We have a group that's shown up at the pickup point. Lookouts are talking to them, and have confirmed that they were sent here by Lieutenant Collins. They're from Ashland."

"Any red flags?"

"Not that we've seen." The man—Artie, if Richard remembered correctly—shook his head in emphasis. "Looks like they came straight out of a retirement community, though. They're almost all jerries."

Richard snickered, flipped his notebook closed, and followed Artie out of the longhouse. The messenger jumped on his bike and headed back to the location that intersected the parking lot. As part of Bill's and Monica's paranoid machinations, Collins was giving any refugees the address of a different warehouse complex a half-mile away. Richard headed to the left shed, where Bill's Mad Science Lab was located. If Bill wasn't there, one of his assistants would know where he was.

He found Bill and Monica just outside the shed. They waved as he walked up.

"That's a very determined walk," Monica said. "Something up?"

"Refugees at the pickup point. This will be our first large group since we took on the Guard and their charges. You guys set for the onslaught?"

"Anything special about them?" Monica asked.

"Doesn't seem to be." All three began walking toward the Outland-side location of the pickup point. "I think the average age is up there a little, judging from the message."

Monica screwed her face up into a scowl. "Hmmph. On the other hand, most of the people from the Guard refugees have settled in nicely, so"—she glanced at Bill—"we might be looking for trouble where there isn't any."

"On the other other hand, the Guard's refugees had had the crap beaten out of them emotionally by the time we showed up, and were more grateful than anything. If this group was doing okay where they were ... " Bill was silent for a moment. "On the fourth hand, I might still be overthinking it. Not *everything* is a movie plot."

Richard and Monica stopped dead and stared at Bill. "Who are you?" Monica said.

"And what have you done with our friend?" Richard added.

"I can't be realistic once in a while?"

"Nope," Richard and Monica replied in sync.

The friends shared a laugh, then continued to their destination.

When they arrived, the personnel on site were in the process of shepherding the new group of refugees through the gate. Since they only had one of the six-footers available to them, it was a slow process. People would come through, then stop dead, slowly rotating in place, an almost universal stupefied look on each face. Rivendell personnel had to constantly chivvy them along so that the line could continue to move. And guards stood around the perimeter, maintaining a watch against any local wildlife that still might think bipeds were a food group.

A small contingent split off from the mass and walked toward Richard and company as they approached. Richard wasn't sure if his group's determined walk signaled them as officialdom, or if one of the guards had pointed them out to the others. Either way, these were most likely the spokesmen for the Ashland group.

And spokes*men* was the right word. Four older men, three in suits and ties—and why the fuck would anyone be wearing a suit and tie nowadays? The fourth had a certain—Richard snickered a little at the thought—resemblance to a certain sheriff from a certain Burt Reynolds/Sally Field movie. And a holstered pistol on his hip. Richard glanced at Bill. From the slightly widened eyes and barely suppressed grin, it was obvious that Bill had picked up on it too. Hopefully he would keep it under control and not start things off with a snarky comment.

The two groups met at a mid-point, and one of the suits began speaking right away. "Good afternoon. I'm Donald Brady, acting mayor for Ashland. These"—he pointed as he made introductions—"are Councilors Crenshaw and Knowles, and this is police chief Cummins. We appreciate the hospitality that your Lieutenant Collins offered us. We'd like to meet with your mayor or council or whatever you're using here as soon as possible."

"Well, that'd be us," Richard replied. "We use a committee of eight people, but the three of us are capable of making any non-apocalyptic decisions. I'm Richard Nadeski, this is Bill Rustad, and Monica Albertelli is our police chief."

Cummins snorted, and the other three got surprised and disbelieving expressions on their faces. Monica turned to face Cummins squarely and shifted her AR-15 to alert position, her face stony. "You have a problem with that, Mr. Cummins?"

"It's *Chief* Cummins, missy."

"Not here it isn't, Tinker Bell."

Cummins's face flushed with anger and he placed his hand on his holstered pistol. "You watch your mouth, young lady—"

Monica's weapon was up in a flash, the point of the barrel one foot from Cummins's face. "You watch *yours*, motherfucker. Let's get this straight right from the get-go. You have no authority here. You are a refugee. You are hat in hand. We have an existing structure, and you will respect it and the people running it or you can go back where you came from. Any of that the slightest bit unclear, *missy*?"

Cummins was silent for a few seconds, as the two had a stare-off. Then he said, "You're a bit quick with the weapon. You sure you can pull the trigger if it comes to it?"

"I haven't had a problem so far."

Richard intervened. "She's not kidding, Mr. Cummins. She has a higher body count than most of the Guard troops. Not"—he gave Monica a hard look—"that we consider that something to brag about." She grinned back at him and lowered the rifle.

The other three men, who had gone rigid during this exchange, exhaled noisily. Brady spoke up, evidently trying to further defuse the situation. "We'll be happy to talk to whoever we need to, as appropriate. We have a hundred and some-odd people that we need to get settled."

Richard glanced at Bill before replying. "Collins did radio us that he'd sent a group our way, so we've made some preparations. It's not like we're short of land..." He made a gesture at the surrounding countryside and smiled. "But we do have to keep everyone inside the construction fences for safety reasons."

Crenshaw looked around. "Lots of wildlife, but it seems to be all grazers."

"The predators have learned to avoid the area, sir. In fact, the grazers have figured out that this is a particularly safe location for them, for just that reason. Of course, the occasional grazer ends up in the stew pot, but I think the herds still consider it a lesser evil."

Cummins looked around and nodded, his face neutral. The tension seemed to have evaporated, but Richard wasn't willing to relax. He had a bad feeling this might be an ongoing thing.

The four Ashland officials sat around one end of the long table. The rest of the table was taken up by the seven regular members of the committee, plus Bea Chavez, who was filling in for Lieutenant Collins.

"A hundred and five people," Brady said. "All that's left of a town of twenty-five hundred or so." He looked crestfallen for a moment, then pulled himself together. "Most of the rest headed east or south over the course of the first week. I'm not sure whether they were the smart ones or not."

"Probably not, Mr. Brady," Richard replied, and Brady swiveled his head to face him. Richard noted, again, that the Ashland people all had a tendency to direct their remarks to Sam, who was the oldest member of the committee. It would definitely turn into a problem if it kept up.

"Radio contact with the Omaha expedition is spotty, but we're getting enough for a reasonably clear picture of the state of the highways. Combine that with news from

Bill's jury-rigged satellite receiver, and it looks like there's nowhere to go, and no way to get there anyway. I hate to say it, but there's a good chance a lot of the people who left Ashland in the first days are dead now, unless they managed to get picked up by a military patrol."

Brady winced, then directed his next question to Sam again. "I'm concerned about some of our older people, though. Tents are fine for the rest of us, at least until winter sets in, but you can't expect someone in their sixties to sleep on the ground."

Sam pointed to Richard. "Mr. Brady, I'm in charge of Animal Sciences. You really have to address these issues to the chair."

Brady put his head in his hand for a moment, then looked up. "I'm sorry. I'm sure I'm coming across poorly, but it's very difficult to have this kind of discussion with people in their twenties. No offense, but you're unlikely to have any direct experience with running large operations."

"Maybe not, Mr. Brady. But we created Rivendell, we brought over several hundred students, and we've kept them not only alive but thriving for months now. Call it trial by fire if you want, but it's a bit late in the day to be questioning our experience or competence." Richard spoke calmly, but he could feel his internal temperature starting to rise. Apologizing for being an asshole didn't cut it if you then continued to be an asshole. "Plus, and this is the real issue facing you, we *are* the people you have to deal with. So you'll have to adapt."

Brady sighed and nodded, then hitched his chair slightly to more squarely face Richard.

41. AT THE UNIVERSITY

September 19

The convoy took several days to evaluate the situation in Omaha. Collins had sent a Hummer ahead to check out the situation, but the scouts had quickly determined that Omaha wouldn't be as big of a problem to get around in. For whatever reason, the exodus from the city had resulted in fewer abandoned vehicles—or at least fewer per block. They compiled a list of useful businesses and resources that could be salvaged if time and cargo space permitted.

The most important target though was the university. After that, they would check out the scientific supplies company that Matt and Richard had ordered parts through. No one knew if it would be a warehouse or just someone's basement.

Matt had a map of the university, drawn from memory by someone in Rivendell. They headed immediately for the Engineering Center. Upon arrival, they found a situation that they'd encountered many times in Lincoln. In multi-story buildings, the flat roof tended to collapse first. Most of the time, this dislodged enough ash so that the rest of the building remained standing. No civil engineer with an ounce of sense would declare it safe for entry, but no civil engineer would have an interdimensional portal capable of accessing the interior without disturbing the structure.

Matt went overside with one truck, and one Hummer for coverage. With the pole-cam active, both sides would be in continuous radio contact.

It was midafternoon before Matt finally called it. They had checked every accessible room in the building, and had scored several significant finds. Matt was ecstatic. Not only had he found many parts and raw materials for gates, but he'd located a supply of controller cards and a PROM-burning rig.

He was about to instruct the soldier with the radio to let the convoy know they'd be coming through, when the radio started squawking. Matt couldn't believe what he was hearing.

The convoy was under attack.

42. MISDIRECTION

He waited until the last possible moment, then walked up to the Southpointe group and waved a hand to get the attention of Jeff, the crew leader. "Can you use one more?" he asked.

Jeff's eyes darted around, which momentarily mystified him, until he remembered that it was a tell for discomfort. So even here, in a group where no one knew him, he was a pariah. He had a momentary urge to break the man's neck on the spot, but held his face immobile.

Finally, Jeff nodded. "Sure, okay. You can work, uh..." He looked around. "Actually, we need someone to check around for anything we missed. You okay to do that?"

He nodded. It was fine. They didn't want him around, he didn't want any of them around.

As the group headed for their pickup truck, he swung by the Home Depot group. "I'm changing to the Southpointe group," he said to Harvey, gesturing to the pickup truck. Without waiting for a response, he turned and hurried to catch up. But he saw, out of the corner of his eye, an expression of surprise on Sean's face.

The work was routine. An advance group would identify all useful items to be found in the chosen location, then another group would bring a gate and collect it. This allowed the scavenging groups to prioritize their efforts. Today's work would collect the identified items into a central location, and tomorrow they'd carry them through to the Outland side. It minimized the amount of time that a gate was committed to any one location, an important consideration now that they were down to just a few of the devices.

He had wondered how he was going to separate himself from the rest of the group for the half-hour or so that he needed, but Jeff had helpfully solved that problem. He waved to the others as he left in a random direction. He didn't check to see if anyone waved back.

As soon as he was out of sight, he jogged around to where he'd left his bike. From here, he'd be able to leave without being spotted, even if someone was watching. He checked his watch, did the essential calculations. He'd make it with several minutes to spare. Sean and his friends were so predictable in their routines. Sean would be alone for up to fifteen minutes as he took his morning nature break and botanical break. The other two would be more of a risk. If they insisted on staying together, he might have to take them both out at the same time. Surprise would be on his side, but he'd have to be quick to prevent either one from yelling for help.

He made it to the Home Depot right at his estimated time, hid his bike behind the dumpster, and retrieved his kit and a vicious-looking Bowie knife. Glancing around reflexively, he headed for the bathrooms.

The bodies went into 55-gallon drums at the back of the lot, and the drums went to the back of the stack. While it was theoretically possible a search would find them, it was far more likely that opening the first couple of barrels would dissuade anyone from continuing. The contents, a corrosive cleaning agent, were eye-wateringly unappealing.

He paused to savor the feeling of triumph, then shook himself. Too soon. He wasn't done until he was back at Southpointe, unobserved. Tonight, safely back in his tent, he would take the time to glory in his victory. But right now, he had a hard pedal ahead.

43. Earthside: California

California had been spared most of the effects of the eruption, the ash having reached only to the Mojave and parts of the Sierra Nevada. In addition, the steady airflow from the Pacific had ensured that ash would tend to drift eastward once settled.

But California was, like Las Vegas, a highly artificial environment, largely propped up by technology. In particular, a major portion of the water supply for most of the densely populated areas was pumped in from central and eastern California, using systems powered by imported electricity. One of the first emergency acts of the province of British Columbia was to halt all electricity exports. Almost overnight, most of Southern California went dead.

Calls to the state government were met with stonewalling and vague promises, which most Californians instantly saw through. Runs on grocery and bulk food stores were immediate and predictable—the fights and running gun battles even more so. By the end of the first week, most of the West Coast had been balkanized, reduced to protection zones zealously defended by the residents or by local warlords against all comers.

The inhabitants found themselves facing a quandary. Almost infinite water was literally within sight, but without power, desalinization plants were useless. The warm, sunny climate would be perfect for growing your own crops, but not without water.

And a new economy, based on a different exchange medium, was born.

Eduardo carefully examined the flat of bottled water. Thirty-five bottles in a thick plastic wrapping lay on the sidewalk between him and the other man.

"Ten pounds, dude," the man said, pointing at the bag in Eduardo's hands. The bag contained potatoes. Not great potatoes, but still edible. But you could live without food longer than you could live without water, and Eduardo was almost mad with thirst. The price of water was undergoing inflation, too. Last week he could have bought this flat with half the weight of potatoes. Next week, what would they be asking?

The plastic wrapping looked good—like something done at the factory. But people had been sold counterfeit water—seawater repackaged into bottles. Eduardo leaned in close. The seals on the screw caps hadn't been broken. If this was bogus, it was a masterful job.

Eduardo carefully placed the bag on the ground beside the water. As the man reached out to pick it up, Eduardo pulled a knife and flicked the edge of the plastic wrap, just enough to allow a bottle to be extracted.

The other man swore and grabbed at Eduardo, but not fast enough. With a twist, the cap was off and he took a mouthful.

And spit it out in disgust. Seawater.

The other man grabbed the bag of potatoes and broke for the car that was waiting by the curb. Someone pushed the door open from inside.

Eduardo reached around behind his back and pulled out the Saturday Night Special that he always kept there. One, two shots and the man was down, dropping the bag. The car pulled away from the curb with a screech of tires, the door slamming shut from the acceleration. Pedestrians and bystanders scattered or hit the deck.

As the car roared past him, someone inside stuck a pistol out of the passenger window. Without hesitation, Eduardo emptied his gun in the direction of the passenger seat. The hand dropped the pistol and flopped, limp, against the side of the car.

As the vehicle fishtailed down the street, avoiding other cars, Eduardo strode over and picked up the pistol. Huh. Nice piece. Automatic. Not sure about the make, but it seemed well taken care of. He turned and aimed it at the bystander who had been about to pick up the bag of potatoes. "Uh-uh, old man. That's still mine."

Unfortunate. There'd be no water today, beyond the slow drip of the solar still he'd managed to set up in his apartment. But he now had a much better weapon, and he still had potatoes. Not the worst day.

44. BATTLE

"What's the situation?" Lieutenant Collins huddled behind the truck with Private Andrews and several other soldiers. Everyone had gone to ground when the first shot was fired. The second shot had been directed at the head of a soldier who was attempting to spot the attacker.

"Sir, whatever they're using, it's big!" Andrews exclaimed. "That thing sounded more like a cannon than a rifle. I'm concerned they might be using armor-piercing rounds. The shots are coming in consistently high, so I'm thinking the shooter is not an expert, or Bradbury over there would be dead."

Collins considered for a moment. "An impasse is pointless. Therefore, they are going to try to bracket us. Send a couple of men out to our flanks to intercept any attempt. Have you contacted the scavenging team?"

"Yes sir. Matt is going to try to use the pole-cam to reconnoiter."

Collins nodded. The portals were their best chance of getting out of this situation. But he was concerned about the large ordnance. A big enough weapon could go right through the vehicles and pick off personnel one at a time. And even if a round didn't hit someone, it could do crippling damage to the equipment. Meanwhile, his men had no options until they could get reliable intel.

Then there was a voice from nearby, projected over a loudspeaker. "Come out with your hands over your heads, and you won't be harmed. Continue to resist, and you will all be killed. We have you surrounded."

Collins glanced at Andrews, who picked up the radio. A few seconds of conversation, and he shook his head. "Pretty sure that's bull, sir. Flankers are still in play, and anyone with two active brain cells would have taken them out if they could."

Collins nodded. Matt and company would be investigating from overside. His best bet was to draw this out as long as possible. He would sit tight and wait for the next move from the opposition.

Matt and the small group of soldiers on the Outland side were using the pole-cam in quick bursts, to avoid being spotted. With the tablet, they could examine the short video clip at leisure after each snapshot.

Then they got lucky. They had just activated the pole-cam for a scan when the unknowns made their loudspeaker demands. The camera microphone was highly directional to begin with, and being mounted at the mouth of an inter-dimensional interface amplified the effect. Within seconds, they were able to estimate the direction of the speaker to within a few degrees.

They continued to move cautiously, taking quick snap-shots, until they found themselves looking down at a couple of men, crouched behind an ornamental wall made of concrete blocks. One of them was aiming what looked to Matt like the biggest damned rifle ever made, using a scope proportional to the rifle. The other was holding a portable loudspeaker. The two were conversing, but too quietly for the pole-cam to pick up.

Quickly turning off the pole-cam, Matt turned to Corporal Timminson, who was holding it.

"What the friggin' hell is *that*?" he said.

Timminson looked at the image on the tablet, and said, "950 JDJ, I think. I saw a YouTube video of one once."

"What do you hunt with that?"

"The Hulk. Godzilla. Cthulhu. Stuff like that." Timminson gave the image a swipe. "They aren't fooling around. Any other actors in the area?"

Matt motioned to the pole-cam, turned it on again, and they did a quick 360. There was someone a short distance away, but that person was lying down in a heap on the ground. He appeared to be unconscious or dead.

The soldiers quickly set up the six-foot gate. After taking a quick last shot through the pole-cam to confirm that nothing had changed, they swapped the connections to the bigger gate.

As they readied themselves to go through, Timminson turned to the two soldiers. "This is a live battle situation. No hesitation. If they give any indication of resistance, pop them. Clear?"

They both nodded. Turning to Matt, Timminson gave the 3-2-1 finger-count. At zero, Matt hit "OK," the interface popped open, and all three soldiers rushed through.

The two men on the ground were taken completely by surprise. The soldiers started yelling at them to lie flat, show their hands, and not resist. Instead the two rolled in opposite directions and attempted to reach for holstered weapons. The exchange of gunfire was one-sided and brief.

Timminson looked down at the two bodies, watching for any signs of life. After a few moments, he looked around.

"Doesn't appear to be anyone else involved. Not sure what the story is with this guy over here." He motioned to the man lying on the ground nearby. As they moved toward the individual, he slowly turned to face them. Timminson brought up his weapon for a moment, then lowered it when the man spoke.

"There's no one else. Just those two. Are they dead?"

"Yes, they are," Timminson replied.

"Thank God," the man said, and started to cry.

Matt bent to examine the man, who was visibly trying to regain control. He realized that the man was chained to the backpack he was wearing, and was also in leg chains and arm chains.

"Oh, this is just getting weirder and weirder," Timminson said, and raised his radio to report.

Lieutenant Collins detailed several soldiers to make sure that all vehicles, personnel, salvage, and equipment ended up back on Earthside. Then he headed over to the scene of the takedown.

On arrival, he found Timminson and two other soldiers talking to a man in arm and leg chains. The man was wearing a backpack, which also appeared to be chained to him.

Timminson stood as the lieutenant approached. "Sir, this is George Handlerson. It appears that he and some other civilians have been held against their will by this group"— he waved at the two corpses—"who appear to be some kind of survivalists. They call themselves the Brotherhood. They captured George's group a while back and have essentially made them into slaves."

Collins looked at George, who was thin, dirty, dressed in rags, and eating an MRE with apparent relish.

"So, George, think you could show us where this group is located?" Collins said.

George smiled, nodded enthusiastically, and took another large bite of MRE. Collins shuddered. He turned to Matt, who had a finger up, about to interject. "I know, Matt, but this can't wait. Lives are at stake, and this *Brotherhood* will start to miss their members soon. We need to take care of this now. We can come back to the university afterward."

45. ANOTHER DAY

September 19

Suzie smiled as she and Richard left the tent. He'd been particularly amorous this morning, and she was pretty sure she was going to be late for work as a result. Well, tough.

She gave Richard a quick parting kiss, and walked quickly toward the facilities, toiletries in hand.

As she started making her way, she realized that Creepy Guy was standing nearby, with an odd look on his face. *Was he WAITING for me?* Suzie was particularly creeped out at this thought. *Definitely going to talk to Richard about him. Creepy fuck.* She deliberately didn't look at him as she walked away.

The morning breakfast routine was going well. There would be omelets again today, so attendance would be high. The last egg breakfast had gone exceedingly well. Everyone had gotten some, there'd been no complaints—except about there not being enough—and the mood around Rivendell had been especially good for the whole day. People were still in a good mood, enough so that the normal complaints—*Beefalo AGAIN?* —were conspicuously less common than usual.

While she was setting up, Maddie sidled up and said in a sing-song tone, "Somebody's got a boyfriend..."

"Well, about time," Suzie said. "I was beginning to worry about you."

Maddie laughed. "Not me, you nitwit! I've got *three* boyfriends, and that works just fine for me! No, I mean Frankie. He seems to have met someone."

Suzie nodded, pleased. Frankie's boyfriend, Darren, hadn't been part of the crowd of refugees when Yellowstone erupted, and there'd never been any sign of him Earthside. Frankie had put up a brave face, but anyone could tell he took it hard. She was glad that her friend was rebuilding a life now.

"And in other news, they're organizing a hoedown tonight," Maddie added after a moment.

"Oh. Will the Booze Brothers be supplying that swill that they laughingly call 'beer' again?" Suzie had tried the stuff—one sip—and sworn off all liquids for life.

Maddie scooped all the organics into the box for composting. "I tasted a sample of their latest. It's actually not bad. Still kind of weak, but getting there. And Krista has declared it not instantly lethal, so that's a bonus." The two shared a laugh. There had been a lot of effort put into providing a supply of alcohol in Rivendell, since all attempts to find any sources Earthside had failed. There was a group trying to make wine as well, but they hadn't been able to locate enough grapes to make more than a token amount.

The two women kidded and gossiped as they prepared breakfast, and the episode with Creepy Guy faded from Suzie's memory.

46. RECON

"Everyone had different reasons for not having left Omaha," George was saying, "but none of us was inclined to judge. We ended up kind of banding together into a community. It was working. We were starting to talk about getting some vehicles and heading south once the ash stopped."

He hesitated, and his voice shook when he resumed talking. "Then the Brotherhood attacked. That's what they call themselves. Arrogant blowhards. They'd apparently been watching us for a while. They knew how many people were in each house, when we came and went, even what weapons we had. I guess we were just concerned about fighting nature. It didn't occur to us that we'd have to protect ourselves from other people, especially not that long after the eruption."

George paused to take a sip of water and another bite of MRE.

"A couple of the guys kicked up a fuss, and the Brotherhood killed them. Just like shooting a dog in the street. *To make a point,* they said. They've been keeping us in their underground shelter. It's one of those things you can order online. I get the impression that Burton—the leader—had more money than brains. He sure had more than his share of toys."

Collins glanced at Matt and noticed that he was blushing. "I'm aware of the irony," Matt muttered. The lieutenant smiled just slightly.

"Anyway, they've been keeping us in one of the rooms, chained up most of the time. We do their labor, cleaning, carrying, cooking. Or else. The men have it easy. The women have to tend to their other needs. Again, or else.

"A couple of our group who pissed one or another of them off for some small reason have been killed, slowly, for their amusement. I wouldn't even consider these scum *human* anymore."

George had finally run down, but it looked like he was starting to tear up again after this last statement.

"So why were you and your two keepers in town?" Matt asked.

"Hunting. Literally. There are other individuals and small groups in the city. Or were, anyway. We hadn't seen anyone at all this trip. Dumb and Dumber there"—he waved in the direction of the two corpses—"like to go hunting. Fredericks likes to try to shoot them with the big rifle from a half-mile away. I'm along as the pack mule, of course.

"When they saw you guys, they thought they could get you to give up, then they'd get the lion's share of the loot. I think the idea was that Fredericks would shoot off his big gun a few times and you'd all roll over."

"It's a nice piece," said Collins. "I'll take pleasure in adding it to our armament. It might be useful against those Albertosauruses." He grinned at Matt, who laughed.

George looked at both of them. "Alberto-what?"

Matt shook his head. "You don't want to know."

"When you're ready, George," Collins said, "you can show us where this Brotherhood is holed up."

❧   ❧   ❧

Collins scanned the area with binoculars. George had led them to a property just outside the city. It had been a large property back when such things had meaning. It was mostly trees, but there was a cleared area at one end, with a small cinder-block building in the middle of it.

Collins, George, and two soldiers had spent the last half hour carefully approaching the area. Collins had enough experience with survivalists to expect traps, surveillance devices and alarms. So far, they'd found nothing. This group was either not very smart, or far smarter than the Guard.

"That's the entrance to the underground bunker," George said.

"It can't just be the single entrance," Timminson said. "I bet there's an emergency exit tunnel or something. It'll be capable of being opened only from the inside."

Collins nodded. "We're going to wait until after dark, then we're going to examine the area using infrared. Chances are that any underground structures will change the heat signature of the ground."

47. Things Are Looking Up

He woke up abruptly. He felt panic, as if he'd just woken from a nightmare, but he couldn't remember anything about it.

He went through his usual routine, ending with his morning meds. He went through the routine because he needed to *finish* things, but it didn't seem nearly as important.

He was feeling especially upbeat today, so he decided to treat himself. Leaving five minutes early, he stopped to take deep breaths of the crisp morning air. This also helped to relieve an unaccustomed overheated feeling that he couldn't explain.

Several of the *normals* stopped to watch. He was slightly surprised that the half-conscious clods had enough mental ability to notice the change in routine.

Finally, he started on his morning walk.

As usual, the dance of humanity proceeded on its clockwork path. He could have almost navigated with his eyes closed. All too soon, he was approaching Suzie's tent, where she and the dolt were just leaving. He smiled at her, and she gave him a look of warning. Of course, silly of him. The dolt was still in view.

Next was Amy, who returned his smile with her usual affectionate one.

Life was *good*.

❖ ❖ ❖

He joined the crowd waiting for assignments, and shuffled his way forward until he was close enough to read the lists.

His name was on the Southpointe list. He'd have whooped for joy if he let himself. They had accepted his change of groups without question.

"Where's Sean?" someone said, looking around. "And Merv and Ivan, for that matter."

The group leader shrugged. "Well, this *is* voluntary. Maybe they're taking a day off. Val, can you work their group instead for today?" Someone, presumably Val, gave a thumbs-up. And just like that, the gap was filled and life went on.

This *would* be a good day.

48. EARTHSIDE: TAKEOVER

It was one of the wealthiest neighborhoods in Corpus Christi. Huge mansions, each with fences, security systems, and in many cases, security personnel. The residents of this neighborhood hadn't been immediately affected by the eruption. There was a little ash, but the staff took care of cleaning it away. There had been some concern when the power went off, but emergency generators running on natural gas took up the slack. When the natural gas finally quit, they'd switched to the gasoline generators. Eventually, that had run out as well.

This was the point when reality started to intrude. It was simply not possible to buy more gasoline—not for any price, not anywhere. The same for food. There had been some bartering between families, but that had been only marginally helpful.

Then the owners had announced to their staff that they could no longer pay or feed them. In some cases, the former employees simply left. In other cases, the former employees indicated to the owners that *they* would be leaving, usually at the point of a gun. Threats, pleas, imprecations were ineffective. Promises to come back with law enforcement were met with laughter; there'd been no sign of anything resembling law enforcement for more than a month.

Now came the last straw. The waves of migrants fleeing the eruption were now arriving in large numbers. Most were armed, none was interested in putative property rights. The large acreages were perfect for growing crops, even if the sunlight was a bit sketchy. The former owners were invited to pick up a hoe if they wanted to stay. Some did.

Martha Pells looked over the small patch of land. It was hers, to the extent that anything belonged to anyone. The Boss had proclaimed that each person would work their own patch and would tithe twenty-five percent for protection. He had also proclaimed that anyone caught stealing from someone else's patch, or doing *anything* that would reduce productivity, would die in the most painful, slow, and public way possible.

Families were given larger patches to work, depending on the number of members. Gordon, Martha's husband of thirty years, had not survived the march south. She teared up, as she always did, with the memory of him lowering himself to the ground at the side of the road and pleading with her to go on and stay with the crowd. He'd died a few hours later in her arms. She ran as best she could to catch up with the only safety she had left, a miscellaneous mob of strangers shuffling their way slowly toward where the sun should be.

Martha began to hack at the lawn with her shovel. It would probably require several days to strip the layer of grass away so that crops could be planted. There would be very little time to grow anything before winter set in, even this far south.

She began to wonder if Gordon had been the lucky one.

49. ASSAULT

September 19 and 20

The National Guard soldiers very carefully reconnoitered the area of the Brotherhood's stronghold. They had both infrared and night-vision equipment available, each of which had its own strengths. They did find two cameras from their heat signatures, but the cameras were set up primarily to monitor the entrance and the immediate surroundings. Since the Guard had no plans for a frontal assault, they simply avoided the area.

A slightly warmer line of earth, leading radially from the stronghold, indicated the possibility of a tunnel or similar structure. A quick investigation revealed a heavily armored hatch, lightly buried under leaves and branches.

The guard took careful measurements of the size and location of the stronghold, triangulating from several points around the perimeter. Then they brought the gates around to each location and transferred to Outland.

When dawn broke on Outland, they started setting up. Matt was everywhere, coordinating. From their survey measurements, they were able to lay out the approximate borders of the stronghold, location of the escape tunnel, and both entrances. Everything was marked with stakes and with spray paint.

George looked over the results. Then he walked to the location of the entrance, and paced out to the marked border. He smiled at Matt. "Feels pretty close. You guys are good! So what now?" George had had a little trouble accepting the explanation for the gate at first, but seeing is believing.

Lieutenant Collins stepped forward. "Now we dig. We need to get deep enough to be able to poke the pole-cam into their living space. It doesn't sound to me like they buried their bunker any deeper than they had to. Three or four feet should do it, at least for preliminary recon." He glanced at a group of soldiers, who were standing by with shovels. Turning back to George, he said, "So, where shall we start?"

The prairie grass had never been tilled or turned over, and as a result the roots were more than a foot deep and heavily entwined. The men were sweating profusely, even in the cool air, by the time they got down to actual dirt. Replacements stepped in, and from that point the work proceeded quickly.

Finally, Collins gestured to the hole. "Okay, Matt. Give it a try."

Matt fired up the gate, and the soldier who was assigned to assist him dipped the pole-cam into the hole.

"I'm going to take a single frame," Matt said. "Don't want to leave the interface open long enough for anyone to notice it. I've got the cam hooded to keep extraneous light out as well." Without waiting for acknowledgement, Matt pressed "OK," and an image came up in the video window.

"Ladies and germs, we are in. Hmm, well, sort of. We'll have to dig down a little more to get the people gate opened."

"Any sign of guards?" Collins asked.

"Nothing in frame." Matt shrugged. "We'll do a better recon once we're deep enough."

It was full dark by the time the hole had been dug down far enough for Matt's satisfaction. The soldiers moved back, and he did another single-frame recon. "It's total darkness in there. George, is this corridor used for anything?"

George stepped forward. He'd been given some spare clothing, but in his emaciated state he looked like a child wearing adult clothes. A blanket was draped across his shoulders for additional warmth. "It's a secret emergency exit. Burton and his cronies were always making up scenarios where someone would lay siege to the shelter, and they'd sneak out this exit and frag them all. Or something." George made a face. "God, the jingoistic chest-thumping got bad sometimes, but if you said anything, a beating was the best-case response. We learned to keep our mouths shut."

"Is there a door at the inside end?" Collins asked.

"Yep. Booby-trapped, too."

"What?" Collins looked up.

"Well, alarmed, I mean," George said quickly. "They tied some bells to it. If someone opens the door, they'll sound."

"You mean like the door to a store or gas station?"

"Yeah, same idea."

"Could we open it slowly enough to not make a sound?"

"Maybe. And if they're partying, they wouldn't notice anyway. Chances are they're wasted by now. Burton stocked up alcohol like it was gold. Probably has several years' supply."

Collins glanced at Matt. "Not like anyone we know."

Matt grinned back. "I have no idea to what you refer."
Then, more seriously, "We could dig the hole into a trench,
get past the door on this side. Either drop directly in or
undo the bells."

Collins shook his head. "Dropping into the main area is
a non-starter. Too dangerous, and we couldn't get people in
fast enough to hold them off if they reacted quickly. Say what
you will about these good-ol'-boys, they won't hesitate to fill
the air with bullets. We need stealth, but we need to do this
quickly. If we wait until tomorrow night, they'll be getting
worried about their missing people, and they'll be on alert."
Collins turned to George. "Where are the prisoners?"

"They get locked in the vault except when they're
needed."

"The *vault?*"

George shrugged. "I think that's what it was originally
supposed to be. It's got a stupid-thick door and a combination lock."

"Okay, then at least they're probably safe." Collins
turned to one of his soldiers. "Got a flashbang?"

The soldier grinned. "Yes sir. I recommend a smaller
one, considering the enclosed space and lack of windows."

Collins nodded. "Then let's do this. We move a squad
into the corridor, open the door stealthily—we hope—and
roll in a flashbang."

"Some of the prisoners might be in there with them,"
Matt said.

"If you ask me, any one of us would consider it a small
price to pay for getting out of there." George shook his head
adamantly. "Don't let that possibility slow you down."

Matt and his assistant set up the six-foot gate and soldiers moved through, weapons at the ready.

"We'll leave the interface open in case a hasty retreat is necessary," Collins said to Timminson. "You know the goal. You're on your own recognizance."

The wait was interminable. Matt was sure hours had passed, but his watch said less than two minutes, when there was a loud *bang* from the gate, followed by yelling. But no gunfire, which was a good sign.

Another minute, and a soldier stuck his head through the interface. "Location secured, sir. We've swept. No other actors."

Collins gave Matt a raised eyebrow, checked his sidearm, and followed the soldier through the interface. Matt hurried to stay with the lieutenant.

Once through the corridor door, they found themselves in a surprisingly large and luxurious space. Comfortable furniture, a couple of TVs with video game consoles attached, and a pair of tables loaded with food and alcohol bottles in various stages of consumption. A scorched area in the center of the room indicated where the flashbang had detonated.

The soldiers had their weapons aimed at four men lying on the ground in disarray. Matt took a close look and had to shake his head. If you wanted to draw a picture of the clichéd stereotype of a backwoods good-ol'-boy, you simply couldn't improve on this lot. Beer bellies, lumberjack shirts and leather vests, Daytons on the feet (even indoors), and scraggly beards. It was so scripted as to be almost cosplay.

"Over here," said one of the soldiers.

They moved to where he'd indicated to find an unconscious woman, naked and spread-eagled, strapped to a ... contraption. Matt felt his gorge rise. There was only one possible use for that thing—to render someone helpless.

Collins called for a medic, and they began to unstrap the victim.

Collins and Matt moved away when the medic arrived. "Have you found the other prisoners?" Collins said to a nearby soldier.

"We've found what we think is the vault, sir. Banged on the door, got thumps back, so someone's in there. We'd have to use explosives to open it, though, unless we can get the combo. And in an underground bunker, with an unknown number of people in an unknown space on the other side, it's problematic."

Collins nodded. "A vault? Like an actual bank vault?"

"Yes sir. It may have actually been intended as a place to lock up valuable items."

"Okay, let's check our prisoners."

The four men seemed to be slowly recovering their senses, although they were having trouble focusing and speaking.

"Dead drunk, all of them," Collins said. "Unbelievable." He turned to one of the guards. "Search them. Maybe someone wrote down the combo. If not, we'll have a conversation."

Matt and Collins scanned the room while they waited. "Corridors down there, there, and there," Matt said. "Pretty standard cross pattern. Probably bedrooms, storage, kitchen, and so on. That's the main exit." He pointed to a circular staircase. "Very advanced. Where do you get something like this?"

"Believe it or not, Matt, you can order these things on the internet. The manufacturer will arrange delivery, excavation, and construction. Apparently, Burton really did have a lot more money than brains."

Matt made an exaggerated expression of shock. "Strange that Bill didn't order one. He's ordered every other item in existence."

A soldier came up to Collins and saluted. "Sir, we've found a considerable cache of supplies, items specifically chosen for long shelf life. These people were prepared for the long haul. Shall we … "

"Oh, absolutely, soldier. We'll be confiscating all of that. Also demoing this structure. Have the vehicles brought in to Earthside, and move everyone over. Use the main entrance to offload everything you find. But set up a perimeter guard just in case there are more Brotherhood out there."

"We should probably check with George on that," Matt said.

The medic, a Private Burroughs, came up next. "The woman is awake. Her name is Maria. She started to sob when she saw us. She's still mostly incoherent, but I think she was unconscious before the assault. She's pretty banged up—it doesn't look like they were trying too hard to keep her alive, long term—but she'll be okay now. Also, Baynes wanted me to tell you, they haven't found anything."

Collins gestured to Matt to follow him. The four men were on their knees, hands bound behind them, and being guarded by several soldiers. Between the inebriation and the effects of the flashbang, they looked much the worse for wear. But they'd recovered enough to have rediscovered some swagger. Collins and Matt were met with hostile glares.

Collins didn't bother with preliminaries. "What's the combination to the vault?"

"Fuck you," said the biggest one.

"Are you Burton?"

"Fuck you."

Collins paused and gave him a once-over. "Your behavior here is going to decide how short and unhappy the rest of your life is going to be. I have no reason to be gentle with you. So let's try again. What's the combination?"

"Fuck you, G.I. Joe. I know your type, all duty and honor and holier than thou. Shoot me, if you think you have the balls."

Again, Collins paused. Then he turned to the medic. "Is Maria strong enough to walk?"

Burroughs looked surprised, then nodded. "Yes, she's already up and moving about. Trying to work out the cramps from her, uh, bonds."

"Bring her here, would you?"

While they waited, Collins drew his sidearm, checked the magazine, and deliberately and conspicuously inspected it. When Burroughs returned with the woman, who was now dressed in what Collins had to imagine were her regular clothes, the lieutenant addressed her. "Maria, do you know how to use a handgun?"

Maria was momentarily taken aback by the question, but recovered quickly. "Safety off, point, shoot," she replied. "I'm not an expert, but I've been to the range. I can hit the target."

"Excellent. These men—" he gestured to the four on their knees—"are refusing to tell us the combination for the vault. I want you to hold this gun to this man's head, and if he doesn't tell me what I want, you do whatever you feel is necessary. Interested?"

Maria's eyes grew wide. "I can't guarantee I won't shoot him anyway."

"That's a chance I'm willing to take." Collins safetied then handed her the weapon.

Maria looked at Burton and a grin slowly spread across her face. There was absolutely nothing friendly or humorous about the expression. She took the gun in a confident two-handed grip, Collins couldn't help noticing, and aimed it at Burton's head. There was a click as the safety came off. "Don't tell him anything," she said. "Please."

Burton started sweating. Literally, beads of moisture popped out on his forehead. No question, he knew she would pull the trigger. "38-12-42-30," he said, barely moving his lips.

A soldier immediately double-timed in the direction of the vault. Collins held out his hand. "Thank you, Maria. Can I have my gun back, please?"

Maria looked at him out of the corner of her eye, then back at Burton. Her face contorted and she gave a wordless snarl.

"It's not like they're going to be just walking away from this," Collins continued. "I have plans for them. Do you really want to miss the fun?"

That got her attention. She couldn't have any idea what the lieutenant meant, but her curiosity was piqued. With an obviously herculean effort, she safetied the gun and handed it back.

Meanwhile, a series of clunks in the distance was followed by loud exclamations and sobs. Five people staggered out of the vault, helped by soldiers. Their clothing was barely more than rags, and they were as emaciated as George, who hugged each person as they exited the room.

50. MISSING

Monica paced through the common area, threading her way between the groups. She catalogued faces as she moved, matching people up with their work groups. Most people were pulling their weight. Most people were decent individuals and would contribute where they could. Others worked because the alternative was boredom. Some put in the minimum effort that they thought they could get away with. They would be in for a surprise when they realized that people noticed. Rivendell wasn't so big that you could get lost in the faceless hordes.

Then there were the malingerers. The freeloaders. There'd been a dramatic drop in those numbers since the performance with Josh, but doubtless they'd just moved into the minimum-effort camp for the moment.

Monica turned as she heard her name being called. It was one of the regulars from Matt's reclamation crews, although she couldn't remember his name offhand.

"Hi, Monica. Listen, have you seen Sean? Sean Fulton. I don't know if you know him..."

"I know the face. He plays a lot of three-on-three with you guys, right?"

"Yeah, he never came back from scavenging yesterday. We were hoping maybe he came back early or through another gate or something, but nada." The man paused and frowned. "Come to think of it, I haven't seen Merv or Ivan around either. They hang together a lot."

"Was his bed slept in?" Monica asked.

"Uh…" The man—Scott was his name, Monica now remembered—looked embarrassed. "I'm not sure how we'd tell. It's not like we, you know…"

"Right. Bachelor style." Monica chuckled. "Don't sweat it. I'm not exactly a neat freak myself. Okay, just go to work. I'll keep an eye out and ask around. If we haven't found any of them by end of day, we'll look at a search party or something."

Howie nodded and walked off. Monica shook her head, amused at how long it had taken to dredge up his name. For the hundredth time, she promised herself she'd get more sleep.

51. NEXT STEPS

He'd had another dream about the dead cat. He re-ran the sequence in his mind, then shrugged it off.

He skipped his normal morning walk; the decision caused him to break into a sweat, but he needed to make an early start. It was time to start preparing his hideaway— a bolt hole to use if worst came to worst, or if he simply couldn't take living here anymore.

He went to the second shed, where the scavenging group would be organizing. There'd been far fewer excursions lately; Lincoln was getting close to being picked clean. He *had* to get some of his materials before things were shut down entirely.

The Southpointe location had been cleaned out, and the former members were being reassigned or picking different groups on their own. It would be easy to sign up for any convenient location; they were used to him, and they didn't want to talk to him any more than he wanted to talk to them. It would also be easy to make an excuse to go check out a pharmacy or medical lab. Maybe he'd bring back some innocuous items so he'd look like he'd been busy and useful. But he'd keep the good stuff.

Sean and his friends were still missing. Of course. But no one had figured it out, or found the bodies, so that was okay. More important, no one seemed especially suspicious.

It was being written off, at least so far, as a case of some guys having decided to stop working.

But that wouldn't last long. And concern would rise. They'd do searches. The first thought would be predators, of course. But if that produced nothing, suspicions would develop. He'd have to forestall that. Maybe some misdirection was in order. A victim completely unrelated to him.

He'd work on it.

But what if he screwed up? What if, despite all his planning, suspicion fell on him? Where would he go? He had the whole of Outland to escape to, of course, but what kind of existence was that? Alone, no support structure, surrounded by predators. Death might be preferable.

Unless he had a support structure already set up. And company. It could work...

52. VICTORY

Seven emaciated people stood in clothing far too large for them, greedily stuffing MREs into their faces. Four fat members of the former Brotherhood stood a short distance away, hands on their heads, covered by as many soldiers.

"Strip," said Collins. The captives just stared, not comprehending. "It's not a complicated order. Take your clothes off, leave them in a pile on the ground. Refuse and I give the gun to Maria again."

Slowly, reluctantly, the four stripped. In the midday fall sun, they weren't quite getting goose bumps, but by sunset Matt was certain they would be feeling the chill.

"Now, leave. You have ten minutes to get out of range. At that point, my soldiers will be ordered to engage in target practice." Collins took a deep breath. "*Move!*"

The prisoners jumped in surprise, then turned and began walking. After several glances back, they began to pick up their pace.

Collins gestured to Corporal Timminson. "If they're still in view in ten minutes, start taking shots. Try more to scare them, but if they don't take the hint, go for body shots. How are we on the supplies?"

"All loaded, sir. Jeffries is wiring up some explosives to take down the bunker. Twenty minutes or so for that. We'll set fire to the above-ground buildings."

Collins nodded. "It's wasteful, especially in these times, but we don't want to give the Brotherhood any way to re-establish here."

Burroughs said, "They'll die of exposure anyway, sir."

"No, we're going to leave their clothes here for them. If they have any sense, they'll come back after we're gone, to pick through everything."

Collins looked around. "And speaking of leaving, let's get this done. It's going to take a day or two just to decide what we should take with us."

53. MORE PLANNING

He watched, and continued to take mental notes. Movements, schedules, habits, and routines. People moved in well-established ruts. Learn the patterns and they were ridiculously predictable.

This one always has a coffee in the morning. That one always stays up late. This one leaves the keys in the ATV. *Idiot.* But useful.

The patterns formed a dance, and the dance could be modified with a simple movement, or you could walk through the middle of it without affecting anything. The trick would be picking the time.

He casually packed some supplies into a backpack, then requested an ATV. Not the one with the keys. Don't want to break that pattern. As usual, there was no problem. Geological studies were a sideline in terms of survival, but still an important one. Recognizing his importance, the man in charge of the equipment was always quick and efficient, getting him on his way without delay.

He drove off, as usual picking a different direction until he was out of sight of the colony. At that point, he turned and headed for his cache.

Once there, he carefully transferred his purloined supplies into the ever-growing collection, and re-buried the cache.

Creating the cache had been a challenge. Some of the contents were inevitably going to smell like food, and wildlife would be interested. The traditional bear-proof cache hanging from a rope would be fine on Earthside, but the first giant sloth that came along would take it down. He had finally built a cache out of large rocks, combined with wooden stakes to keep animals at bay. It was a thorough pain to get into each time he visited, but so far it was working as designed.

Soon, he thought. *Soon, we can be together, the way we have all been wishing for.*

54. EARTHSIDE: EAST COAST

The East Coast of the U.S. was one of the most hard-hit areas on the planet, only exceeded by the devastation experienced immediately downwind of Yellowstone. In New York, Washington, D.C., Maine, and surrounding areas, the ash had settled in for the duration, leaving no ecosystem, no transportation system, and a collapsed electrical system. The technological collapse was near total.

But the East Coast had a spectacularly profuse boat culture. From fishing boats and other working vessels to pleasure craft to ferries, cargo vessels, and anything else that could float, there were many opportunities for the public to get out of town. Initially, most departures were at the hands of the rightful owners. However, as the days went on, confiscation and piracy became a real thing. By two weeks after the eruption, there were no seaworthy vessels left at moorage anywhere north of Florida.

The East Coast being the most densely populated part of the U.S., the watery escape routes afforded an opportunity for only a small percentage of the population. Trains and other forms of mass transit moved the masses southward for as long as they remained in service; the highways and interstates lasted perhaps a few days longer. But in the end, as every form of transportation ground to a halt or clogged up beyond usability, people found themselves stuck.

Motorcycles were useful for a tankful of distance; more if the owner packed some jerricans. Bicycles were slower but more dependable, until the ash in the air rendered the cyclist too ill to continue. And very few seriously considered walking.

Looting as a career choice enjoyed a brief popularity. However, it was a high-risk occupation, and suffered from the additional problem that looters often found themselves defending their hard-won gains from other looters. Attrition was swift and brutal.

After this point, many East Coast cities settled into a waiting pattern, almost a hibernation, hoping for the air to clear or the government to appear, or *something*.

There would be no rescue. The population density on the eastern seaboard, even after the boat exodus, guaranteed that all the food and water was consumed within weeks of the event. The Atlantic weather, combined with lack of any warming sunlight and a consequent cooling of the Gulf Stream, resulted in what would be the most brutal winter conditions that humanity had ever experienced in that geographic region, beginning in late summer.

The Great Dying had begun.

55. University of Nebraska at Omaha

September 22

Matt examined the Agriculture building in chagrin through a pair of 10x50 binoculars. The structure had been right at the edge of a fire that had swept through the Omaha campus. Very little was left, and what there was didn't look stable.

"We won't be exploring that, I think," Collins, beside him, said.

Matt brought the binoculars down to his chest and let them hang from the strap. "Not much point anyway. I'm more disappointed in the damage to the medical buildings. Krista won't like that."

Collins grunted. "We can't spend too long on this. And unfortunately, if we come back in six months, it'll probably be even more trashed. We still need to check your hardware supplier. And follow up on your heavy equipment idea."

Matt nodded. If the company that supplied their gate components was trashed, that would be a huge blow. They could probably scrounge up some PC parts from local computer retail outlets, but the lasers and interferometry equipment were very much specialty items. Those would place a hard limit on the number of gates that could ultimately be built, at least until civilization bootstrapped back up to that level of technology. If it ever did.

"We'll make a stop at George's community on the way, but I don't have a lot of hope," Collins said. "There's been nothing on the radio from them. They may have bugged out, or the Brotherhood might have finished the job before we got here."

Matt nodded without comment and re-cased the binoculars.

George guided the convoy to his neighborhood. When they arrived, he stepped out of the truck and looked around while the truck drivers honked their horns. Thirty seconds of honking produced no results, however.

George, looking crestfallen, shook his head at Matt and Collins. "They're either gone or dead, most likely because of the Brotherhood. I know you can't do a full search through the city, but is there anything you *can* do?"

"We can put up a sign," Matt said. "If someone has a radio, they can contact us. If they don't, maybe they can make their way to Lincoln. We can include the address of the storage facility."

Collins nodded in agreement. "Not really much we can do beyond that. Sorry, George. How many people might have still been here, best case?"

"Up to a dozen." George hung his head. "I guess we should consider ourselves lucky that seven of us survived. But if I ever see one of those fat fucks, and I have a weapon..."

"Yeah, can't blame you," Matt said. He turned to the lieutenant. "Time to check out Bill's vendor, I guess. Then, unless something else comes to mind, I think we're done with Omaha."

Ironically, the company that Bill and Richard had been using to order their equipment operated out of a storage unit. Matt grinned at the lieutenant as he gestured to the tall, blue rollup door. "There's something poetic about this."

Collins snorted, then gestured to the soldier holding the bolt cutter. The padlock took only a moment to cut, and they were looking into a large warehouse space.

"No lights," Matt said. He activated his rechargeable spotlight and scanned the room. "Wow, they were into a lot of stuff. I may be here a while."

"Let's find the items you're specifically looking for, okay? Once we load them, we can determine how much more equipment you can salvage."

"You got it." Matt gestured to Timminson, who had a pad and paper ready, and they began examining shelves. Meanwhile, Collins turned to Burroughs.

"Perimeter?"

"Sentries set up, sir. No one will be sneaking up on us."

"Good. Any of that coffee left in the thermos?"

Matt strode up, Timminson in tow, just as Collins was finishing off his cup. "I have good news, and good news," he said.

Collins frowned. "That can't be right. Doesn't sound like the way the universe normally works."

Matt laughed. "I know, right? But we double-checked this stuff." He gestured at Timminson, who held up the pad. "Not only did the distributor have our order ready, but it looks like he over-ordered, either expecting us to order more or thinking someone else might want the same stuff. But either way, we have enough equipment for two extra truck gates, over and above what I was expecting."

"That *is* good news."

"Yeah, and on top of that, we've got a bunch of high-quality industrial-grade items, including Linux and Raspberry Pi cards. And PROM burners."

"Was that English? It doesn't mean a whole lot to me, but you seem pleased, so that's good news. Can we load it all?"

"Uh ... " Matt's face fell. "I guess there is some bad news after all. And the universe is back in balance. We could have just loaded it all if we still had all the vehicles. But... "

"Ashland."

"Yup. Plus loading up on all that stuff at Nebraska Crossing."

Collins sighed. "How does this building look? Can we do anything to improve the chances of it still being upright in the spring?"

Matt thought for a moment. "Actually, if we can just make sure that there's no ash clogging any of the drainage or downspouts, we're probably good. Maybe shovel some of the excess off the roof."

"Is that necessary? It's held up so far, and the ashfall has pretty much stopped."

"True, but what's there is kind of caked on. Very little of it is going to be washed off unless there's the granddaddy of all rainstorms. And when the snow starts falling, that'll be the normal expected winter load on top of the unexpected ash load. I doubt it'll survive until spring."

"Right." Collins turned to Timminson. "Looks like we're doing roof cleanup. Set it up." And to Matt, "Triage what we have already versus what you want to bring. Everything that doesn't have a limited shelf life can potentially stay behind. Leave the least valuable items for next time, and re-lock the unit."

While some of the soldiers began roof cleanup, Matt and Timminson grabbed the bolt cutters and went to check out some of the other storage units. But as they were about to cut the first lock, Matt hesitated. "Uh, I'm probably being silly..."

"What?"

"If we cut these open, we're basically making them available to anyone who comes along—"

"What, you think we're the only people with bolt cutters?" Timminson asked. "If someone else does come along, whether or not we cut them open won't matter. Unless we've already grabbed all the good stuff."

"And almost all the units will be pre-opened, except one. Ours. You don't think they'll notice?"

Timminson hesitated. "Huh. Good point. So you want to..."

"Leave the locks on. The chances of there being anything here that's more valuable than what we've already got is pretty low anyway."

Timminson paused, then looked up. "On the other hand..."

Matt followed his gaze as Timminson turned and marched away from the building. Then Timminson about-faced and began yelling instructions to the soldiers on roof duty. In a few moments he was back. "The common-sense thing to do is shovel the ash off at points where it won't interfere with the unit doors. But if we abandon common sense, any other scavengers that come along will have to shovel piles of ash out of the way before they can check out the contents."

Matt smiled. "Without knowing in advance what they might be getting. If anything."

"Of course, *we'll* have to do that shoveling if and when we return, but at least we'll know we're digging out un-looted units."

It took the rest of the day to clear the roof to Matt's satisfaction. Several huge ramps of sticky volcanic ash were piled along the sides of the warehouse, wholly or partially blocking most of the roll-up doors. "That will absolutely dissuade looters," Matt commented. "No one's going to want to shovel that crap. *Way* too much like real work."

"No kidding," muttered a soldier leaning on a shovel. Matt grinned at him.

"We'll overnight here," Collins said. "The roof will make a good sentry post." He turned to Timminson. "Send a couple of people over to Outland to do a little hunting. We might as well eat well tonight."

"Yes, *sir!*" Timminson said with enthusiasm and began giving orders.

56. Earthside: Vancouver

The Lower Mainland of British Columbia mostly got off easy, at least in terms of direct effects from Yellowstone. As with the Mount Saint Helens eruption, there had been virtually no local ashfall. Despite the exponentially larger Yellowstone eruption, the winds were all simply going the wrong way.

However, Vancouver and its environs was a major Canadian transportation hub and gateway to the Pacific Rim, and the citizens had been in the habit of having immediate and constant access to goods from every corner of the globe. Yellowstone put an end to that.

The descent into anarchy had been gradual and typically Canadian. In the Fraser Valley, a heavy farming area, there had been no die-off of livestock. It took several weeks for the general public to really begin to notice lack of specific items, and another month to begin to feel the bite of hunger. At that point, Canada geese suddenly found themselves on the menu. These fat, stupid, ornery fowl had been breeding out of control for decades, protected as Canada's national bird, and most of them no longer bothered to migrate. Or flee.

A massive increase in goose dinners staved off the specter of hunger for most of the second month, before the geese finally developed a belated survival instinct. But it had not been lost on the citizenry that there had been no consequences for this very unpatriotic act.

There were town hall meetings, heated words were exchanged, and votes were taken. In the end, municipalities declared themselves to be sovereign entities, at least until the provincial or federal government started making an appearance. Local RCMP detachments were invited to convert to a local police force or relocate. Most elected to stay where they had a home—and an ongoing paycheck. And all roads in and out of each municipality were placed under border controls. By general agreement, Highway 1 was considered neutral territory with safe passage guaranteed.

Trade continued between municipalities. The farmers continued to farm; the industrialized areas figured out how to gear down and produce equipment and goods more suitable for a nineteenth-century lifestyle. Electricity continued to flow from the Peace River dam in northern B.C. Local skiers and snowboarders celebrated the record early snowfalls on the local slopes. Grouse Mountain was finally able to put their wind turbine to good use. And life went on.

Adèle Savard looked through the basket of groceries, doing some mental addition. She was over budget, but couldn't see skipping any of the items. She glanced around the farmers' market, hoping for inspiration. The market, an open-air setup in Langley, British Columbia, was sparsely populated today. Not just shoppers; even the merchants seemed to be staying home. The weather had to be the motivation. The Lower Mainland had been feeling the effects of global warming the last few years, resulting in sweltering summers, long, warm autumns, and tumultuous, unpredictable winters.

This year, early autumn was already outdoing most recent winters for low temps. Adèle pulled her sweater sleeves over her hands to bring some life back to her fingers.

She and Marcel had settled easily into life in the Vancouver area. The eruption and subsequent governmental collapse meant immigration and employment rules were obsolete, at least for the moment. People who had skills or a strong back could find work. But most jobs now involved far more manual labor than most people were used to, and many of the pickier job-seekers were starting to feel the pinch. For Adèle, a general laborer job at a local farm was no biggie, and gave her first pick of some of their produce.

Marcel had managed to get a job in a garage, which paid considerably better. He'd aced the job interview, such as it was, by fixing a truck that wouldn't start, using literally nothing but a screwdriver. Adèle smiled at the thought. All those years of tinkering with old vehicles were now paying off.

Her smile vanished as she thought of her daughter. All she had was that last phone message from Erin. She could be dead. She could even be here in the Lower Mainland, having taken her own advice. There was simply no way to connect up in what was effectively a nineteenth-century society.

57. Morning Rounds

As he did every day without fail, he walked his habitual route through Rivendell. It was important to remind the clods that he was around. And even more important to keep close track of the girls that he'd selected. He smiled at that thought, and a few people near him recoiled.

He mentally went over his inventory. Medication, syringes, cloths, cuffs, Taser (for emergencies). The ATV was in place. He'd finally trained that idiot in charge of inventory to leave it in the same spot all the time. He had a spare key; that had taken a surprising amount of subterfuge.

He just needed to map out the human dance a little better, and then decide on the best time to move.

It was actually going to happen. Pretty soon he'd have his own colony, his own family, and he'd no longer have to put up with these small, petty beings.

58. FIRST TESTS

September 27

A wide but shallow hole had been dug in the prairie grass just outside the Rivendell fence. Bill, Kevin, and Charlie stood in the hole, accompanied by the gate hardware and a couple of volunteer guards with weapons. A crowd of onlookers, including Richard and Monica, stood around the periphery. A buzz of conversation rose slowly in volume as the crowd waited for some action.

Finally, Bill gave a loud whistle. "Ready to go, everyone. Remember, if a T-Rex comes through, run. And keep in mind you only have to be faster than the other guy." He grinned to the scattered return laughter.

Charlie held up the tablet, nodded to the guards, and pressed "OK." The interface shimmered into focus, showing a dark, dank space—the interior of the culvert on the Dino Planet side.

One of the guards looked through both sides of the gate, poked his head through, gave a thumbs-up, and walked in. Then there was a scream of pain and surprise from the interface, and the crowd stepped back in alarm.

The guard, grinning, stuck his head through from the other side. "Just kidding. It's clear."

There were titters from the spectators, and multiple comments of "asshole."

Bill called out, "Harry, when we go fishing for T-Rex, you're gonna be the bait." He stepped through the gate and found himself inside the upended culvert, standing on a loose-dirt floor. The ceiling, a large circle of steel plate, had been bolted onto the top of the culvert with multiple angle iron brackets. Light shone through four slits in the side, each covered by a bolted-on piece of plexiglass. Around the periphery, below knee level, posts were driven through holes into the surrounding dirt, anchoring the whole structure in place. In the center of the space, a construction scaffolding had been set up, with its top level about fifteen feet off the ground in the culvert. That would put the gate about ten feet above the natural ground level, ensuring no conflict with the surface of other timelines.

"Not bad. Needs furniture, though," Bill said.

"Har de har," Harry answered.

"No, seriously. A table to work on, a chair or two. Nothing fancy, but I'd just as soon not sit in dirt."

"Huh. I'll see what I can do." Harry stepped through the interface to Outland, just as Kevin and Charlie came through the other side, lugging the pressure vessel and small-gate equipment.

Bill went up on his toes and tried to look through one of the wall slits, but couldn't quite reach. "Dammit. I need a step-ladder. No way I'm going to waste the opportunity to look out."

"Is there anything you can see that you couldn't see through the pole-cam?"

"It's real out there, Kev. Watching a video window on a tablet just isn't the same."

"If you say so," Kevin replied.

"Say, anyone care to help me move this stuff?"

Bill laughed and went to help Charlie lug the equipment up to the top of the scaffolding.

In a few minutes, everything was moved and set up. Kevin activated the tablet and looked at Charlie, who gave him a thumbs-up.

"So, we're going to check for other Earths," Kevin said in lecture mode. "Hopefully the pressure vessel will be enough protection if we make a connection."

"Second that." Bill stepped over to watch the tablet screen over Kevin's shoulder. "Let's do this."

Charlie called down to someone on the other side of the large gate, and the aperture disappeared. "They'll check back in five minutes," he said.

Kevin nodded and tapped the tablet. For a few seconds nothing happened. Then with a *whoosh*, water flooded through the small gate and filled the pressure vessel to the top of the gate's circumference.

"Wow. I don't think I ever checked if the camera was waterproof," Charlie commented.

"After our experience with Greenhouse Earth," Bill replied, "we made sure we bought units with diving cases." He glanced at the video window on the tablet. "Hmm. Pitch-black. It actually looks like the only light is coming from our side."

Kevin pointed at one of the readings on the tablet. "Two degrees Celsius. That's cold. That's glacial meltwater cold."

"Like that lake under Antarctica?"

Kevin shook his head. "No, thank the universe. If we'd tapped into that, we'd probably be dead. The water in Lake Vostok is around minus three, but it's liquid because of the weight of all the ice above it. That kind of pressure would have ruptured the pressure vessel. This is probably just meltwater at the base of some glacier on the other side."

Charlie rolled his eyes. "Kevin, you are as usual both a font of information and a bit of a downer. How do you remember this stuff?"

Kevin frowned at him. "How do you not?"

"Okay, guys." Bill held up his hands. "We've dodged a bullet. But it looks like this isn't going to be a terribly useful timeline."

Kevin poked the tablet and the interface closed. "Now, how do we drain the bell?"

The three men stared at the container for a few moments, then Charlie suggested, "Greenhouse Earth?"

Bill nodded. "Good idea. It's not like cross-contamination is going to be an issue."

Kevin poked at the tablet and the interface re-opened. The water poured out, replaced by a yellowish mist. Soon, the remaining water in the bell had evaporated, and Kevin closed the interface.

"Is that our only option from here?" Charlie asked.

"Good question. Kev, there's no theoretical reason we couldn't connect to multiple timelines, is there?"

"No. The geometry of n-space is complex. Each timeline would have its own surrounding topology that would determine how many possible neighbors it might have."

"But we can reach them from Outland?"

"Yes, once we have the coordinates."

Bill pointed at the tablet. "Then let's try again."

Again, Kevin played with the tablet, and after a short delay, the interface opened up.

Bill's eyebrows went up as he stared at the video window. "You didn't accidentally connect to Outland, did you?"

Kevin shook his head. "No Rivendell. No fence. Just animals."

Now Charlie came around to gaze at the tablet's video window, which showed a pastoral scene that could easily be mistaken for Outland. He pointed at one corner of the video. "Are those buffalo? They look smaller."

Bill nodded slowly. "Interesting. Actually, the species distribution looks different from Outland. We're going to have to get Monica to look at this. Kev, you have the coordinates?"

"Locked and saved."

"Okay. Disconnect and let's try for another one."

Kevin nodded and went through the usual process. As the interface re-opened, the bell made an audible *thunk* and a blindingly bright light shone through the gate.

"What the eff?" Bill exclaimed.

Kevin pointed at one of the readings. "Atmospheric pressure—zero. Aborting." Without waiting for a response, he shut down the gate.

"What the hell was that?" Charlie said slowly.

"Actual hell, I think," Bill replied. He tilted the tablet toward him. "Without atmosphere, we couldn't get an ambient temperature, but the light level was plenty scary. I'm going to go out on a limb and declare that version of Earth a poor candidate."

"Noted," Kevin said, and made a few keystrokes. "I'm honestly getting a little worried, guys," he added. "I'm beginning to think we're playing with matches here. I'm not sure we should continue—"

Before he could finish, the interface from the large gate opened in mid-air and Richard stuck his head through. "I see you guys survived. Find anything interesting?"

Charlie, Bill, and Kevin exchanged glances, then Bill said, "We're going to need a meeting, I think."

The committee was gathered around the table, with the addition of Kevin, who normally didn't attend. Richard gestured to him. "Please summarize what you told me for the group, Kev."

Kevin blushed and stammered, but swiftly got it under control. "I'm not liking the odds. Two out of three timelines we accessed were unlivable. At best, fifty percent of all the timelines we know about are unlivable. Two-thirds, if you count Earthside as unlivable. What if we connect to something even more dangerous than Greenhouse Earth? We could wipe ourselves out."

Bill looked around the table. All eyes were fixed on Kevin. "You have a suggestion, Kev?"

Kevin shook his head, hesitated, then shrugged. "Um, sort of. Look, what we really need is to be able to search around dangerous timelines like Greenhouse Earth without having to actually go there. Building the fortress on Dino Planet was enough risk and effort. Trying to do that on Greenhouse Earth or Vacuum Earth or Glacier Earth would be even harder and more risky."

"So…"

"If we had something we could stick through the small gate into Greenhouse Earth that would allow us to scan from Greenhouse Earth without actually going there, then that removes a lot of the risk and almost all of the difficulty."

Bill's eyebrows went up. This was the first he'd heard of this. Of course, Kevin wasn't the most talkative person. "You have an idea for something like that, Kev?"

"Um, yeah. I've been playing around with the equations—I never stopped, really—and I have some ideas on improving the interface."

"The tablet G.U.I.?"

Kevin shook his head vehemently. "No, no. That's an implementation—completely irrelevant. I mean the interface between timelines. I think I can control it better. I should be able to scan for other timelines without actually needing a gate. It would just be a sensor rig."

Bill nodded slowly. He opened his mouth to ask a question, but Richard jumped in. "What do you need to test it?"

"Uh, that's also Applied Physics. Your turf. So I need some of your time."

Bill waved a hand to get attention. "Any idea on hardware requirements?"

"Probably a couple of diffractors. And a controller card, of course. I'm guessing this will be one of those head-exploding moments."

Bill laughed. "Uh huh. We're down to two gates and the pole-cam, until the Omaha expedition gets back. We can't afford to lose any of those."

"We could work at night."

Bill frowned. "Come again?"

"Work at night." Kevin gestured vaguely upward. "We can borrow the equipment at night and put everything back before morning."

Richard turned to Bill. "He ain't wrong. You have any qualms about constant disassembly and reassembly of a gate system?"

"Nope. Modular design is our friend. Even more than expected, it seems."

Richard smiled at Kevin. "Looks like we're in business. Let us know when you're ready to start."

59. EARTHSIDE: AUSTRALIA

Peter narrowed his eyes as he gazed over the sunbaked Kamilario landscape. Full summer was coming to the land formerly known as New South Wales, and even the plants and trees seemed to have given up trying to maintain their color.

Koa smiled as he mentally corrected himself. He was no longer Peter, he was Koa, a citizen of Kamilario. The colonialists were all gone now, some under their own power, some with an assist from a spear-tip to the behind. Metaphorically, of course. You couldn't win battles without guns, these days.

Most of the colonialists had started running for the coast when the storms hit and the power went out. Koa's people had merely given the stragglers an assist. And without the trappings of civilization, the colonialists would be gone soon, even from there.

He'd picked up snippets of news before everything went down for good. The northern hemisphere had taken a much heavier blow than the south. The common belief was that most everywhere was back to pre-industrial levels by now. But there was some concern that more colonialists might come by boat to Australia's shores, looking for sanctuary. That would be bad. They'd try to take over, just like the last lot. Not this time, though. Now Koa's people had guns as well, and knew what to expect from the invaders.

Koa let his eyes sweep the land one more time. So much land, so few of his people left. There'd be no problem claiming a patch, maybe build something semi-permanent. The elders would disapprove—that was the colonialists' way. But Koa had grown up with a heavy European cultural influence, and he couldn't just toss it off overnight. Some of the imported ideas were good. Comfortable, even. There would be adaptations.

And eventually, the wildlife would come back, once all the fences were down.

60. THE ROAD HOME

September 24 to 29

The trip back to Lincoln was far less eventful than the trip out, although considerably more fun for the troops. As Matt had hoped, they'd found a John Deere dealer with some heavy equipment in stock. There had been a lot of argument, some of the personnel wanting to bring back one of everything. But common sense had prevailed, and they'd settled on two wheel-loaders and a big backhoe. No semi tank trailer had been found, but a couple of five-thousand-gallon Freightliners would fill the bill for the moment. Too big to fit through the existing gates, unfortunately, but Bill might be able to build a bigger one with what they'd been able to scrounge up.

One of the trucks was half-full, the other nearly empty. The obvious ploy, refilling them from gas stations, turned out to be a little more complicated since the whole system was designed to move the fuel in the other direction. Some hasty kludges with pumping equipment and an overnight stay eventually solved the issue.

"This will actually make life in Rivendell a lot easier," Matt said. "Although if I remember right, we're going to have to start filtering the diesel for sludge buildup."

"Fortunately, the military has been dealing with that issue for years," Collins replied. "We got this."

Although they'd cleared the eastbound road on the way out, they decided to take the westbound side back to Lincoln and clear it as well. "Might as well do things right," Collins commented.

"And your people are just itching to do some damage," Matt replied with a smile.

There was always the chance of running into another band of refugees, but Collins felt it unlikely. "People will have mostly stopped moving by now," he said. "Anyone who hasn't found a place to stay by this point is probably dead of starvation and exposure. You simply can't live off the land on this side."

After almost a week on the road, they pulled into the warehouse parking lot in Lincoln that formed their Earthside base. Some recent disturbances of the ever-present dust and ash gave them hope that the Ashland group had already arrived.

As Matt climbed out of the Hummer, a loud "hello!" from a nearby rooftop made him look up. A soldier was standing and waving at them. Another soldier came out of a warehouse door and saluted. "Glad to see you back, sir. *Real* glad."

"Well, that's not ominous or anything," Collins said in an aside to Matt. Then to the soldier, "Something significant happening?"

"Erm, well, not so much *happening*, sir. But Ms. Albertelli has concerns about the Ashland refugees, and she's got us doing drills and scenarios. Even Corp—er, Ms. Chavez is involved."

Collins consciously avoided rolling his eyes. "Uh huh. And if Monica and Bill are good for anything at all, it's making plans for the most outrageous situations." He glanced at Matt. "My money says all the weapons are now somewhere else."

"No bet," Matt muttered.

The convoy was back through the gate in Rivendell, and Corporal Timminson was seeing to stowing their equipment. Collins took a moment to enjoy the sunshine and the fresh, slightly crisp air. There was a definite feeling of autumn in the air, and a coolness in the shade that foretold falling temperatures in the near future. While cooler than a normal Nebraska day for this time of year, it was warmer than Earthside at the moment.

The air was mostly clear of ash on Earthside, but it still tasted faintly of dirt or smoke. And the sunshine was still wan and half-hearted. Something about stratospheric contamination, according to Erin Savard.

"Afternoon, Lieutenant."

Collins turned at the voice. It was Chief Cummins from Ashland. The brief discussion back in the parking lot hadn't given Collins a lot to work with, just the general feeling that the Ashland refugees might not be integrating smoothly. Collins kept his face neutral. "Hello, Chief. Settling in well?"

Cummins hitched his pants and made a face. "Mostly. They've made room, and it looks like there are enough tents for everyone. Lots of food, too. I'm impressed at how well your people have set things up. Some of our more elderly are being settled in one of the longhouses early. Nice construction there too, by the way. You have some good people working here."

Collins smiled and nodded. "There's a lot of motivation when your life might depend on doing it right."

Cummins looked down at his boots for a few moments. "Sir, I do have a concern that I'd like to discuss with you. I'm sure these are all fine young people, and certainly with a lot of book-smarts, but they're *kids*. And they're running the show. It seems to me that we have to put folks with more experience in charge, and quickly. As you say, lives depend on this place working properly."

"Just how would we do that, Chief?"

Cummins frowned. "What do you mean?"

"I mean, exactly what process would we use for putting your people in charge? I assume you're talking about your people. Just march up to the committee and tell them they're out?"

"Well, I'd expect if we presented a united front and simply laid out the cold, hard facts, I'd hope they'd do the sensible thing. But if it came down to it, I don't think they'd want to take on the military."

"So, a military coup. I always wanted one of those on my resumé. Tell me, if we'd marched into Ashland and just announced we were taking over, how do you suppose you and Mr. Brady would have reacted? Stepped meekly aside? Didn't think so. I understand you and Chief Albertelli already had words."

"*Chief* Albertelli. What a joke. Girls used to play with dolls, now they play soldier."

"Mr. Cummins," Collins replied, his voice dead even, "Chief Albertelli participated in a night op with my people to remove some insurrectionists around six weeks ago. She was professional, she did not freeze, and she pulled her weight. You dismiss her at your peril. She's also handled several altercations in town with people far bigger than you or I. She's earned the position, and earned the trust of the population." Collins paused. "As for the Rivendell committee, I answer to them. So there will be no 'united front,' as you put it."

"You can't be serious. By what authority? Myself and Mr. Brady, we may be just small-town folk, but we at least represent an official chain of command. It seems to me that you should be answerable to us, not to them."

"I'm sure if we had a half-dozen lawyers here, we could get a half-dozen different opinions on that. But it's moot. Here and now, Rivendell represents the best hope for American citizens that I can see. And the people who put it together and are keeping it running are who I answer to."

Collins turned to leave, then stopped and turned back, remembering the latest news. "There is, of course, a constitutional convention and subsequent election in the works. You could try to get yourselves *elected* to the positions. I'd support that." Without waiting for a response, he marched off.

61. PLEBISCITE

September 30

"Are we all having fun?" Richard grinned and stepped back from the mike, and felt the crowd's response wash over him. There was no way to pick out any content from that inchoate roar, but it seemed to be good-natured in tone.

He stepped back up as the noise settled. "We're going to vote on a couple of referendum items today. One is to confirm the authority of the current committee until such time as we are able to vote for and form a new government. The alternative, if this is voted down, is that everything stops until we get a new government installed."

Richard paused and gauged the crowd. People seemed to be mostly paying attention, although there were a lot of sidebars going on.

"The second item is to confirm Monica Albertelli as the leader of our police force. There's been some internal debate about whether Monica is a sheriff or a police chief. The short answer is, we don't really care. She maintains order, she upholds the rules of Rivendell, and she has the authority to shoot people. And you know she will." Laughter and catcalls greeted this last statement. Monica's reputation had grown after the Josh McAllen event, and several stories had recently circulated about her confrontation with Cummins, not all of them exaggerated beyond belief.

"As an aside, Beatrice Chavez, formerly of the National Guard, will serve as her official deputy, something she's been doing on an informal basis up 'til now. So this will be a package deal. Again, once we have a new government, it will be their job to define how our law enforcement will be set up." Richard pointed to one side of the lawn where a number of tables had been assembled. "Voting happens over there. Details are on the whiteboards. No speeches today. This is pretty straightforward."

He stepped back from the mike. There was an amplified *pop* as Bill turned off the PA, and the crowd began to mill around as people tried to form lines for the tables.

"Well, that was, as usual, the highlight of my day," Richard said to Monica as he stepped away from the podium.

"Hey, my *job* is on the line here, big guy. Little respect?" Monica grinned up at him as they fell into step.

"Sure, sure. I think the important thing is that we're getting people used to the whole process. I don't know how much the eventual government will want to settle through plebiscites and how much they'll just decide in committee. Or whatever. But I get the feeling that the citizenry wants a large say in how it gets put together."

"You know this is going to end up nothing like the old American system, right? At *any* level."

Richard stopped and turned to her. "This is bad, how? The state and federal systems were each a dog's breakfast of overly complicated rules and procedures that seemed to be designed specifically to insulate government officials from accountability. We've actually seen—"

Monica held up a hand. "You're preaching to the converted, Richard. Let's keep it simple, keep the people involved, and make sure the politicians are *always* answerable."

Richard nodded and started walking again, consciously relaxing the frown off his face. "I wonder what it will look like."

The committee members were sitting around the long table, except for Bill, who was off somewhere working on one of his projects. Richard was just reaching for the carafe to refill his mug when Frankie walked in, waving a sheet of paper.

"Got the results," he said. "You all still have jobs, at least for now."

"Damn," Richard replied. "I almost half-hoped they'd toss us out."

"Yeah, wouldn't *that* be a mess," Sam said. "We'll be out on our asses soon enough. No point making it messier." He pointed at Monica. "What about Buford T. Justice here?"

Monica made a face at Sam as Frankie glanced at his paper. "She's in. 95 percent in favor. Total landslide."

Now Monica made a face at Frankie. "Wait, I was running *unopposed* and I didn't get all the votes?"

This comment was met with general laughter as people visibly relaxed. Richard realized that there had actually been some subconscious concern about the outcome of this first voting round.

Krista sighed and hitched her chair up to the table. "Well, at least we can make decisions with some assurance that they'll be accepted. Let's get this meeting rolling."

Richard flipped open his notebook. "Right. First item ... "

62. Constitutional Convention

October 2

Two days later, the committee was again discussing politics. Richard looked around the table. "Is that really the right term? Constitutional convention?"

Sam replied before anyone else. "I don't think it matters, really. Everyone knows what you're talking about when you say it. I suppose whatever we decide on will form the basis of a constitution. We just need to get the practicalities laid out first."

"What do we have, so far?" Krista asked.

Richard gave her an eye roll, then glanced at his notes. "Well, let's see. Um ... " he paused. "Pretty much everything. We've got communists, socialists, libertarians, anarchists, capitalists, to the extent you can have capitalism without a monetary system, greenies, city-state advocates, even—I kid you not—some people advocating an elected monarchy."

"That'd be the *Star Wars* fans, I expect," Bill said, grinning.

"But all systems involving elected positions, right?" Krista said.

"Except the anarchists," Bill replied.

Collins sat forward. "I've made it pretty clear that the Guard will not support the implementation of any system that doesn't involve free elections. I think it sank any thoughts of alternatives before they even got off the ground."

"I have an idea on how to handle the anarchists," Bill said with an evil smile. "We declare anarchy as our form of government, shoot the anarchists, then hold another vote."

"Hmm." Richard shuffled papers for a moment, studiously ignoring Bill. "I have here, for instance, a green manifesto that I received a while back, which has gone through a revision or two. It's not a suggestion for a government type, but a list of demands in regards to how a government should behave."

"Involves a lot of tree hugging, I expect," Matt said.

"You have no idea," Bill replied. "I'm as sensitive to environmental concerns as the next person, but that"—he pointed at the papers in Richard's hand—"is over-the-top looney-tunes. We would literally never be able to build another building in our lifetimes if we took that whole thing at face value."

"Ask for the stars, settle for the moon."

Bill grinned at Richard. "Yeah, except if you overdo it, you end up alienating people."

"What kind of demands?" Erin asked.

"Like placing severe limits on tree-cutting. Or outlawing manufacture and use of concrete." Bill hesitated. "I'm ambivalent about that last one, honestly. Concrete was actually the second-biggest generator of CO_2 on old Earth, after fossil fuels. Not that we're anywhere near having to worry about it, yet. But still—"

Krista waved a hand, interrupting Bill's meandering explanation. "What exactly is a socialist government?"

Richard chuckled. "It's not. I mean, it's not a system of government, it's a policy. Just like you can have capitalist totalitarianism as in China or a capitalist democracy like America, you can have a socialist democracy or a more-hands-off democracy. Based on the speeches I've heard so far, most people seem to be more concerned about the policies we'll pursue than they are about the actual structure of the government. So we're getting all these side issues being argued."

Erin spoke up. "I've been just wandering around, talking and listening, and trying to avoid looking or sounding official in any way. I'm finding some interesting things." She paused and smiled at the other committee members, drawing the moment out. Finally, Matt growled at her.

Erin gave him a laugh and a small dig with her elbow. "I think there's pretty much no chance we're going to end up with anything that looks like the old American system. Almost everyone is thoroughly disillusioned with it."

"Almost everyone?" Sam asked.

Erin looked at him for a moment as if judging what to say, then shrugged. "It's roughly along age lines, Sam. Below maybe forty to fifty, you'll get little or no support for the old system. At or above that, there's more support, although it's not unanimous either."

"So what *do* we have that's actionable?" Nick asked.

"Election of officials is universal. Popular vote is *almost* universal. There'll be no electoral college or voting districts, unless I'm seriously misreading the mood," Erin replied.

"Which means alternatives like proportional representation and ranked balloting are out," Bill added.

"Fine by me," said Richard. "I'd rather keep things simple."

"Monarchy, president, parliament, committee," Erin continued. "Again, we're not big enough for anything complicated, and I think Richard's right about keeping things simple. Most people just don't have the patience for the level of BS required to support anything more complex."

Richard put down his notes. "That's about the way I'm reading it. So I think we have enough to present the masses with a preliminary set of ideas. Shall we stick our collective neck in the noose?"

The grunts around the table were at least supportive, if not particularly enthusiastic.

"I suppose you're all wondering why I've gathered you here," Richard said into the mike. As usual, the crowd was raucous in their response. He waited while a couple of people chivvied some whiteboards into place.

"This is what we understand are the main alternatives. If enough people think something should be added, we will do so. But for now, we've divided things into government structure, electoral structure, and policy." Richard pointed at the first board. "Alternatives for government structure are elected monarchy"—he had to pause for the laughter to die down—"committee, which is basically what we have right now; presidency, which for most practical purposes is pretty much an elected monarch; and various types of parliaments and senatorial systems, which all just pit a president against a committee of some kind."

The roar of the crowd swelled as the audience started debating on the spot. Richard put his hand to the bridge of his nose for a second, then yelled into the mike, "Shut up, for fuck's sake!"

The debates cut off like a switch had been thrown, followed by general laughter. Richard had to admit that the mood was upbeat, and enthusiasm was certainly a good thing.

"Electoral structure comes down to direct voting or some kind of republicanism; popular vote or vote by district; and first-past-the-post versus some kind of proportional representation. Some of these alternatives are incompatible with each other, so watch that."

Richard paused for another mutiny, but the crowd now had itself under control. "And last, policy. Will we place an emphasis on green values? Socialism? Free-market capitalism? Libertarianism? Social contract? Communism? How will we balance individual freedoms against the needs of the society as a whole? I think we've seen that particular question played out the last couple of years, so I won't beat it to death."

This time the mutiny did start up. As the arguments swelled in volume, Richard gestured to Kevin, who handed him an airhorn. He held it in the air and let out a loud *blaaaaaaaat.* The uproar cut off cleanly.

"The last thing to remember is that nothing we're doing here is irreversible, although I think we'd need a good reason to change course further down the road. What will work for us as a single small town of less than a thousand might not be so good if we grow to tens of thousands. It's important, though, to keep the long view in mind. We will be making decisions that will affect our children and their children. Let's try to get it right. Argue, debate, make speeches. The mike will be available, but Kevin will be enforcing a five-minute maximum per person. Tomorrow we will do a non-binding test vote. Then more arguing. Then a final vote." Richard paused and grinned. "So let's have some fun!"

He switched off the mike and stepped back before the crowd could get their suggestions organized.

"How'd I do?" he said to Monica.

"You've created a shitstorm, big guy." She grinned back. "Which is a typical weekday around here."

Richard turned to glance back at the podium, where people were already lining up to make speeches. "Is it actually a weekday?" he muttered. "I've lost track."

63. FLYOVERS

October 3

Bill looked around the table. The entire committee had shown up for today's session. Not surprising, considering the first item on the agenda.

Richard broke the silence. "Okay, Bill, let's hear it."

Bill gave him a mock salute. "The new scanner is a success. Not a perfect success—there are shortcomings—but for the main concern, keeping us alive, it's doing the job." He paused to take a sip of coffee. "And the sensors I've added should protect us from most things."

"Most things?"

"Well, there are still some theoretical dangers. A laser, for instance, or gamma rays, or even light from a nuclear explosion. But we can avoid those by just not standing in line with the spy-cam when it's active."

Bill gestured to Erin. "At Erin's request, I've also rigged a good LED flashlight onto it so we can illuminate pitch-black locations like Glacier Earth."

Erin sat forward. "We did a quick session, looking at Glacier Earth, and it was very interesting. Kevin was right, it is an underground river running under ice. Probably not a huge glacier, or it would have crushed the river flat. Bill's talking about flying over it—"

"What?" Richard sat up straight, shocked. "Are you nuts? You want to go across to Glacier Earth?"

Bill waved his hands. "No, no, nothing like that. I'm going to do a flight on this side, with Goro piloting, and I'll take the spy-cam up with me." He grinned. "It'll probably be a little cramped, with the UPS and the server sharing seat space with me, but anything for science, right?"

Richard nodded. "Ah. And get a scan from above. Makes sense. And unusually sane, for you."

"Oh, hah hah."

"So when are you planning on doing this?"

"As soon as possible. Goro is figuring out how to carry the portal equipment on the ultralight. I have to rig up a version of the small gate that won't suck all our air out to Vacuum Earth."

Richard rolled his eyes. "That'd be nice."

"What about more timelines?" Monica asked. "Have you done further checking?"

"We have several to check right now. Later, we'll need to look for new timelines, using *those* as a base. But this process, based on results so far, has an *R* greater than one, so we'll always be discovering new timelines faster than we can examine them. At some point we're going to have to get organized. I don't think we can just keep winging it."

"Cool." Richard nodded. "I agree. Let's look at what we've got, then at least we'll be able to make a decision on next steps."

The takeoff was significantly more uncomfortable than usual. Bill had rigged slings and brackets for the various components, but he still felt like he'd been wedged into a storage closet with a bunch of computer equipment.

"She's sluggish," Goro said over his shoulder. "You need to go on a diet. Or shrink the equipment."

"I'm already on a diet. It's called the *no snacks in Outland* diet, and a lot of people are on it. As for the equipment, there's not much—" Bill hesitated and frowned. He'd been about to say there wasn't much that could be done about it, but on reflection that might not be true. He'd have to talk to Matt.

"Up to altitude," Goro said a minute later. Bill grabbed the tablet and went through the startup sequence. Then he picked up the spy-cam and began panning with it.

"Wow. I mean, like really *wow!*" Bill said after a minute.

"Care to fill me in?"

"It's like the Arctic in early spring. All snow or ice— probably ice, since it looks pretty pitted and rutted."

"So, glacier?"

"Yep. We're up, what, a thousand feet? It's maybe a hundred or so below us. So not a deep glacier. Nothing like what we had on Earth during the ice ages."

Goro hesitated. "You sure about that? I seem to remember hearing that Nebraska had very little glaciation."

"Really? Well, I'm not an expert. I'll check with Erin when we land."

"Cool. Gonna do the other Earths?"

"Yessir. Up next, Vacuum Earth. Prepare to kiss your ass goodbye."

Goro snorted but otherwise didn't comment. Bill pulled down the dropdown list, on which the new Earths had already been added. He selected Vacuum Earth, then hesitated before hitting "OK." He was certain his gate mod would preserve an atmospheric seal—well, fairly certain— well, pretty sure. Sighing, he pressed "OK." No immediate doom and destruction being apparent, he went through the scanning routine again.

"Definitely not prime real estate," Bill said after a few moments. "Looks like the moon."

"What about the supposedly bright sunlight?"

"I think that's just a result of not having an atmosphere to filter it. There's nothing unusual that I can see—I mean, other than the obvious."

"Okay, so we won't be going there on vacation," Goro quipped. "But we still have to think about using it as a jump-off point for further searches, right?"

"Well, at least we don't have to physically visit it. Just stick the scanner through. That ought to be safe. Relatively. Meanwhile ... " Bill clicked the dropdown again and selected Pastoral Earth. The name was kind of weak, but given that it looked like a toned-down Outland, no one had been able to come up with anything better.

A few seconds of scanning, and Bill said, "Oh, shit. Start circling, Goro. To the left."

"Aye, Captain. *Arrrr.*" Goro got the ultralight into a slow banking turn, then looked over his shoulder. "What do you have?"

"People. I think. A village, anyway. Or some kind of structures."

"Oh, wow. Not a city? Not a Rivendell kind of thing?"

"No, more like a"—Bill squinted at the video window—"like a Native American kind of thing, I think. Teepees? Again, not an expert."

Goro completed a circle, then asked for further instructions.

"I think we can head back now."

Goro acknowledged and banked the plane in the direction of Rivendell.

❧   ❧   ❧

"Glacier Earth and Vacuum Earth, totally useless," Erin said, peering at the video windows, all of which had been paused. "But Pastoral Earth … that's definitely a human village, and almost certainly Native American."

"Uh, you're a geologist … ," Bill said.

"I can't have minors?" she shot back.

Bill grinned and shrugged. "Don't know that it matters, because we won't be visiting anyway."

"Why?"

"Remember way back when, we were asking Monica about cross-timeline contamination? This is exactly the scenario she warned against. A population that very possibly has never been exposed to European-based diseases. We pop over for a cup of tea, and we could kill millions. I think we have to mark this one off-limits except for the spy-cam."

Erin nodded. "Yeah, you're right. I'll talk to Monica. I'm sure she'll be excited, but I'm also sure she'll agree with you as well." She sat back. "So this is all very interesting, but we really don't have anything useful, do we?"

"Well, not directly useful, but these are all jumping-off points for more scanning." Bill paused and frowned. "Anyway, I'm not sure what *useful* looks like at this point. What are you hoping for?"

"Honestly, anything that looks like old Earth pre-eruption. At minimum, we could get supplies from there. Like coffee."

Bill sat up straight. "Damn. Sold. Okay, this is now a high-priority project."

Erin laughed. "No argument, Bill. Not from anyone, I bet."

64. Executing the Plan

October 4

It was time. He had verified all the dance steps, and had done a couple of dry runs.

The utility ATV was in place. It had required a careful balancing act to get it out of the equipment pool late enough that it wouldn't be expected back, but not so late as to be suspicious.

First up was Amy. She'd be coming from the longhouse, having completed her late-evening cleanup. There she was, now. And as she entered that darker patch of the lawn...

He came up behind the girl and stuck a cloth over her mouth and nose. Amy gasped in alarm, and thereby took a lungful of halothane. The effect was virtually immediate. The girl slumped in his arms.

The effect would start to wear off in seconds, however. Halothane was only useful as an anesthetic if breathed continuously. He swiftly pulled out the syringe that had been pre-filled with the correct amount of etorphine for Amy's weight. A quick injection, and she never got a chance to get more than semi-conscious.

It was a matter of two minutes to get the unconscious girl to the utility ATV. He laid her carefully in the back, then prepped for his second target.

Suzie would be at her tent already. However, Richard would still be at the longhouse for another hour. He had to time his encounter just right.

He came around the tent from the back, just as she was exiting to perform her evening ablutions. The halothane and etorphine worked their magic again. He took a moment to gather her dropped toiletries, then picked her up and carried her toward the opening that he'd made in the fence. This was his moment of greatest exposure. There was just enough light for an inconvenient passerby to notice something and yell out. His shoulders itched, waiting for the outcry, but he made it to the fence with no alarm being raised.

Drop Suzie off at the ATV, handcuff the two girls, back to the fence to reconnect the panels, then he would be home free.

Then he stopped. There, walking through the tent area. That was Erin Savard. That bitch had rejected him, and it had eaten at him. Here was a chance for revenge. Her martial-arts-expert boyfriend was nowhere around, so there would be no problem handling her. He'd have to get rid of the body afterward, but there was room on the ATV.

He pulled out his kit and carefully loaded the syringe. He knew where her tent was, of course, so he was able to catch up once he'd finished his preparations.

Quickly, he moved up behind Erin and grabbed her around the neck. Before she could react, he stuck the syringe into the side of her neck and—

A blinding blow to his forehead made him see stars. As he staggered with surprise and pain, something struck him in the stomach. His vision cleared just in time to see Erin's angry expression as she drove another blow into the side of his head. He swung blindly and made contact, but not with any real authority. It seemed to be enough, though, to drive her back, and he took the opportunity to flee. Hopefully in the darkness, she wouldn't be able to keep up. But if she yelled for help, it could be the end of everything.

He had positioned the ATV facing downhill. Now he donned a pair of night-vision goggles and, taking the ATV out of gear, he was able to roll more than a hundred yards before needing to turn the engine on. The nightly wildlife concert was more than adequate to drown out the vehicle. Nevertheless, he drove slowly, with minimum throttle, until he was far enough away from Rivendell.

At that point, he started to drive as quickly as he dared. He had a good idea of how long the girls would be out, and he needed to be at their new home before they were completely conscious.

What had gone wrong with the Savard woman? Had someone else stepped in? No, there'd been no indication of anyone else in the area. He had deeply underestimated her, and gotten his ass kicked for his trouble. And worse, tipped his hand. For better or worse, he was now committed to his own colony.

The thought brought a smile to his face, despite the immediate urgency. His girls would be so pleased that the lying and pretending was over. Now finally they could all be together in their own home.

65. ATTACKED

Erin woke slowly to the sensation of being shaken repeatedly. She could hear her name being called. A wave of nausea momentarily overtook her, then her head cleared. It was one of her tent city neighbors, Andrea.

Erin sat up carefully, holding her head. "Um. What happened?"

"I don't know," Andrea replied. "I found you lying on the ground in a heap. This hypodermic was on the ground beside you." The woman held a syringe in her hand.

As Erin gazed at it, everything came rushing back: the attack from behind, her instinctive reaction, the sharp pain in the side of her neck...

"I was attacked. Can you get Matt?"

"Archie's off looking for him right now. Do you know who it was?"

"I..." Erin tried to remember a face, but it had been dark, and everything happened so quickly. "No. Just a general impression."

At that moment, Matt came running up, trailed by Andrea's boyfriend. Wordlessly Matt gathered her in his arms. The warmth felt good, and helped to clear her head a little more.

Finally, he held her at arm's length. "We need to get you to the longhouse. I've sent someone to look for Krista."

Leaning heavily on Matt, Erin was able to climb to her feet.

⚜ ⚜ ⚜

Krista held the syringe in the air. "There's still liquid in this. Whatever he was trying to inject you with, you only got a partial dose."

"What do you think it is?"

"If I had to guess, and without a lab that's really all I can do, I'd guess etorphine. It's an animal tranquilizer, so not too terribly difficult to get. And it's very potent. It'll knock you out immediately."

"Which is probably what our mystery attacker was going for," Matt added. "This sounds like an attempted abduction."

At that moment, Richard and Monica arrived, both out of breath.

"What happened?" Richard said.

It took only moments to update them. At the end, Monica asked Erin, "And you can't place who it was?"

"No. Male, obviously, maybe six feet tall. White, I think, although I wouldn't swear to it. He attacked from behind. I kneed him in the face, then applied a couple of elbows, but by then I think I was already starting to go under from the drug."

Matt flashed a quick smile. "Men tend to underestimate women's flexibility. That's not a move you'd expect from a male opponent, unless you're attacking Jet Li."

Richard frowned. "Huh?"

"One of the *Lethal Weapon* movies," Bill said as he entered. "I could tell you which one after a coffee, but then I'd never get to sleep. What happened?"

Matt brought Bill up to date, then said to the group, "What do we do now?"

239

"I don't think we can do anything before morning," Monica replied. She prodded the syringe with a finger. "Even if we had the equipment to take fingerprints, too many people have handled this thing now."

"Plus, we don't have fingerprint records for the citizenry of Rivendell," Richard added. "And asking everyone to supply prints would be a non-starter."

"Like it or not, we'll have to hope Erin remembers something else, or some other clues surface. Otherwise we have to wait for this person to strike again." Monica grimaced. "Fuck. This is a part of being a cop that I *don't* like."

66. REALIZATION

Richard sighed wearily as he unzipped the tent flap and entered as quietly as he could. The meeting had gone late, and Suzie would have long since fallen asleep. He scrunched over to his side, feeling his way in the dark, then reached over to lightly touch her sleeping form. He was still shocked by how quickly and how deeply he'd committed to this relationship. For a lifelong loner like him to—

His hand met air. Frowning, he felt around. No Suzie. That was not normal. Her duties were strictly daytime, and no one would ever accuse her of being a night owl. A sudden sense of unease gripped him, and he grabbed for the flashlight.

"Weren't we just here?" Bill said, blinking at the others.

Richard gave him a hard look. As much as he'd grown to like Bill, the guy could still be a jerk. "Suzie is missing." He looked around the table, where the rest of the committee members sat in various stages of exhaustion.

"You've checked all the usual spots?" Monica said.

"This time of night, there really aren't any usual spots," Richard replied. "On the other hand, there aren't that many places she could be, and those places would all have lights on."

They were interrupted by someone entering the long-house. Richard recognized the man as one of the Agro crew.

The man addressed Monica immediately. "I can't find my girlfriend, Amy. Anywhere. There's no reason for her to be somewhere else right now. And after the business with Erin Savard earlier—"

"That's one attack and two missing, then." Monica's lips compressed as her expression clouded up. "We can't dismiss this as coincidence now."

"There really isn't anything we can do until morning, though," Bill said. "And I think that's only a couple of hours away. Richard and, uh … " Bill gestured at Amy's boyfriend, and he said, "Trey."

"Okay. Richard and Trey won't be getting any sleep, so you guys can discuss contingencies. Me, I'm not going to be good for anything unless I get at least a couple of hours. In the morning, I'll take the ultralight up and we'll see if we can spot anything."

"And I'll go check inventories," Monica replied. "No one is going to get rid of two bod—" She cut herself off quickly, then resumed. "Victims without some kind of transportation. It might give us a clue."

"And we'll try to do a roll call of some kind. We have the lists from the votes. Unless our mystery person didn't register at all." Matt made a sour face as he finished.

"It's still a start," Bill said to him.

No one had anything else to add. One by one, they shuffled out of the longhouse until only Richard was left, staring at the opposite wall.

※　※　※

Richard woke with a jerk. Despite everything, he'd nodded off, his head on the table. He worked his shoulders, trying to stretch out some of the stiffness. The window showed full daylight. It was time to get started, and if Bill hadn't gotten enough sleep yet, that was tough shit.

He almost ran into Monica at the door. She stepped back and did an about-face to walk with him. Not bothering with pleasantries, she launched straight into a report. "We've got people working a call tree with the voter lists. They'll be through it by mid-morning. Meanwhile, there's an ATV missing. The guy in charge says it's one that Jenson Hildebrandt normally uses. And he doesn't always bring it back the same day, so that could be unrelated."

"If we find this Jenson character, we can ask."

Matt, who had just joined them in their march across the lawn, said, "What about Jenson?"

"You know him?"

"Erin does. Bit of a creepoid, apparently."

"Hmm, that's two connections." Monica hesitated. "I don't want to jump to conclusions, though. It would be too easy to get into a lynch mob mentality. Let's see if we turn up anything more."

The informal census was completed more quickly than expected. A town-wide sense of urgency ensured that everyone cooperated. Monica and several others spent a few minutes going over the list.

"Hmm. A couple of people that we couldn't find, but other people swear they've seen them today. A bunch who went out early on work crews, but again, we have the names. Suzie and Amy, of course. Then there's the three guys who went missing recently—Sean and his friends and, surprise, surprise, Jenson Hildebrandt. That's three connections."

"Four, I think. Maybe," said Matt.

Monica looked up at him. "How so?"

"Sean and his friends. Ivan and Merv. I didn't have any real reason to make the connection before, but they got on Jenson's case a lot. Nothing really bad that I could see, otherwise I'd have separated them, but the point is—"

"He knew them, and had reason not to like them. And they've disappeared."

Richard rubbed his eyes. "Oh, fuck. So we could have a serial killer on our hands? Some kind of psychopath?"

"More likely a sociopath than a psychopath, big guy." Monica considered for a moment. "I'd like to be able to check the definitions, but I think a serial killer is generally going to be the second one. This guy is sloppy and reactive, and that's more like the first one."

"So he might not have killed Suzie and Amy."

"That's my hope."

Richard sighed. "Mine, too."

67. Held Captive

October 4 and 5

The camp was a little crude, Jenson had to admit. A tent, camp grill, fire pit, and an animal-deterrent fence. That last item had been very hard to get through the gates without anyone catching on. It would only work because of the steep sides of the hill, both uphill and downhill, that kept the larger predators away.

But it would keep him and his girls safe. They'd be waking up shortly. He wanted to have everything homey and comfortable for them. The ankle restraints were only a formality, of course. They would never run away. But best to avoid accidents.

He touched his face and forehead gingerly. There would probably be bruising, but no permanent harm. If an opportunity ever presented itself, though, there would definitely be payback.

Suzie watched Creepy Guy—*Jenson*, he'd said—out of the corner of her eye as she cooked the rabbit over the fire. Amy, across the firepit, was barely keeping it together. She probably couldn't be counted on if things started going to hell, so Suzie was essentially on her own.

She seethed, but tried to keep it from showing on her face. What was it about her that every nut job with an axe to grind had to grab *her*? Okay, with the thugs, she was just in the wrong place at the right time. Still, once was too much, and twice—well, if this latest whacko left her an opening, he was going to lose some very important body parts.

Suzie smiled to herself. She would have generally been considered the shy and retiring type back in Lincoln, but Outland seemed to have brought out the warrior in her. Beating people with heavy sticks didn't seem nearly as foreign an idea as it would have pre-Yellowstone.

Jenson came over and sat in front of the fire. Wordlessly, he held his hands out to warm them. Amy cringed and moved as far from him as she could get without leaving the circle of warmth herself.

From what little Suzie already knew of Jenson, he was a weird duck with no social skills, and based on results so far, no conversational skills either. Although watching his face and his occasional gestures, it seemed as if he was having entire dialogues with her and Amy, but only in his head. It was creepy in the extreme.

When they'd first woken up, suffering from what felt like massive hangovers, Jenson had explained that they were finally free of their former lives and would be starting their own colony and living under their own rules. The leg restraints, he said, were just a formality to ensure that they stayed within his area of protection.

Yeah, right.

The restraint, actually a lightweight metal cable rather than a chain, stretched from a manacle on one ankle to a large common ring set in the ground. It looked to be somewhere around thirty feet in length.

Jenson stood and announced, "I'm going to get the tents set up. I'll be back when dinner is ready." Suzie glanced at him then looked away, unwilling to acknowledge him any more than necessary. So far, he had made no demands, other than delivering the rabbit and ordering her and Amy to cook it.

"What does he want with us?" Amy whispered.

"Normally I'd say that's obvious," Suzie replied, "but with this guy, maybe not so much. Just keep quiet and wait for him to fill in the silences. At some point, he'll monologue or something."

"Where are we, do you know?"

"No idea. I was out cold during the ride. We can't be too close or people in Rivendell might see smoke during the day or the fire at night. But we can't be too far, or Jenson wouldn't have been able to set this up with day trips."

"What makes you think he only used day trips?"

"The ATV. If someone didn't return with an ATV or bike at the end of the day, Jonesy would have had a fit."

Amy returned a small smile. "I'll take your word for that. Does it help us?"

"Not sure..." Suzie stared into the fire. "If they start a search, even a half-day's radius is a lot of ground to cover, and we're not exactly exposed." Suzie looked around, paying close attention to the layout of the camp and the immediate geography. "They could easily miss us with a visual search. We could jump up and down, but I have a feeling that Jenson might put a violent stop to that."

"Do you think they'll even look?"

"Oh, pretty sure. Richard will be frantic once he realizes I'm missing. I don't know if you know Richard, but when he gets a notion, you'd best not try to stand in his way."

"But what can he do?"

"That's a good question, Amy. And a better question is, what can we do to prepare for whatever they do?"

Amy frowned, trying to untwist the logic of Suzie's statement. Finally, she nodded. "A signal fire?"

"Hah. I don't see Jenson not noticing that." Suzie paused and glanced over at the camp grill. "However... "

The camp grill was one of those items you find in public campgrounds. A metal box with an open front and a grill on top, it was pretty much the minimalist's cast-iron stove in outdoor form.

"Amy," Suzie said, "we're going to start using the camp grill for all our cooking, and we're going to cook as late in the day as possible. Understand?"

"Not really, but okay."

At that moment, Jenson walked up to the fire. "Dinner ready?"

Suzie removed the skewer from the fire and began to separate the meat from the carcass.

"I have to answer a call of nature," Amy announced.

Jenson gestured with one hand as he accepted a plate from Suzie. "The cable is long enough to get to the outhouse. And to the tent."

Suzie measured the distance to the small structure, then inspected the cable. Long enough, but just. And thoroughly spiked down at the end. She doubted she could get that anchor out of the ground without mechanical aid.

"Why do we have to be chained?" Amy asked.

"It's a formality," Jenson said. Then his face contorted in a series of facial expressions, although *seizures* wouldn't be implausible either. It was like he was having a whole conversation in his mind. In the end he smiled and said, "You understand."

Wow. You really are a freaky deaky, aren't you? Suzie thought. She would play it cool, both to avoid setting him off and to avoid giving him any cause for concern or suspicion. But if she got the chance, she would cave in his skull without a second thought.

For a kidnapper and general whacko, Jenson seemed oddly respectful of Suzie and Amy. They had their own tent, which was within chain distance of the outhouse. Suzie noted that Jenson's tent was outside chain range, though. Whacko maybe, but not stupid. He also took the only visible weapons with him.

68. SEARCH

October 5

Goro was piloting today, while Bill scanned the landscape with binoculars. He admitted to himself that this was a low-probability play. Any encampment would be at least minimally camouflaged, and it wouldn't take much to fool the eye from this height.

The real problem was that Outland was not the flat monoculture that Nebraska had long since been converted to. Forests and copses, large and small, alternated with plains, bogs, swamps, and all of it covered with a seemingly infinite carpet of running, grazing, and flying creatures.

Goro took advantage of every updraft with a level of skill that Bill had to admire. The ultralight, never loud in any case, was completely silent when gliding. It was a slim chance that it would make a difference, but they needed every advantage they could get.

All the silent running also stretched the fuel reserves, allowing them to spend most of the day in the air. But finally, by mid-afternoon, Bill was ready to call it quits.

"We should anyway," Goro replied to Bill's comment. "Refuel and inspection, then we go up again after dark with the night-vision and thermal-vision equipment."

"True. And gives us time to hit the facilities and get some food." Bill sat back and put the binoculars back in their case. "Okay, Goro. Take us home."

❧   ❧   ❧

While Goro tended to the ultralight, Bill took care of the necessaries then went looking for Richard. He spotted Monica, stomping along in full marching mode, a thunderous expression on her face. "Hey, Mon. Seen Richard?"

She looked in his direction and her expression softened slightly, but she didn't alter her vector at all. Bill had to jog to match trajectories.

"Richard's out in an ATV. He's got all of them doing a circle around Rivendell at a three-mile radius." She waved a hand vaguely *out there*. "He figures if they find any tracks out that far, they'll have a good chance of being Jenson's."

"They'll have to drive pretty slow to be able to spot anything."

Monica shrugged. "At this point, we don't have anything better to work with. Either you and Goro spot something, or the ATVs spot something. Until then, we're just thrashing around."

Bill nodded without response, and slowed to let Monica pull away. He wasn't helping, and in fact was probably distracting her from whatever mission of destruction she was pursuing.

Then there was a shout, and both Bill and Monica looked around to see a runner sprinting their way, waving his arm sporadically. The man staggered to a stop and placed his hands on his knees for a moment to get his wind back.

"You've got all day to breathe," Monica growled impatiently. "What?"

The man straightened up with difficulty. "Radio message from Richard. They think they've found something."

Bill had never been a sprinter. Or a runner of any kind, except perhaps in video games. But he found himself feeling an inappropriate level of pride that he was able to keep up with the other two. They arrived at the impromptu command center, a folding table set out in front of one of the longhouses, to find Erin giving orders as people came and went.

"What's the sitch?" Monica asked without preamble.

"Richard found a fresh set of ATV tracks, south-southeast of here. Plus, evidence of older tracks, coming and going, all in the same direction." Erin pointed to Charlie, who was in discussion with several people over a hand-drawn map spread out on the table. "Charlie can't think of a single op that anyone has done in that direction, that far out. It looks like our best clue so far."

Monica nodded, then glanced at Erin. "You holding out okay?"

"I'm fine," Erin replied, her face stony. "Don't worry about me. Find this fucker."

"I'll go talk to Collins," Monica said. "He was prepping a truck, for when we found anything."

"And that's my cue," Bill added. "The plane should be just about ready. Time to fly."

69. RESCUE

Suzie turned the skewer over the camp stove, careful to ensure no singeing. This morning's confrontation when she'd slightly burned the breakfast bird made it abundantly clear that this creepo was truly warped. The expression on his face had been terrifying, almost inhumanly contorted. He literally vibrated in place for several seconds before waving the skewer in her face and yelling.

Well, okay then. Mustn't piss off the looney-tune. Tonight's dinner would be very carefully cooked. She didn't want him on edge.

"Why are you using the camp stove?" Jenson asked, pointing to the cast iron appliance.

"Keeps the fire concentrated," she said, "and lets me do the cooking with less danger of burning either myself or the food."

Jenson nodded, apparently mollified. Very probably that part about not burning the food appealed to him, so he'd want it to be true.

The real reason was that the camp stove would retain the heat for hours. Jenson had them put out the fire before going to bed, probably to prevent any telltale light. But without a lot of water, they had to do it by burying the coals. If, as Suzie suspected, Rivendell would be searching by ultralight using the night-vision and thermal-imaging goggles, then the stove should stand out like a beacon.

Well, that was the theory. She'd also try to leave a few hot coals out if she could.

And she hoped they'd come soon. This situation with Jenson was not sustainable. Whatever fantasy world he was living in was going to collide with reality, and soon. He'd already started talking about "populating their new colony." She hoped he didn't mean what she thought he did. Even assuming—no, never mind. She wasn't going to even think about it, even in theory.

She and Amy did their evening cleanup and ablutions, then zipped themselves into their tent, the cables trailing out through a small gap in the tent flaps. Jenson watched them settle in, then headed for his own tent.

Suzie opened her eyes. Something had woken her, but she couldn't remember what. She held her breath, as still as she could be. And there it was—a droning sound, barely perceptible over the nocturnal cacophony of calls, screams, and roars.

She nudged Amy, then began carefully unzipping their tent flap. But before she could get the zipper up more than a foot, Jenson burst out of his tent, brandishing his rifle. She couldn't make out his expression in the dark, but she could see him turning, looking for the source of the sound.

Suzie put a hand on Amy's shoulder, then whispered, "We've been found, but Jenson's about to fire on the ultralight. Then he'll move us. Or worse. We have to make a stand."

She couldn't see Amy's face, but she distinctly heard the *gulp* as Amy processed her statement. Without waiting, Suzie finished unzipping the tent flap. Between the sounds of the night wildlife and his concentrating on pinpointing the location of the ultralight, Jenson didn't notice the small noise.

Suzie looked around. There was nothing within reach that was usable as a weapon. Then she looked down at her restraint. Grabbing up about six feet of cable, she handed a loop to Amy. "Run at him and trip him. Hold this taut."

Jenson was facing away from them and looking up, and now bringing his rifle up to bear. Amy and Suzie charged straight at him from behind, holding a length of cable between them. As they reached him, they brought the cable low and hit his legs mid-calf.

The effect of yanking his legs out from under him was not just equivalent to falling from a standing position. The cable sweeping Jenson's legs at a running speed created a rotation of his body around his center of mass that added acceleration to what gravity naturally supplied. His head and back struck the ground with the force of a ten-foot fall.

Suzie ran back and grabbed the rifle, which Jenson had dropped. "Check him for any other weapons. Quickly."

Amy poked and patted but found nothing. Then she jumped back as Jenson made a feeble attempt to grab her.

Suzie aimed the rifle. "I will fucking shoot you if you even blink wrong. Stay on the ground."

They both stepped back to make a lunge and grab impossible, and made sure their cables weren't within reach. Suzie admitted to herself, though, that Jenson didn't look to be in any shape to do anything. It was hard to tell in the dim light, but that might be blood pooling around his head. Well, no loss if so.

It couldn't have been more than a half hour before the cavalry arrived, in the form of several military vehicles. Between the headlights and the auxiliary light bars, the area lit up like daytime. The night life, thoroughly intimidated, went silent. After months of getting used to the constant nighttime cacophony, the silence gave the whole scene an eerie feel, almost like a weird form of horror-movie background music.

Richard jumped out of the passenger side of one of the trucks before they'd even come to a stop. Suzie teared up, seeing him. She called out to him, "You're late—*oof!*" Richard wrapped her in a bear hug and lifted her right off the ground. Suzie had a moment of fear that Jenson might pick that moment to bolt, or grab the rifle, or something. But no worries—several soldiers had followed and were restraining him.

❖ ❖ ❖

It was hours before they were ready to go. No one had thought to bring a cable cutter, and Jenson appeared to have intended the restraints to be permanent. Or maybe he just hadn't thought that far ahead. Jenson did in fact have a head wound, and a concussion, apparently. He was still groggy when they loaded him into the back of a truck in handcuffs.

They packed what they could of the camp supplies into the trucks, and bundled the rest to be as critter-proof as possible. And Suzie found herself sitting in a personnel carrier between Amy and Richard. Going home.

"This is not going to be comfortable," Richard said to her. "Although we'll probably drive a lot more slowly on the way back. Still, I hope your bladder is empty."

One of the Guard leaned forward. Suzie saw in the low light that it was Lieutenant Collins. "We've pretty much figured out, in broad terms, what was going on. This Hildebrandt character kidnapped the two of you and brought you here, correct? Do you know why? Did he say?"

"He wanted to start his own colony. I guess we were breeding stock." She paused. "He's, uh, not quite right in the head, I think."

Collins frowned. "That's going to complicate things."

"You mean in terms of a trial?"

Collins nodded. "Questions of intent, *compos mentis*, and so on."

"Listen to you, sounding like a lawyer and all." Richard leaned forward. "Now you listen to me. He kidnapped two women. He chained them up. He did all this stealthily, with massive planning. You've seen the camp. We have reason to believe he's killed three people who pissed him off. Also with sufficient pre-planning to make sure he didn't get caught. He knew what he was doing. Having a mental illness is not automatically a defense."

Collins held up both hands. "Hey, I am not the person you want to argue with. I'd just put him in front of a firing squad if it was up to me. But we have this whole 'birth of a nation' thing going on. There will be people who think we should give him some consideration for this."

Richard crossed his arms and frowned thunderously. "Fuck that. If he gets off because of any 'consideration,' I'll kill him myself."

Suzie put her arms around his arm and rested her head on his shoulder. "And then Monica will have to arrest you. I don't want to be a prison bride."

The comment broke the tension, and they all chuckled. But the central problem remained. What would they do with Jenson? And would they be able to live with it?

70. ANOTHER TRIAL

October 6

The news of a kidnapper and possible serial killer in their midst spread through the town like wildfire. And tempers were still short from the recent Jimmy Korniski trial, which resulted in several mobs in front of the longhouse, demanding an immediate and dramatic resolution.

Richard peeked out the door. "It's getting kind of ugly. I don't *think* they'll storm the building, but I don't want to bet my life on it."

Monica gave Jenson one last glare. Handcuffed to a chair, he had steadfastly refused to answer any questions, or even acknowledge anyone's existence. Every once in a while, his face would go red and he would shake a little, as if he was having an internal battle. But otherwise, for all his reaction, he might as well be the only person in the room.

She sighed and stood. "I'll go talk to them." Monica grabbed her AR-15 and made for the door. Curious to see how she'd handle this, Richard followed.

The crowd noise increased as they stepped out onto the porch. Unlike with the conventions and the trial, this was not a good-natured sound. This crowd was angry, and wanted blood.

"Hey!" Monica yelled. As always when she cut loose, Richard was amazed that anyone that size could produce that many decibels.

And as it so often did, the shout shocked the crowd into silence. Or almost silence. A low muttering continued, until Monica yelled, "Shut the fuck up!"

She paused just the right amount of time, then said, "How many people here think I'm some kind of bleeding-heart liberal?"

The question was met with laughs.

"How many people think I'm gonna let someone who attacked my best friend just walk away?"

This time, there was no laughter, just a low growl.

"Understand this, people. There will be a trial. And if he walks, it'll be because YOU voted that way. Is that going to happen?"

The mob responded with cries of "No way" and "Fuck no!"

"Then go home, do your laundry or whatever can't wait, because the trial is tomorrow. Be there."

It took a few moments before a rising buzz of conversation and argument rose in the slowly dispersing crowd. Monica slung her rifle over her shoulder and grinned at Richard. "And done."

"God, woman, you scare me sometimes."

She gestured to the front door. "Let's see what we can do with Jenson. Maybe he's ready to start talking."

Setting up was considerably easier this time around, with the experience gained from Jimmy's trial. The crowd knew what to expect and settled in quickly.

Richard, as usual, did the intro via PA. "Your attention, please." Pause. "We're going to keep the same format as last time. Sam will preside, Bea will be prosecution, and Fred will be defense." Richard paused again and glanced sideways at Fred. "And Fred is having just as little luck this time, too. But I'll let him tell you about it."

Fred took the mike from Richard. "What Richard means is that the defendant won't talk to anyone. He won't make eye contact, he won't even acknowledge our existence. I frankly think an insanity defense is a real possibility here. Or at least a consideration. Other than that, I got nothing, until and unless the defendant starts cooperating with me."

He stepped back and handed the mike to Richard, to an overwhelming roar of boos.

"And now, the prosecution." Richard handed the mike to Bea. Cheers erupted.

"What we know...," she began. "We found the defendant at a remote camp that he had obviously spent considerable time preparing. He had two kidnap victims with him, chained to prevent escape. Based on what they report of interactions with him, this was intended to be a permanent state of affairs."

Bea paused and looked at Richard for a moment. "What we are pretty sure of... Erin Savard was attacked by someone who attempted to inject her with a substance that knocked her out. The two victims show physical evidence of similar injections, at the same location on their bodies. A vial of etorphine was found in the defendant's personal effects. That's a horse tranquilizer. So now we have two kidnappings and a third attempted one."

Again, Bea paused, taking a breath. "What we are speculating on... three men who used to bully the defendant all disappeared at the same time. It happened right after the defendant abruptly changed work crews, which we think was an attempt to give himself an alibi. We haven't found any bodies, and with two worlds to hide them on, I don't expect we will. But I'll add that if the three men had died of more-innocent causes, we would probably have found some traces of at least one of them. Having three complete disappearances is, in itself, suspicious."

Bea hesitated, then glanced at Sam before continuing. "We're re-inventing a judicial process as we go here, and we shouldn't cut too many corners. I'd like to have the victims give their testimony for the record. Fred can cross-examine if he wants." She gestured to Erin to step forward.

Erin gave a short, concise, and clinical description of her experience. When Fred declined to cross, Bea gestured to Amy, but she shook her head vehemently. "Suzie can speak for both of us."

Suzie stepped up and took the mike. Her testimony was longer and far more passionate. Sam had to interrupt her several times as she seemed determined to descend into a rant.

"We get that you don't like the defendant," he said on the third interruption. "But speculating on his ancestry, species, and mating habits is outside your area of expertise. And not useful as evidence."

Suzie glared at him but nodded after a moment and handed the mike back to Bea. Again, Fred declined to cross.

"You sure, Fred?" Sam asked.

Fred took the mike to reply. "The facts as stated really aren't in dispute, Sam. I think back on Earth, a lawyer would have plea-bargained in these circumstances. Or gone with insanity, maybe." Fred made a gesture of helplessness. "I don't think that'll fly here." He hesitated, then handed the mike back to Bea, who passed it on to Sam.

"This won't be as easy as the last one, folks. Last time, Jimmy loudly and gleefully admitted his guilt and bragged about his motivations, which made it completely open and shut. This time, we have someone who may not be all there, if you get my drift, and who refuses to say *anything*. All we have is two kidnappings and one attempted kidnapping. If and when we find bodies, we can re-try him, but until then, we have to go on what we have." Sam took a breath. "Like last time, we will first decide if he's guilty, then we'll decide on sentence. So, you all know the drill."

Sam handed the mike back to Richard. The crowd, now that the formalities were over, was becoming boisterous and loud. Without a word, Richard gestured to the tables where volunteers waited to record people's votes.

Monica sidled up to Richard as he watched the residents queue up to vote. "How's Suzie doing?"

He turned and gave her an uncertain smile. "Seems okay, overall. I wouldn't go so far as to say *no worse for wear*, but no obvious problems, anyway. Baby seems okay, which is a huge relief."

Monica blew out a breath. "That's good. I think we'd have to hang a homicide rap on him if she'd lost it."

Richard nodded, and let the silence stretch for a few moments. "Sentencing is going to be a bitch."

"He'll be dead in a week."

Richard glanced at her. "Prediction, or promise?"

"Yep."

He nodded. "Well, let's see what happens."

The results were a surprise to no one. Guilty as charged.

"Now comes the hard part," said Sam to the crowd. "Sentencing. On the one hand, kidnapping doesn't and has never had as harsh a sentence as murder. On the other hand, we have to be aware of the logistics of our decision. If we choose incarceration, we have to supply the jail cell. And the guards. If we choose repatriation—"

"Exile."

Sam stopped in mid-sentence. Jenson had stood and uttered the one word, the first time since his arrest that he'd acknowledged anyone else's existence.

"Exile," Jenson repeated. "Or death. You don't want me, I don't want you."

Sam cleared his throat and looked at Richard, uncertainty plain on his face. Richard shrugged back at him to indicate that he had no more clue than Sam how to handle this.

Finally, Sam spoke into the mike. "Okay, the defendant has chosen exile to Dino Planet as his preference. Uh, take that into account when deciding. Keep in mind that it is essentially a death sentence."

As before, the crowd knew what to do, and was lining up before Sam had even called time out.

❧   ❧   ❧

The votes were counted and the results posted in record time.

1- DO NOTHING:	2
2- INCARCERATION:	1
3- FORCED LABOR:	14
4- REPATRIATION:	56
5- EXILE TO DINO PLANET:	324
6- FIRING SQUAD:	87

"Looks like people want to give Jenson what he asked for," Richard commented.

"Except for the ones who still want to shoot him," Bea added. "Pointing that out for a friend."

Monica snorted. "And what is it with the do-nothings? Are they just trolling?"

No one replied to her question. Instead, Richard said, "Well, let's get this done."

It was a virtual repeat of Jimmy's sentence. The gate stood ready, Kevin at the controls. Monica, Bea, and several soldiers stood with their weapons, ready for any moves from the prisoner or from the gate when it was opened. Jenson stood, hands zip-tied, a bundle of supplies at his feet.

"We'll cut your bonds," Richard said, "then we'll open the interface. Pick up the supplies and walk through. We're not interested in a monologue. Clear?"

Jenson returned Richard's glare for a moment, then said, "Sean and his friends. They're in barrels at the back of that environmental cleanup company beside the Home Depot." Then he held out his wrists.

Richard was momentarily shocked into immobility. Then he cut the zip tie and nodded to Kevin. The interface shimmered into a scene from another, more primitive world. As the air wafted through the interface, Jenson picked up the bundle and walked through without a backward glance.

Everyone exchanged baffled looks as Kevin closed down the gate. "That was just weird," Richard finally said.

"I wonder," Bea added, "was he being helpful, or was that some bizarre kind of boasting?"

"I'm going with the latter," Monica replied. She shook her head. "But yeah, this was just…bizarre. I thought he might have been an Incel, but this was more than just frustration with women. Based on what Erin's told me, Jenson had trouble with *everyone*."

Richard sighed. "We'll never know. And it doesn't matter, does it? Would it change anything that happened?"

"No. Actions and intent. Case closed." Monica adjusted her weapon strap to take the weight of her rifle, then glanced at Kevin, who was just finishing up packing the gate hardware. "Let's go. We're done here. We're going to have to go to Earthside and open a bunch of chemical drums. I hope we have some gas masks."

71. Campaigning

October 8

Bill walked alongside Monica, glancing right and left to take in the circus. Or zoo. Either description worked. Groups were congregating all over the lawn, some with whiteboards, some with flipcharts. Bill smiled, thinking that Charlie's head must have exploded at the requests.

Over here, a group was discussing Communism versus Marxism versus Socialism. Over there, someone was advocating Libertarianism. And over there, a fistfight was about to develop over who the hell knew what.

Monica spotted the problem at the same moment and veered in that direction. Bill hurried to keep up as she dropped into marching mode.

"This doesn't look like voting to me," Monica called out as she arrived. The participants and onlookers turned to her in apparent surprise. "You know the rules," Monica continued. "No violence. No threats. No attempts at intimidation. If you can't persuade people to your point of view, maybe it isn't all that valuable."

One of the crowd gave her a dark look. "Just because a majority chooses a system doesn't make it the *best* one. That's just—"

"Wrong, Chucky," Monica interjected. "If the majority chooses a system, it by definition *is* the best, since the definition of 'best' is *The system that the majority chooses.*" She smiled, but not in a friendly way. "We hold these truths to be self-evident, and all that."

She glared around the group, but no one seemed inclined to challenge her. Bill snuck a glance at the flipchart and realized that the subject was separation of church and state. He was taken slightly aback. He hadn't realized there was much in the way of strong religious feeling in Rivendell. But maybe he just hadn't been paying attention. He gestured at the flipchart. "What's the beef, anyway?"

One of the two would-be pugilists, a man Bill remembered as Paul, replied, "Dean here wants religious principles to be embedded in our new constitution. Of course, he meant *Christian* principles. I suggested we adopt Pastafarian principles instead, and he got butt-hurt."

Bill grinned and turned to the other guy. "Honestly, Dean, if it came to a vote, I think Pastafarianism would win over fundamentalism. So maybe insisting on one religion—"

"Exactly why this shouldn't be decided by a vote. It's way too important—"

"Jesus," Monica exclaimed. "You don't want a vote because you know you'll lose, so you figure you'll just shove your religion down our throats? And you want us to stand meekly by and let you do it? Not gonna happen. But thanks for making it real clear how you feel." She stepped forward until she was within Dean's space. "No violence. No intimidation. Not negotiable. Deal with it. Or I will." Before Dean could mount a rebuttal, she turned and stalked off.

"Wow, that was fun," Bill muttered as they continued on their way.

"Thing is, Bill, we've got *way* too many people with *way* too many ideas of how things should be done. Right now, it feels like we'll be voting on fifty different questions before we can even decide on what we should be voting on. This is gonna take forever."

"Yeah, we need a referendum. Multiple questions." Bill paused to do a stutter step to keep even with Monica. "Just some basics at first, to establish fundamentals."

She interrupted him with a gesture. "Here's one of our potential flashpoints." She made an abrupt vector change, once again requiring Bill to scramble to keep up.

This crowd was large, and their attention was directed to the speaker, who was literally standing on a soapbox. Well, a box of some kind anyway. Did soap still come in boxes?

Bill's eyebrows went up in surprise. It was Goro, the town's chief aircraft pilot and Bill's occasional instructor. Goro was venting passionately, and it took Bill a few seconds to pick up the thread.

"...You've heard the claims, even recently from the Ashland politicians. We're too young, we're too inexperienced, we're too blah blah blah. So I guess the implication is that the jerries can do a better job. Tell me, does anyone here think they've been doing a good job for the last umpteen centuries? Every country on Earth has been run by jerries since countries were invented. Anyone remember any good jobs being done? Wars, famines, corruption, pogroms, environmental destruction, totalitarianism, institutionalized racism and sexism, ghettos, and on and on. In exactly what way have the jerries ever done a *better* job? Or even a *half-decent* job? Would *you* put that crap on your resumé?"

Bill sidled up to a woman he recognized, Anna, and prodded her lightly on the arm. "What's the deal here?"

She replied in a low voice, "Goro seems to think old people, jerries, shouldn't be allowed to hold office after a certain age. Kind of the reverse of the Age of Candidacy rules."

"Because…"

Anna snorted. "Because, according to Goro, jerries have been doing a truly shitty job of running anything and everything back on Earth since forever, and it's time to recognize that and take the keys away from them. He's actually made some very good points. I think I'd support him."

"What's that word he's got scrawled on there?" Monica squinted. "Neoatomocracy?" She made a couple of attempts at pronunciation, then settled on her first attempt.

"Yep, that's how Goro says it," Anna replied. "He says it's a neologism—at least he can't find anyone who's ever heard of it."

"Wonderful," Monica said, rolling her eyes. "This won't be an acrimonious election *at all*."

72. New Interface

October 10

Bill held the assembly and turned it around in his hands. It looked somewhat like a camera, except for a lack of lenses. "So how does this work?"

"The gate generates a probability interface," Kevin replied, "which connects to another timeline and then allows light and matter to step through. This design does the first part of that, but never actually opens the connection. But it can be used to find new timelines, just like the small gate."

Bill and Richard stared at each other for a few moments before turning back to Kevin. "Wow," Bill said. "That's, uh…pretty impressive." Then he frowned. "And we didn't bother making this before now because…"

"Give it a rest, Bill," Richard growled. "We've been kind of busy."

Kevin shrugged. "I had it at the back of my mind for something to look into someday. Until our last couple of connections made it a priority."

"Got it. Sorry, Kev." And Bill admitted to himself that this bit of gadget-mongering was a welcome break from all the arguing over governments and economic systems. If he was sick and tired of it, how much more weary would Kevin be? Doubtless that figured at least somewhat into Kevin's sudden interest in hardware design.

Richard sighed. "And it doesn't really change much. This will give us new coordinates to check, but won't tell us anything about the level of danger in those timelines. At some point, we will still have to open a gate and actually look."

"I might have a few ideas on that front," Bill replied. "We have the pressure cut-out on the pressure vessel ever since our first adventure back in the lab. I can add sensors for other conditions. It'll take some work, but should adequately address the safety issue."

It took only a day for Bill to make the modifications. He and Kevin presented a summary of their plans. When they were done, Richard gazed at Bill in perplexity. "I don't understand. You're going to be accessing Greenhouse Earth from Dino Planet? Isn't that like two jumps away?"

Bill and Kevin both said, "It doesn't—" at the same time. Bill gestured to Kevin, who continued. "It doesn't matter where you access a timeline from, once we have the coordinates to connect with it. It's just the initial blind fishing for new timelines that's limited to the immediately adjacent ones."

Bill took over as Kevin finished. "And there's still some risk with what we're doing. Let's face it, any connection with Greenhouse Earth carries risk. So we'll do it from Dino Planet to reduce the risk to Rivendell."

"But increase the risk to Dino Planet," Erin muttered.

"Hey, in any conflict between people and dinos, I vote people," Bill replied.

"An excellent philosophy for any political situation," Richard said. "Okay, guys, let me know how it goes. Although I guess if it goes badly, this is probably good-bye."

"Oh, great, thanks for that," Bill grumbled, as he and Kevin stepped into the waiting gate.

They found themselves, once again, in the upended culvert on Dino Planet. Charlie had arrived earlier and had the pressure vessel set up.

Bill gestured to the mechanism, which had some obvious recent modifications. "I've added a couple of ports so that we can have two devices operating inside the vessel, namely the small gate and the scanner. I've also added this high-pressure sliding shaft seal so we can push the scanner through the small gate, once it's connected to Greenhouse Earth. Then we'll scan for any timelines from there. That's the plan, right, Kev?"

"As far as you know."

Bill did a double-take, then laughed as he saw that Kevin was smiling. While the Yellowstone event may have been bad for humanity in general, it was turning out to be good for Kevin, at least. And Richard, come to think of it.

"Okay, Charlie, fire up the small gate."

Charlie complied without comment, and the small gate's interface shimmered to life. Immediately, a yellowish haze invaded the interior of the pressure vessel.

"And, inserting the scanner," Bill said, and began pushing on a rod outside the bell. Inside the bell, the scanner, attached to the other end of the rod, moved smoothly through the interface to Greenhouse Earth. "Okay, Kev, begin scan."

"I'm not going to linger on any connections," Kevin replied as he worked his tablet. "I'll just record the coordinates as fast as we get them, and we can decide what to do about it later."

He tapped at the control interface a few times, then grunted. "Done. Only two connections. That's disappointing."

Bill pulled the rod back, and the scanner retracted out of the small gate. Charlie pressed some buttons and, with a thud, the yellowish haze in the vessel disappeared from the interface. At the same time, an extremely bright light shone through the gate.

"What … ?" Bill started.

"I've decided as a matter of policy I'll evacuate the vessel to Vacuum Earth before shutting down," Charlie replied. "It seems unlikely that anything there will be harmed."

"Huh. Good thinking." Bill looked at Kevin, who waved the tablet in confirmation. "Okay, decision time. Do we want to see what we've got?"

"You've rigged some safety systems?" Charlie asked.

"Yeah," Bill replied. "Temperature sensors, pressure sensors, radiation sensors, even a trip switch if something solid tries to come through the interface. It will shut down the portal within ten microseconds of detecting an out-of-bounds condition."

"Damn." Charlie nodded in appreciation. "Okay, you got my vote."

Bill looked again at Kevin, who shrugged. "I'll take that as a yes," Bill said, and began disassembling the pressure vessel again to swap in the camera. "You know, there's no real reason we can't put the camera and the scanner on the push-bar. It would save time."

Kevin shrugged. "You're the engineer."

"Selecting first coordinates," Kevin said, and jabbed the tablet. The interface faded for a moment, then re-solidified into a scene of devastation. Charred stumps alternated with blackened rock and drifts of ash.

"Forest fire? Grass fire?" Charlie said, looking at the hellish landscape.

"Any or all of the above," Bill replied. "On the other hand, it looks to be long over. Temperature readings aren't higher than normal. I guess that's another one that'll need a review."

Bill pulled the rod back again, to retract the scanner. Charlie pressed some buttons and again evacuated the contents of the pressure vessel onto Vacuum Earth.

Kevin operated the controls, and all three men said "oh" in unison. On the screen, an image of a wheat field held their collective gaze. And a field it was. The wheat, clearly a variety bred for high yield and of a uniform height, moved slowly in the breeze.

"Oh, wow." Bill looked at the other two. "Obviously inhabited, and by people—"

"*Maybe* people," Kevin interjected.

Bill laughed. "Yeah, true, might be intelligent meerkats. But whoever or whatever they are, they have agriculture." He hesitated. "We should probably keep this quiet for the moment, guys."

"State secrets already?" Charlie said mockingly.

"Do you really want the barrage of demands if everyone thinks we've found a way back home? Or some reasonable facsimile, anyway?"

Charlie thought for a moment, looking down at the ground. "No, you're right. We don't really know what we have, and a lot of people will want to go off half-cocked. I'm fine with waiting until we have more info."

Bill gave Charlie a thumbs-up, but he couldn't help a moment of internal disquiet. Classifying something like this *always* resulted in trouble for the inner circle, in every movie he'd ever seen. He hoped he wasn't about to get eaten by pterodactyls or something.

Bill began to slowly rotate the pressure vessel. "Anything?"

"No ... no ... wait. Something in that direction."

Charlie looked up at the camera, consulted a compass, and announced, "North north-west. Can you estimate a distance?"

"No, it's just an interruption to the horizon line. So not close, I guess. Maybe a farmhouse?"

Bill grunted. "I'm supposed to be going up in the ultra-light with Goro again tomorrow. I'll add this to the list of things to investigate." He slowly blew out a breath. "Keep it quiet, right? I admit, I'm even feeling hopeful. And I know better."

"Murphy?"

"Murphy and his bitch wife, Payback."

73. EARTHSIDE: ANTARCTICA

As the clouds of ash from Yellowstone moved across the equator, they created the same disruption and destruction as that suffered by the northern hemisphere. Operating equipment was destroyed within hours or days. Transportation systems such as rail became unusable. Ships and boats that took on too large of an ash load capsized from the weight. Airport runways were buried and couldn't be cleared without heavy equipment.

And human beings, more concerned with their families and their own lives, abandoned their jobs as they fled, imagining better conditions elsewhere.

The geography of the southern hemisphere is such that anything other than local movement was impossible without modern technology. Overnight, every human habitation was isolated.

The dozens of nationally funded stations scattered across Antarctica in particular are highly artificial environments. One hundred percent of their supplies and resources come from their parent nations or organizations, and almost entirely by air. And to place additional pressure on their resources, the ash blocked light from the early spring sun that would otherwise already have begun the long, slow process of raising the continent out of its winter deep freeze.

Marianna Spana gazed morosely at the monitor, not really registering the contents of the video windows. They were nearing the end of Antarctic winter, and the sun was making an appearance over the horizon for about half of each day. In theory. By now the temps should be coming up and the brutal winter winds dying down.

Not that Marianna would know it, looking at the video feeds from the outside cameras. It was midday. Even if overcast, it should be recognizably daylight. And the temperature was at least ten degrees Celsius below normal.

Radio comms had been spotty since shortly after the Yellowstone eruption, but now they hadn't heard from Hobart base in almost a week.

One of the other staff members stuck his head into the room and silently raised an eyebrow. Marianna shook her head, and he grimaced and walked away without ever uttering a word.

The station survived on stockpiled supplies through the brutal Antarctic winter, but they were reaching the end of those stockpiles. By now, Hobart should be scheduling flights to Casey station to begin to replenish their depleted supplies. And with the temps well below normal for this time of year, they were burning through their heating fuel faster than expected. Freezing to death was becoming a distinct danger.

Marianna pushed herself away from the desk and glided across the floor on the office chair, expertly swiveling just in time to catch herself as she rolled up to the radio. She donned the headphones and flicked through all the official frequencies. Nothing but static. Some of the other Antarctic stations were close enough to communicate with, but none of them had heard from their mother nations either.

"Still nothing?"

Marianna looked up. Brian Hall, her boss and the station manager, stood at the door. Marianna glanced up at the clock. She was due to report in ten minutes, but apparently Brian hadn't been able to wait.

"Nothing," she said, shaking her head. "I guess it's time to start discussing alternatives." Slowly, feeling like her legs each weighed a ton, she followed him to the common room for a very difficult staff meeting.

74. ROUND ONE

October 12

Richard looked up as Bill approached, plate heaped high with something-chili stew. Richard hitched himself over on the bench, making room, and Bill sat with a grateful sigh.

"Frontier life hasn't dulled your appetite," Richard said, nodding at the plate.

"No, but it's sure made a dent in my middle." Bill patted his stomach. "I used to have a spare tire. Now I could almost pass for a jock."

"I wouldn't go that far." Richard grinned, then changed the subject. "Did you watch the circus today?"

Bill shook his head in disbelief. "If I may borrow one of your phrases, fuck me! I've never seen so many heads exploding at the same time. And some of the fine details they're arguing about..."

"Makes Lutherans sound like pragmatists?"

Bill snorted. "Yeah, like that." He hesitated before continuing. "Brady made a speech."

"Oh?"

"It didn't go well. You heard about the lieutenant's conversation with Cummins when they first got here, right? Well, Brady's a little more politically savvy, so he did more of a soft sell, but essentially the message was still that we should all go back to playing with our toys and let the adults take over."

"That seems like a bad tactic in a field composed largely of university students."

"You'd think, wouldn't you?" Monica said as she slid in across the table from them. "But I think Brady and company are aiming their sales pitch at the older demographic. If enough of the Lincoln refugees that came with the Guard support Brady, we could be in trouble."

"And Brady's cause was probably helped along by Goro's speech right after him. Same one as the other day, but with maybe an extra helping of derision." Bill chuckled and gave Richard the eye, waiting for him to comment.

Richard instead stuck a spoonful of stew in his mouth, then waved the utensil at Bill like a wand. Bill continued, "You know we've got this anti-jerry attitude going around—"

"That's not new with Rivendell, Bill," Monica interrupted. "It didn't even start with Thunberg, although I think she gave it focus."

"Yeah, I know, but I think the nickname *jerries* started here." Bill paused to roll his eyes. "Anyway, Goro's been pushing the idea that most of the problems of Earthside in general and America in particular derived from governments always being primarily gerontocracies. So he suggests that we flip the American minimum age requirements for certain positions by setting a *maximum* age for holding office. And suggested forty as a nice, round number."

Richard chuckled. "Bet that went over well."

Monica smiled back at him. "Strangely and purely by coincidence, support was divided mostly along age lines. Who'd have thought?"

"Brady also took a few swipes at socialism," Bill added.

"Seriously?" Richard exclaimed. "He's going for lone-wolf, free-market capitalism?"

"Yeah," Bill replied. "Talked about the incredible opportunities with this untouched land, building a civilization to rival the ages, yadda yadda."

"And?"

Bill sighed. "Jerries can't seem to get it through their heads that they aren't fooling anyone. You'd think at least the boomers would understand the concept of a demographic bulge having exceptional power. I think maybe they still think *they're* the bulge, even here."

Richard waved his spoon again. "Look, none of this matters. We're going to do it right, we're going to allow speeches and choice and free votes, and we're all going to accept the results."

"Well, *we* will," Monica said. "But that doesn't mean everyone else will."

⚜ ⚜ ⚜

Richard was doing his rounds, checking on the statuses of various projects, when he heard his name called. Turning, he saw Brady approaching. *Oh, great,* he thought.

"Mr. Nadeski…"

"It's Richard, please. Not for any reason other than that's what I'm used to hearing. Do you prefer Don or Donald?"

"I prefer *Mr.* Brady, honestly."

"Just a bit of advice for you: You'd better ashcan that attitude. You're not in a position of authority, and the general attitude here is that age doesn't bring you any particular entitlement. I'm sure you heard Goro's speech. I myself didn't, as it happens, but I've been told what was in it. On the other hand, we call Tom *lieutenant* because he's earned it, and continues to do so." Richard paused. "I have to say, for people who've supposedly been in politics all your lives, you're really badly misreading the room."

"Mr. Nadeski, people are people, overall. You kids may consider yourselves adults, and oh so much smarter than us, but *every* generation does that. Including mine in my day, much to my embarrassment. It takes decades of beating your head against the establishment walls before you start to realize that you have to work with the system, rather than trying to tear it down."

"The system has a lot of inertia—" Richard cut off what he was saying as Brady simply turned and walked away. Richard felt his face flush and gritted his teeth, then stopped and frowned. Cummins and another Ashland resident, whose name Richard had never learned, were hovering at just about talking distance, and both had pistols on their hips. They were also very carefully not looking in his direction. Was this a set-up? Had Brady been deliberately trying to provoke a reaction?

Interesting.

"So you think he was *trying* to get you angry?" Monica tilted her head in a disbelieving expression.

"That's what it feels like. And Cummins and his deppitty were waiting to intervene. Presumably the narrative would be that I'm too volatile to be in charge."

Now Monica was grinning. "You and Bill haven't had a personality transplant, have you? Because I have to tell you, on the paranoia scale, that's … "

"About a nine-point-five. Yeah. But I betcha if we ask around, we'll find that someone's been having casual conversations with people to find out about me. All of us, probably."

"Wow. Okay, I *will* ask around." Monica chuckled. "Bill will love this."

75. OVERFLIGHT

October 14

Bill waited patiently while Goro did the preflight. He'd had enough in the way of lessons to know better than to try to hurry the pilot.

Eventually, Goro announced he was done and climbed into the pilot's seat. Bill maneuvered himself into the back seat with all the equipment, with some help from Charlie. In moments, they were airborne.

"First one," Bill said. "Forest Fire Earth. You can straighten out." He made the adjustments on the tablet, then watched the video.

After several minutes, Goro said, "Uh, Bill? You still alive back there?"

"Yeah," Bill said, his voice sounding distracted. "Do a wide turn, okay?"

"You going to fill me in?"

"I'm not sure what I'm seeing, Goro. I'll need to discuss this. Let's just move on to the second one for now."

Bill tapped at the tablet, then raised the spy-cam in the air. The video window on the tablet shifted as he rotated the camera. "The farmstead is just a hair to the left of your current heading," he directed. The ultralight shifted slightly as Goro adjusted.

"Okay, start bringing it lower. Whatever you feel comfortable with." Bill began shifting the spy-cam, trying to get as much of the panorama recorded as possible. He wouldn't even try analyzing it until they were done and back on the ground.

"We're past the farmstead. Get some altitude and I'll do a 360 sweep."

The ultralight rose slowly, and Bill slowly turned the camera. Then he stopped. "Hey, I think I found downtown Lincoln. It's just a little farther away. Northeast."

Goro again turned the ultralight, and they made for the city, Bill providing occasional advice for adjustments in their heading.

"Okay, Goro, give us a couple of low sweeps at right angles, centered on this location, more or less. We'll settle for that for today."

Once again, they gathered around the tablet to watch the video of Bill's flight. This particular timeline was especially interesting, as it could conceivably be an alternate, civilized USA.

"The farmstead looks pretty normal," Erin commented. "Equipment's maybe kind of old, but that could just be what they own."

Bill pointed. "People. So not meerkats. That's good." He grinned at Richard's snort.

When they reached the flyover of Lincoln, Bill put the video into slow motion. The viewpoint crawled over the city, passing buildings and parks, until the view seemed to be zooming in on what might be City Hall. "I don't think that's where our City Hall is on Earthside, so that's another diff... oh, fuck." Bill hit pause, then zoomed the still frame.

Two flags flew on either side of the main entrance to the building. The flags were identical, and they weren't the Stars and Stripes. Bill looked at his friends, his expression grim.

"Swastikas."

Richard did a slow facepalm. "Christ. Can we not catch a break?"

The committee was back in session—again. With this latest revelation, everyone felt a need to discuss the progress, or lack thereof, in finding a useful alternative timeline.

Bill had just written a list of timelines on a whiteboard that Charlie had recently liberated.

Earthside
Outland
Greenhouse Earth
Dino Planet
Glacier Earth
Vacuum Earth
Forest Fire Earth
Native American Earth
Nazi Earth

He turned to his audience. "We haven't scanned out from the last four, so we theoretically have more options. I do have cross-contamination concerns with the last two, though."

Monica interjected, "Absolutely. We don't know why Native Americans are still there, but it's a fair bet that they haven't been exposed to European diseases yet."

"I'm not sure that's true."

All heads turned to Erin, who was holding a tablet and staring at something on the screen. She wordlessly passed it to Monica, who peered at the screen, her eyebrows furrowing.

"Shit," Monica said, finally. She passed the tablet back. "I see the problem."

"Going to fill us in?" Richard asked.

"Horses," Erin said. "One of the videos has a herd of horses in it."

"What? Lemme see." Bill almost ripped the tablet out of Erin's hand. He stared at the image for a few moments. "Son of a bitch."

Richard frowned. "I guess I'm missing the point."

"Horses were introduced into North America by the Spanish in our timeline," Erin said. She paused and pointed. "And those are the descendants of domesticated horses, not steppe ponies. So the Spanish have been here. There. Whatever."

"Plausible but not certain," Monica replied. "I see two possibilities. One, the ancestral stock didn't go extinct on this timeline and the Native Americans bred up the horses; or two, the whole 'discovering America' thing happened but didn't go well for the Europeans."

"Like how?"

"What am I, an oracle?" Monica retorted. "But here, just for a working hypothesis, let's say for instance that the introduction of new diseases was more symmetrical in this timeline. Europeans bring smallpox, measles, typhus, and cholera to North America, and pick up the Spanish Flu or the zombie virus or something and bring it back. Pretty sure that would dissuade them from a follow-up attempt at colonization, know what I mean?"

Richard looked surprised for a moment. "Yeah, but by now they'd know how to handle it."

"You're assuming science progresses as fast in this timeline. Maybe the Spanish bring it back with them and it knocks the European population back just like the Black Death and bubonic plague. They might still be a century or two behind old Earth, technologically and socially."

"Is that what you think happened?"

Monica glared at Richard. "I think that's one possible hypothetical. Whatever the actuality, it'll be similar in the broadest sense. Europeans came, Europeans saw, Europeans somehow got their asses kicked. Native Americans continued to live in their ancestral ways. They may or may not have had a population die-back as well."

"But," Erin said, "the Europeans stayed just long enough to lose some horses. Or maybe all their horses, if they were all killed."

Richard put an arm over his chair and gestured to the whiteboard with the other hand. "But getting back to that, there's not much that's useful with the timelines we've found so far. And we really shouldn't access Native American Earth, and I definitely don't want to go anywhere near Nazi Earth."

"Well, depending on their level of technology, they might turn out to be useful," Bill said. "I'm fairly certain they won't have IBM-compatible PCs, or Macs for that matter, but they might have lasers and diffraction gratings and other such-like scientific apparatus. Even just sheet metal or processed aluminum would be cool.

"Also," he added after a pause, "Charlie sort of developed a process that I think could keep us from contaminating the other human-inhabited timelines. We start by opening the gate to Greenhouse Earth, which bakes any germs in two-hundred-degree sulfur dioxide-laden air, then we switch to Vacuum Earth, which exhausts the whole thing out, germs and all. I think anything that survives that deserves to wipe us out."

Monica's eyebrows went up. "I don't see that working out well for people."

"We're not planning on sending anyone through any-time soon," Bill replied seriously. "We're just trying to avoid moving air and germs from one world to another."

Monica grinned. "I was kidding, Bill. And that sounds good. Also, let's open up a gate far away from any settle-ments, just to be safe. And to not scare the crap out of them."

Matt gave a thumbs-up. "I'll talk to Charlie."

Monica paused, then said, "Now, let's hear about Forest Fire Earth, Bill. I know you've been keeping something under your hat."

"Well, not really. Not like a secret. Just a theory." Bill hesitated. "As I've mentioned, it looked dead and scorched as far as I could see. I'm wondering if this is the result of something more global than just a fire sweeping through the area. Maybe something Yucatán-like, but recent. Is there any way we could test my idea?"

Monica's eyes grew wide as she considered. "Wow. That seems like a pretty long leap, Bill. I mean, even from a thou-sand feet up, you're still only seeing the local picture." She grew silent and looked down at her notepad for a moment, then looked up. "It's not definitive, but if we could get a small sample of air, we could test for sulfur compounds. And soil samples would allow us to look for forms of impactites. The Chicxulub impact or something like it would generate a lot of those in the immediate aftermath. The atmospheric stuff would clear pretty fast, but there'd be higher-than-normal background traces for maybe up to a century."

"Can you do those tests?"

Monica grinned. "Me? No. But we have a lot of Chem majors digging latrines and building fences. I bet they'd kill for a chance to actually do something chemistry-related."

Matt groaned. "No doubt they'll need a few things, just a couple of items, no big deal. Charlie can have the job back. I quit."

76. Votes and Elections

October 16

R ichard looked up as Monica walked into the room.

"Hey, Richard." She sat down and flopped back loosely into the chair. "So I asked around, and you were right. A whole lot of questions are being asked about us. All of us."

"What did you tell people?"

"The truth. Or what we think is happening, anyway. It didn't go over well, generally. Brady and company really are badly miscalculating this."

"Same as with Thunberg's movement, right? Remember when they started by trying to ridicule her? Completely backfired. The establishment tries to use the same old strategies, and can't seem to get that they're dealing with a different mindset." Richard stared into space for a moment, rubbing his chin. "So dirty tricks could be on the menu. What about the possibility of a power play or coup attempt?"

Monica snorted. "Bill and I were two of the most paranoid people you'll ever meet, even *before* the Rivendell coup attempt. Now..." She grinned at him. "Even our double reverses have double reverses."

"Don't get overconfident, though, Mon. One thing Brady *et al.* are at least partly right about is that they *are* older and more experienced. Like them or not, they won't make the same mistakes that the failed revolutionaries did."

"And they won't go at it in the same way in the first place. Yeah, Bill's doing backflips trying to outguess them. It's making me a little nuts, to be honest."

Richard tapped the mike on the P.A. and waited for the crowd noise to subside. "Okay, people, here's what we have." He gestured toward the whiteboards behind him. "This is not an exhaustive list of government and economic types. It's just those that have gotten enough grassroots support to justify their being on the list."

Richard walked back to the board, mike in hand, and pointed. "Whatever we choose, it must be an elected form of government. Lieutenant Collins has put his foot down on that point, and there's very little support for anything else anyway. There will be total separation of church and state. As those of you who were pushing for a Christian state have discovered, you're outnumbered. So it's a secular state or a Pastafarian state." Richard paused and looked around. He had everyone's total attention. "Structural options: elected monarch, with almost autocratic powers during their tenure; president, answerable to a congress or senate or parliament; or a standalone parliament or committee, the only real difference being the implied size."

He moved over to the next list. "Next, economic system. This is obviously more of a future thing, but the new government can start working toward it. Free-market capitalism, socialist capitalism, communism."

Richard pointed down to the next list. "Policies. Green, libertarian, social contract. How much do we want to pay attention to ecological issues when building this new world? How in-your-face do we want our government to be? And how much do individual rights trump the good of society? We've seen a lot of that particular debate the last few years on old Earth, so it's worth talking about."

He stepped back to the mike stand and re-holstered the mike. "Today's votes on government types, economic systems, and policies are non-binding and illustrative only. You could say this is more of a poll than a vote, really. We want everyone to get a sense of which way we're leaning. Then there will be more arguing and speechmaking."

Richard flicked off the mike and stepped away. Immediately, people began lining up at the tables.

"Well, this should be interesting," Bill said, sidling up.

Once again, the committee was gathering in the longhouse, even though a formal meeting wasn't scheduled. But by unspoken agreement, all had decided that this was the place to exchange information and gauge the trends.

"Socialism. Boogeddy boogeddy." Monica announced as she walked into the meeting room.

"Eh?" said several people at once.

"The socialist boogeyman. Brady played it. And like most people who freak out about it, he's not clear on the differences between socialism and communism and totalitarianism. Or on the differences between capitalism and democracy. Or maybe he thinks his audience isn't."

Richard sighed. "It's a mindset. And it's one the older generation just can't seem to shake. Is it age, or is it decades of rhetoric and brinksmanship politics?" He sat back and rubbed his forehead. "I'm beginning to think Goro and his group might be right. About not letting jerries into positions of power, I mean."

"Wow, that's a concession, coming from you," Erin said with a smile.

"Neoatomocracy," Bill interjected.

"What?" both Erin and Richard said at once.

"It's what Goro and his group are calling a form of government that's the opposite of a gerontocracy. From the Greek for *young person.*"

Monica chuckled. "And Brady and his crew are calling it an infantocracy at every opportunity."

"Cool," Richard said, sarcasm dripping from the single word. He shook his head, then motioned to Monica with his chin. "So do we have any results yet?"

"Nothing final, but the trend is mostly in support of the current committee structure— elected, of course—with a social-contract constitution and possibly eventual capitalism with a heavy side dish of socialism."

"Wow. And these are *Americans?*"

Monica grinned. "*Young* Americans, big guy. Highly disillusioned post-millennials who see the boomers as having sucked the world dry, and who will automatically oppose anything the boomers favor."

"Yeah. I get that." He flipped his notepad open. "I guess we'd better talk about our official response, then."

77. Reactions

October 18

The news hit Rivendell like a bomb. Somehow, despite Bill's warnings, the news of Nazi Earth and Native American Earth became public knowledge at the same time. And as usual, the lawn became a hotbed of debate and discussion.

Richard wandered around the area, listening but not engaging. He wanted to gauge the reaction before deciding on any sweeping policies.

There seemed to be general agreement that Native American Earth should remain undisturbed. If nothing else, no one wanted to implement the European invasion of North America a second time. And the specter of a two-way disease transmission certainly figured into it. Whether or not Monica was right about that bit of speculation, it was proving invaluable.

Nazi Earth wasn't as much of an issue as he'd expected. As Bill had pointed out, in movies and books everyone immediately wanted to invade the alternate timeline and trounce the Nazis. But a few hundred university students living in semi-Stone Age conditions were unlikely to be able to take on an entire planetary civilization. The result was a philosophical view that each world could go its own way.

The overwhelming emotion seemed to be disappointment that nothing more useful had been found. Everyone acknowledged that there were doubtless many more versions of Earth to be discovered and identified, but what had been found so far was not encouraging.

"People are pissed," Monica said, looking around the table. "It's not fair and it doesn't make sense, and if you ask anyone individually they'll admit that. But collectively, there's a feeling that we're either incompetent or lazy or not trying hard enough to find the useful timelines. Or something."

Bill rolled his eyes. "And what are the useful timelines?"

Richard replied before Monica could get started. He knew she would inevitably go off on a rant. Better to head it off before it started. "It varies a little, Bill, but it's mostly about a timeline that's close enough to our own so that people can go back to a normal life. Maybe even go back to their families."

"That makes no sense. If their families are in this theoretical timeline, then a version of them will already be there. The alternate *them* won't just conveniently vanish."

"Yeah, I don't see it working out either. But as Monica points out, it's not really a well-thought-out stance."

"It's worse than that," Kevin said. All eyes turned to him. "It's extremely unlikely that we'll ever find anything that's anywhere close to old Earth. Even Nazi Earth was a surprise to me."

"Why, Kev? How can you make that prediction?" Monica asked.

"Timeline splits are caused by singular events that cause two or more alternate subsequent histories. But this doesn't happen with every little thing. Smaller disturbances might produce temporary splits, but they'll tend to merge back together. It's like two marbles on the same slope. They might start on different paths, but they'll tend to end up in the same place at the bottom. Only when something major happens that rolls one of those marbles right into a different valley will you get a permanent split."

Kevin paused to look around the room. "But then those marbles will end up *way, way* apart. The point is that smaller splits are unlikely to persist, so we're unlikely to find any timelines that are based on smaller splits."

"Which means no chance of an Earth Two with the same population of Lincoln," Richard huffed.

"'Fraid so."

"It was a dumb idea anyway," Bill said. "What would we do if we found one—kill off our doppelgangers and take their places?" He turned to Monica. "Any progress on gathering some Chem students?"

"Yep, and they're raring to go. Except"—Monica smiled and glanced at Matt—"they needed a few things from Lincoln."

Everyone laughed except Matt, who made a low growling sound.

Erin leaned forward. "Why are you so interested in this, Bill?"

"If I'm right," he replied, "then we're looking at a planet with a usable environment but almost no ecosystem. I've been concerned about what people will do to Outland if we manage to get the gate plans out to the population in general. But overall, people might prefer a planet like Forest Fire Earth with no predators, no weeds, and land just waiting to be claimed."

"The ecosystem isn't completely dead, Bill, or there wouldn't be any homeostasis."

"I get that, Monica, but that might be mostly ocean-based right now. In any case, there's very little there, if there's anything. After Chicxulub, wasn't it all small animals for a long time? So If we can breathe the air, I think it's humanity's best bet for Earth Two."

Richard nodded. "Not wrong. And probably not something we can control anyway. I'd be more worried about some white supremacist bastard giving the plans to Nazi Earth so they can go interdimensional with their fascist bullshit."

Everyone at the table sat back, shocked looks on their faces. "Well, that sucks," Bill said. "So we're back to the question of whether we give out the plans." He paused to rub his forehead. "Y'know, I mostly haven't cared a whole bunch about the whole election and government question, but it's looking more and more like whoever ends up making the decisions will be affecting the destiny of multiple worlds."

Richard nodded. "So I guess we'd better get it right, right?"

78. REFERENDUM RESULTS

October 19

Richard watched as Charlie and his assistant placed the whiteboard, then flipped it over to show the writing. The crowd surged forward to the barrier; there was a moment of electric silence as people read the list and drew breath, then—pandemonium.

He lifted the microphone and spoke over the uproar. "The votes are in, people. Remember, this series of referendum questions just helps us define the broad strokes of the type of government we're going to have. Ninety-six percent support for some kind of elected government, so that's a slam-dunk. I'm worried about the four percent of you that think that's a bad idea, though. Or maybe that's the anarchists. I wonder if you're aware of the irony of voting to not have a vote."

The crowd erupted into general laughter, and Richard paused to let it die down.

"Anyway, the general feeling is that capitalism is out, at least for now, light socialism is in, environmentalism is *way* in, and equality is in. Which means no ageism as well."

There was a loud *boo* that Richard immediately recognized as Goro's voice. That was okay. Goro had already commented that he expected to lose, but was happy to have had a chance to make the point.

"The big surprise," Richard continued, "is the size of the backlash against any kind of party politics." He waved to the whiteboard in an offhand way. "The majority of people seem to think—and I agree with them—that forming a party and voting as a bloc is responsible for most of the messes back on Earth. So all political candidates will run on their own merits. Even attempting to form a party is grounds for disqualification or recall."

This produced another uproar, and Richard had to wait several minutes for it to die down.

"And the last item—for some strange reason, a significant majority of people think our committee structure is working, at least with the size of Rivendell right now. So if you adopt this form of government in the binding vote, we will continue to have a committee of specialists who are in charge of their respective areas. Plus, based on suggestions, we'll add positions for three members-at-large with no specialization."

More uproar.

"A binding vote for all of this happens tomorrow, just to formalize it. Based on the numbers, I don't think there's any doubt what we're going to end up with. Assuming you don't all suddenly change your minds overnight, committee candidates will then declare for their intended seat and can only run for one seat. Voting will be in two days, and you vote for your choice for each seat. Questions? No? Good."

This last was said so quickly that no one could have possibly reacted in time. Some laughter and catcalls rang out as Richard motioned to Kevin to turn off the P.A.

Monica grinned at him as he dropped the mike onto the electronics cart. "Are we still having fun?"

Richard snorted. "I honestly wouldn't mind all that much if I got voted out. This is just so fucking exhausting." He shook his head. "I can't believe some people choose this shit for a career."

79. Election Day

October 21

After all the yelling, arguing, and speechmaking, it was finally time for the payoff. The line-ups started forming right after breakfast, and now at mid-morning they stretched right across the lawn. The election staff worked diligently, consistent with getting it done properly, but the simple fact was that this election would have a virtually one hundred percent participation rate—something unheard of on old Earth.

Election observers milled around, but Monica had been very clear—any attempt to interfere, intimidate, or kibitz would get the miscreant arrested at minimum, and shot at worst. But for the most part, everyone seemed very well-behaved. People could feel that this election would affect their futures on a much more visceral level than anything pre-volcano, and everyone was taking it seriously.

Richard sighed and turned away. He felt like a car passenger neurotically keeping his eye on things to prevent the driver from going off the road. There had to be something else he could do to occupy his mind.

He headed for the big longhouse, worked his way through the newly added airlock porch, doffed his parka, and sat down heavily in his usual spot at the committee table. Erin and Krista looked up and gave him nods, then went back to whatever discussion they'd been having. Richard tried halfheartedly to eavesdrop for a moment, then gave it up as too much effort.

There was no coffee carafe on the table. They'd long since extracted every bit of coffee they could find from Lincoln, and Bill's supply, while huge, had been intended for six people. Bill was talking about going back to Omaha on a coffee-scavenging run. And honestly, he wasn't getting a lot of pushback. What would life be like when the last of the coffee had been consumed? Nothing good, certainly.

Bill came in with a bang of the door, slapping his hands together. "Jeez, it's cold. The temps dropped really fast. Way faster than back in Lincoln. Merry global fucking warming, y'all."

Richard smiled. Bill cursed rarely enough for it to be a significant event when he dropped one. "Yep. Nick is modifying his construction a little. Adding in a layer of that space-blanket material."

"And the enclosed porch," Bill replied. "Which I completely approve of." He plopped himself down in his chair, glanced around the table, and grunted. "No coffee."

"Nope. We'll discuss another Omaha expedition next committee meeting. Assuming it's us, that is." Richard paused. "So how are the special projects going?"

"On track," Bill replied. "I'm glad we didn't advertise the extra gates we were able to assemble from the Omaha expedition. I'm sure *some people*"—Bill made air quotes—"are watching the existing gates very closely, with an eye to figuring out where we might be squirreling stuff away."

"And the controllers?"

"Matt has started putting passwords on them, so if someone steals one they won't be able to use it. Of course, someone with firmware expertise and a burner could remove that function, but I don't see that as a high-probability event."

Richard sighed, and Bill cocked his head. "You're really worried."

"Yeah, I am," Richard replied. "I kid myself that our generation is more realistic about life than the jerries—I'm probably buying into Goro's rhetoric a little bit—but we still have a lot of the extreme, inflexible, no-compromise attitudes that have infected American politics the last couple of years. Monica's heard more than one person say that they won't accept the results of an election that doesn't go their way."

Bill shrugged. "So they can leave. Literally. We are in a unique position here in that you can just hop the fence and start walking if you don't like it here."

"Sure, except it's a death sentence. Even the so-called survivalists depended on modern technologically produced items, like guns, axes, and knives. And any group that wants to leave will want some of ours."

Richard was surprised to see Bill grin as he replied. "Got that covered too, big guy. All those finance people that I organized a while back? They've been spreadsheeting our inventory, and tracking how much work each Rivendell citizen has been doing. If someone wants to leave, we can work out a prorated value of the labor they've contributed, and they can basically buy items with that."

"Wow!" Richard's eyebrows climbed his forehead. "You've really been thinking ahead. How're you doing on the question of setting up gates in other—"

Charlie picked that moment to burst into the room. "Voting's done. Vote counting has been mostly keeping up pretty well, so we're probably a half hour away from an announcement. Monica wants all the G.O. out front for that."

Bill, Richard, and Erin stood. Krista leaned back and said to Erin, "We can continue this later, if we're still in power."

The G.O. stood with the crowd on the lawn, waiting with everyone else for the results to be posted. People up front had made room for them, which Richard found amusing somehow. Since the committee had been dissolved just before the election, he and the other ex-members were currently just common rabble like everyone else.

Then, movement. The crowd noise died immediately as members of the vote-tallying team wheeled out a whiteboard with a sheet thrown over it.

"Here it comes," Bill stage-whispered. "Anyone want to take bets?"

"Where've you been?" Erin replied. "There's been a betting pool going." She smiled at him. "You're a hundred to one against, by the way."

Bill faked an exaggerated laugh, then opened his mouth to reply, just as the board-jockeys grabbed the sheet and flipped it up. Everyone leaned forward to read the board.

One second, two, then a roar from hundreds of voices all trying to yell over each other. "Son of a bitch," Richard said, although he doubted anyone could hear him. The entire existing committee had been re-elected to the specialist seats, even though the incumbents had done little or no campaigning. Maybe not such a surprise, really. There hadn't been much of a concerted effort to overthrow any of the specialist seats, either. That part of the list read:

Bill Rustad (Science and Tech)
Erin Savard (Earth Sciences)
Matt Siemens (Reclamation Services)
Lieutenant Tom Collins (Security and Policing)
Krista Tollefson (Medical)
Sam Benton (Animal Sciences)
Anita Neumann (Agronomy and Horticulture)
Nick McCormack (Infrastructure)

Monica had declined to run, pointing out that they only needed her *or* Collins, and she was quite happy to stick him with the paperwork while she continued as police chief. Both Kevin and Charlie had been asked if they wanted to run for formal positions on the council, since they'd participated in the past. Kevin had declared, in somewhat different words, that he didn't give even the smallest fraction of a rat's ass about being on the committee. Charlie had laughed maniacally when asked.

As Richard's eyes reached the bottom of the list, his eyes grew wide. The three at-large seats were won by himself, Goro Yoshida, and … Donald Brady.

"Oh, fuck," Richard muttered. Life was about to get very interesting.

Bill reached the bottom of the list at that point and began to laugh. He nudged Richard. "I'm positive—in fact, I'd bet real money—that people voted that way on purpose, just to see what would happen. You three are like vinegar, water, and gasoline. I give it a month before one of you is dead. Probably Brady. Hopefully."

Richard snorted. "You ain't wrong."

80. New Government

October 23

"Meeting will come to order." Richard looked around the table, waiting for everyone to settle in. "First order of business is to elect a new chair."

"I nominate Richard Nadeski," Monica said immediately.

"Point of order," Brady interjected. "Ms. Albertelli is not a member of the committee. In fact, I question why she is here."

Richard sighed. "We've been fairly casual about who can and can't attend meetings up until now. But if you think it's a problem, we'll discuss a policy going forward. And Monica, he's right. You can't nominate. So Donald—"

Bill and Brady spoke at the same time, partially running over each other.

"I nominate Richard Nadeski," Bill said.

"It's *Mr.* Brady," said Brady.

Richard smirked. "Thanks, Bill. As to how we will address you, *Mr.* Brady, we're all on a first-name basis here, and we're all comfortable with that. But if you want to be addressed as *mister*, then you'll be addressing each and every one of us as *mister* or *miz* in return. If you have some reason for insisting on the formality, I don't think it's going to work out the way you want, know what I mean?"

Richard and Brady exchanged glares for a few seconds, then Brady broke eye contact. "Understood. And I'm not trying to be difficult—well, not primarily, I guess—but I've been doing this for forty years and—"

"Which is part of the problem," Goro muttered loudly enough for all to hear.

Richard rubbed his forehead. "Goro, for fuck's sake. Let's not start this off with a bunch of sniping. Can we at least pretend we're adults for a few minutes?"

Brady flashed a momentary smile. "Fine. And I nominate myself."

"You can't do that," Bill interjected. "Someone else has to nominate you."

"Actually, I can," Brady replied. "It isn't normally done, but there's no Robert's Rule specifically against it."

"And if no one will nominate you in the first place," Goro almost snarled, "how many votes do you expect to—"

"*Gevalt*," Richard exclaimed. He looked around. "I expect Donald ... sorry, *Mr. Brady* is doing it just to have it on the record." He glanced over at one of Bill's administrative team, who had been introduced as Timothy. "Now that we're going to be keeping minutes."

Timothy smiled back at him and stopped writing long enough to give a small thumbs-up.

"Any other nominations?" Richard looked around. No one spoke. "Fine. Show of hands. For Richard Nadeski? Donald Brady?"

The voting took only a few seconds. Ten votes for Richard, one for Brady.

"Well, that's—" Richard cut off his comment as a roar of noise grew outside. He looked around the table to see surprised expressions on all faces—except Brady's, he noted.

The committee members rushed to the door, to find a smallish mob standing in front of the longhouse. It seemed to Richard more of a rabble than a mob, if that made any sense. Multiple groups with multiple messages, although the people chanting, "Bullshit! Bullshit!" seemed to be carrying the day in terms of raw volume. Some were holding up plywood sheets with slogans spray-painted on them. Nick groaned loudly. There was only one place that plywood could have come from.

"What's going on?" Richard yelled to a soldier who had placed himself in front of the longhouse entrance.

"Protest, sir. Hard to make anything out, but I think they didn't like the election results."

Richard did a quick scan. Possibly forty people. They were already surrounded by Monica and her deputies, along with several National Guard. All armed, if worse came to worst.

"Is there a spokesman here?" Richard yelled. A few people looked like they were trying to answer, but the "bullshit" group increased their volume to drown out any discussion.

Richard shrugged, as obviously as he could, then motioned the committee and Monica back inside.

"Is this wise?" Brady asked as soon as they were inside. Yelled, actually. The volume outside would prevent any normal conversation levels. He continued, "I don't think ignoring legitimate concerns is a good way to start the new government."

"And how do you know their concerns are legitimate?" Richard asked. Brady looked shocked, then opened his mouth to reply, but Richard continued, "They aren't here to discuss, or they'd have done that as soon as we tried to ask a question. They're here to disrupt. So I want to take that from them. We may not be able to actually have a meeting, but they can't see that. So let's sit down, have a coffee, and wait." He turned to Monica. "When they calm down enough or get bored enough, let a maximum of three people in. Until then, try to look as unaffected as possible. Bring a book if you have one."

Monica nodded and headed for the door.

It took almost two hours before the protesters became either tired enough or bored enough to consider alternative tactics. At that point, the Guard let three people in to talk to the committee.

The three protesters looked both uncomfortable and belligerent. Richard had made a point of not offering them chairs. Or coffee. Over Donald Brady's objections in both cases. It was becoming increasingly obvious to Richard that Brady's sympathies, if not his loyalty, were with the mob.

"We demand—" one of the protesters began.

"The *fuck* you do," Richard interrupted. "You have no authority with which to demand *anything*. Try again."

Another protester piped up while the first one was regrouping. "We don't recognize the legitimacy of this government—"

"Tough shit," Richard interjected, cutting her off. "If you had a majority of people who agreed with you, they'd have voted in the government you want. Since they didn't, you don't."

The protestor was persistent. "I don't recognize your right to dictate anything—"

Again, Richard interrupted her. "And I don't recognize your right to not recognize my right to dictate anything. So fuck off."

There was a moment of silence while all three attempted to parse that that statement. Then, "We want to know what would be involved in forming another colony," the third protester said.

Richard gazed at him for several seconds, a slow smile growing on his face. "Finally. So at least one of you isn't just a mindless mouthpiece. Okay, bud, we'll talk about that. The other two of you, hit the road." Richard motioned to a couple of guards, who began to chivvy the first two toward the door.

"You can't just throw us out," the first one yelled.

Richard stood slowly, while maintaining eye contact with the other man. Richard was built like a fullback—a very muscular fullback—and several months of Outland diet had leaned him out without reducing his muscle mass. He walked right up to the man, who involuntarily backed up a step, and stuck his face inches from the other's.

"Wanna bet?" Richard growled. He waited a second for a reply. When none was offered, he backed away slightly and continued, "If you want to discuss something, like this guy"—Richard motioned to the third protester—"then we can do that. If you just want to yell and act like an asshole, I will be quite happy to personally return the favor. If you want to try violence as a tactic, well ... " Richard smiled, and it wasn't a friendly smile. He held up a clenched fist. "I can do that too. I guarantee you won't like it."

He took another step back and swept his gaze over the three. "As has been pointed out too many times to count, this is a survival situation. We don't have the luxury of putting up with a lot of the crap that went on back on old Earth. Especially a bunch of infants throwing a fit because they didn't get their way. If you disrupt things for any length of time, people will start to go hungry. Hungry people are not reasonable. Your right to protest will not be recognized. It'll be you against the entire rest of the colony. Do I have to spell it out any more clearly than that?"

The three protesters exchanged glances. After a moment, by some unspoken agreement, the first protester spoke. "We want more say in how things are run around here."

Richard's eyebrows rose. "You just had a vote on what kind of government you want, then another vote on who you want in that government. How much more input do you think you're entitled to?"

"That's just it," the woman interjected. "The results are a joke. This is a socialist wet dream. It's not a legitimate—"

Richard cut her off. "Are you saying the majority did *not* vote for this government?"

"That's not the point. It's—"

"It's *exactly* the point. The majority voted for this. Don't like it? Tough. Leave."

"I don't believe the majority actually *did*—"

"Yet again, tough shit. Show your proof. Otherwise, fuck off."

The third protester held up a finger, and said in a conversational tone, "Which brings us back to me."

Richard smiled at him. "Yup. And we've actually taken steps to make that possible. I think we should sit down and compare notes." He glared at the other two. "You can be part of the discussion as well, as long as it remains a *discussion*. Start trying to disrupt things just to be an asshole and I will personally throw you out."

The other two glanced at each other, then one said, "This isn't over. You're going to regret your stubbornness." They both turned on their heels and headed for the door.

Richard sighed. "Honest to God, I'm seriously considering suggesting we bring back dueling. I wonder how brave idiots like that would be if they could die from their stupidity." He looked at the remaining protester. "Okay, bud, let's see what we can come up with."

81. Clean-up in Aisle Three

October 24

Charlie surveyed the cavernous space with a sigh. Portable spotlights had been brought in to illuminate the interior of the Wal-Mart, with power cables running through the interface to a generator on the Outland side. This store had been scavenged already once before, but back in the early days when the pickings were still easy. Now they were reduced to scouring old sites for anything they'd missed, propping up and digging out collapsed sections for buried but still usable items. The low-hanging fruit was all picked out in Lincoln. Now it was truly scavenging.

He looked at the piles of goods just on the other side of the truck gate. It wasn't a bad haul, really. Just a lot more work these days. Another month, though, and it would be too cold to continue. And snow on top of ash on the structures in Lincoln would probably take care of anything still standing.

Charlie turned to Norm, who was holding the gate controls. "I think we're going to shut it down for the day. Call everyone in. We can finish tomorrow." Charlie walked through the interface as Norm began yelling orders. He glanced at the workers who were organizing the haul. They seemed to have everything well in hand.

For the fifth time today, Charlie considered telling Matt to take over the day-to-day scavenging operations again. As jobs went, it wasn't particularly onerous, but the responsibility of supplying the colony along with the complexities of juggling all the equipment and locations and staff was a constant headache. Even with the extra gates that Bill had been able to build after the Omaha expedition, there still weren't enough to cover all the places they needed to be.

The last few workers came through the gate, carrying whatever they'd managed to dig up. Norm ticked them off on his list, then turned to Charlie. "Two guys still in there. They say they need to get some support beams braced before they leave. Maybe ten minutes. I can wait for them if you want to head back." He motioned with his chin. "Get the loot into Rivendell before the nocturnal scavengers come sniffing around. We'll take down the gate and bring it back."

Charlie nodded, feeling exhaustion right in his bones. "Thanks, Norm. Sounds good."

Norm watched as Charlie headed for one of the fully laden trucks. Norm waved, then allowed himself a thin smile as the passenger door slammed shut and the truck pulled away. Finally, after weeks of planning, conditions were perfect. A quick scan of the group confirmed his mental inventory. Six patriots, two commies. He made eye contact with Trevor and Mitch, and nodded. Without hesitation, the two men pulled pistols and levelled them at the heads of the commies. His other soldiers followed suit, and in moments the two Rivendell boot-lickers were disarmed, still rigid with shock. One of them finally regained his voice. "What... Norm, what's going on?"

"Shut up," Norm snapped. He gestured with his chin. "Put them through." As the two men were shoved toward the gate, he grinned at them. "What does Gunzilla call it? You're being repatriated."

In moments, the two were on the Lincoln side, and the interface had been deactivated. "Should have just shot them," Mitch grumbled.

Norm sighed. "Mitch, we're not the bad guys. You need to get over this TV tough-guy thing. We're trying to set things straight, not make them worse. Don't become the cliché they want to make us out to be, okay?"

Mitch gave him a sour look but didn't argue. In minutes they had the gate disassembled and loaded onto the truck. Norm felt a surge of pride. Regardless of his motivations, he'd been a good student and had paid attention to everything Charlie had taught him. If the other group had done their jobs as well, his people would now have two gates. That was enough to move between dimensions, taking your gates with you.

It was a tight fit with seven people in the truck, resulting in some of his friends all but sitting on each other's laps. Trevor made some comment about homos, and Norm concentrated on not rolling his eyes. Really, in a lot of ways, the clichés weren't far off. Still, he'd rather live with these guys than be stuck in the communist dystopia that had just been elected in Rivendell.

Norm felt a moment of sadness for Sean, Ivan, and Merv. They were good people, and their deaths had left his group short-handed. There'd been no time to recruit more patriots, though. They'd just have to hope that the element of surprise would be enough.

Mitch glanced at his compass. "Little more to the left, Norm, and pick it up a little. We need to get as close as we can before dark. And headlights off."

Norm nodded and checked the headlight control. They needed to be as close to Rivendell as they could manage for the next phase, but they didn't want the guards spotting them.

It was less than ten minutes from being too dark to drive when the other truck pulled up with five people inside. They'd picked this copse specifically because a slight rise combined with the dense trees would guarantee they couldn't be spotted from Rivendell. And the Earthside location was also out of sight of the warehouse complex. Early scouting had verified that the commies were maintaining a guard there as well. No surprise, really. It was an obvious move. They weren't dumb, after all, just misguided about their politics. And it would be wise to remember that. The last group that had tried to take over had learned the hard way.

Norm made an audible "pfft" sound as the thought entered his head. Adam had had the right idea, but he had been too convinced of his macho superiority. So when the libtards turned out to be smarter than expected, Adam got his ass kicked. And somehow, Norm had managed to escape notice. He still couldn't believe he'd avoided the subsequent roundup, and even more that none of his fellow conspirators had fingered him. So now he had a second chance to make this work, but with a considerably more intelligent plan.

For now, they had to get across to Earthside if they didn't want to spend the night in Outland, twelve people smooshed into two pickups, with no safe way to take bathroom breaks.

No doubt Trevor would have had more witticisms at the ready.

Norm woke with a jerk as his alarm went off. As a member of the scavenging team, he was entitled to a phone and charging privileges. He poked the button to stop the chime and frowned at the thought. Things would be different, of course, when his group was in charge. But there were still only so many phones, and only so much electricity.

Then he shrugged. With the motivation that free enterprise and a lot fewer rules provided, and maybe a lot less dead weight, the colony would blossom. People would die, soon, and that was unfortunate. But no revolution had ever been bloodless.

The men moved swiftly as they set up the truck gate. With both the warehouse on Earthside and sheds on Rivendell being well-guarded, there was no way to execute a surprise attack from those locations. But no one had thought to place guards on the other Earths. Unfortunately, only Bill's tablet had the coordinates for the new Earths, and Greenhouse Earth was pretty obviously shit-useless, but Dino Planet was completely open. They'd only be on that side for a short time, and as Bill and Monica had mentioned, the wildlife wasn't anything like *Jurassic Park* level, at least in terms of numbers. Norm snickered. He'd seen the second movie, and the T-Rex rampaging through L.A. had been priceless. But he didn't want to run into one of those things in real life. He still remembered the scene in the ship's hold, where the supposed bad guy was fed to the baby T-Rex. Typical left-wing moralizing. Still, a lousy way to check out. Norm shuddered.

The operation went smoothly. Set up the truck gate. Open a portal to Dino Planet. Drive through, carrying the smaller gate. Set up the smaller gate and connect to Earthside. Shut down and disassemble the truck gate and move it through the smaller gate to Dino Planet. Turn off the smaller gate. Set up the truck gate right where the shed would be. Tune it to Rivendell.

Norm stood with his finger poised over the button. "Okay, you guys ready? We have to take control of the shed in minimum time. As little bloodshed as possible, but if anyone slows you down, pop 'em. Then we start grabbing stuff. The gun safes are probably red herrings, but they've been keeping the weapons somewhere, and they hand them out from the shed. So check everything that looks big enough to hold a rifle." He swept the group with his gaze and received calm, alert looks in response. "Then let's do this, guys. For freedom!"

82. ATTACK

October 25

Bill sat up with a jerk. Gunshots were ringing out, and close by. There were also cries of anger and fear. This wasn't guards taking potshots at dire wolves. Unless the wolves had gotten through the fence somehow?

Didn't matter. However you parsed it, something bad was happening. He glanced to his left where Monica would be, if she ever actually slept. Bill snorted. Okay, slight exaggeration, but the woman seemed to survive nicely on four hours a night. If Bill didn't get eight and a half, and coffee at the end of it, he was useless.

He'd been intending to sleep a little extra this morning, maybe get in on the tail end of breakfast. He could smell the meal preparations, which gave him a good indicator of the time. Chances were there'd be no relaxed, casual dining this morning.

Dressing quickly, Bill scampered out of the tent and hurried in the direction of the shots. They seemed to be coming from the center of town—from the storage sheds. That couldn't be good.

As he rushed toward the shed, he saw Monica prone behind an overturned picnic table. She was waving frantically at him to get down or get low. Discretion being the better part of staying alive, Bill hit the dirt and crawled the rest of the way.

Krista was there, tending to someone with what looked like a bullet wound. Charlie. Bill's heart sank. A couple of soldiers were scanning the area with scopes.

"What happened?" Bill said to Monica.

Charlie replied before she could say anything. "Someone gated into the shed. I don't know how or from where. Norm was leading them, I think. I can't believe I trusted that asshole." Charlie sucked in a breath and moaned as Krista started suturing him, battlefield style.

"Sorry," she muttered.

"Where did they get the gate?" Bill asked.

"I left Norm at the Wal-Mart site yesterday end-of-day. He said he'd pack it up. Bastard."

"A truck gate. Not a coincidence, I'll bet." Bill looked at Monica.

"This has the smell of a coordinated, well-planned operation," she replied. "In order to make it work, they'd have had to steal a second gate. Wouldn't have to be a big one, though."

Bill nodded. "We have so many systems in so many different places right now. I can think of two that they could have grabbed. Stuff left out in the field to save time. Shit." He looked at Monica. "I guess we weren't paranoid enough."

She gave him an affectionate smile and patted his hand. "Can't stay ahead forever, Bill. They start to expect the double-reverses."

Suddenly, there was a scream from the direction of the shed. Then more screams, and men came pouring out, running frantically. *From* something.

Bill looked carefully over the edge of the upturned table. "I think I just figured out how they snuck up on us."

"Oh, fuck," Monica replied.

83. BREAKOUT

Norm counted down from five, then hit the button. His men poured through the interface the moment it formed, spreading out in all directions. He could hear yelled commands and cursing through the gate, followed by several shots. Then a pause, then more shots.

"Shit!" That was Trevor's voice. "The little prick got away."

Norm sauntered through the interface, his feeling of triumph only slightly muted by Trevor's complaint. "Who got away?"

"Charlie. Winged him, though. I really wanted to teach that arrogant darkie a lesson on who's boss and who's not."

Norm suppressed a sigh. Notwithstanding Trevor's rabid racism, Charlie would have made a good hostage, and might be needed if they found one of the new gates, which he understood were now password-protected. Still, on the grand scale of things, it was a minor issue. They had the shed, and could clean it out at their leisure. No doubt the commies would set up guards in the other one, but it was a lot less strategically important anyway. Mostly food and clothing.

Trevor and Mitch set up a defensive crossfire position near the shed door. At a gesture from Norm, most of the rest of the men began moving items through the truck gate, while the few remaining started searching the shed for weapons.

The men had done several laps through the gate when Harvey strode up to report. "We've found a few filing cabinets that seem heavy. I'm having trouble visualizing any actual need for filing cabinets on the frontier, so my bet... "

Norm grinned at Harvey's innuendo. It sounded like just the kind of geeky thing that Bill Rustad would think was hilarious. He was just opening his mouth to supply a humorous rejoinder when there was a scream and one of the crew ran past him from the truck gate in an apparent panic. Harvey looked up past Norm's head and his face went slack. Then he said, "Oh, shit!" and reached for his pistol.

Norm turned and just had time to get an impression of teeth—far, far too many teeth—and fetid breath. He managed only to say, "Oh, you have *got* to be—"

84. Yeah, That's Just Great

Bill felt his eyes grow wide as several dinosaurs sprinted out from the shed and then stopped to scan the lawn. The theropods seemed to vary from three to five feet high at the hip, small front limbs dangling relaxed. Teeth and claws left very little doubt about their preferred diet. "What the ffffff— Monica, weren't real velociraptors supposed to be much smaller than the movie versions? Those—"

"Aren't velociraptors, Bill. No killing claws. Those look more like small T-Rexes than big veloci—oh, shit."

As Monica had been lecturing, a much larger version of the dinosaurs suddenly made an appearance at the shed door. The entrance, designed to accommodate large vehicles—the shed had originally been marketed as a truck storage unit—was almost but not quite big enough to accommodate the beast. The dino gave a shove with its head to expand the opening, ripping the roof half off. The smaller versions looked up, then moved aside, but seemed otherwise unafraid.

"Juveniles," Monica commented. "Mommy and her babies, out for a Sunday hunt, I think."

"So that is a what? Albertosaurus?"

"How the fuck would I know? Sixty-five million years of evolution we know nothing about, Bill. A whole lot of tax-onomy needing to be done to answer that, and I'd just as soon worry about surviving the next five minutes, thank you very much."

One of the juveniles abruptly took off after a fleeing human. The acceleration and speed of the animal were unbelievable, almost video-game-level impossible. In less than a second, the prey was down and being disemboweled. The screams were mercifully brief.

Bill recognized the victim as Trevor, one of Charlie's group. Not one of his favorite people, even before he turned out to be a seditionist. Still, it was a shitty way to go.

Bill's ears began to ring as Monica ripped out burst after burst from her rifle. She had switched to auto, a sure sign of the seriousness of the situation. Monica normally would be disgusted at the waste of ammo and lack of precision.

He tried to count the juvenile raptors, but they were moving too quickly. It was an overlapping attack pattern, probably intended to confuse and contain prey. And it seemed to be working so far. Several more people were dragged down, even as the defenders poured shot after shot into the predators. Even as two of the dinos went down, the rest continued to attack. The mother, or parent, or whatever it was roared in apparent rage as some of the juveniles fell onto their sides and kicked frantically, then went still.

"Uh oh. Mommy mad," Bill said.

"This thing isn't big enough to take her down," Monica replied, glaring at her weapon. "And I think she's figured out that the shooting sounds correlate with her babies dying."

Indeed, the mother dino had focused her attention and her rage on the picnic table, Bill, and Monica. She wheeled her considerable bulk and accelerated toward them. Monica released burst after burst of gunfire, and Bill could see the red dots as the bullets impacted, but it was having no more effect than a bunch of bee stings.

Was this it? Was this the way he would go?

Then one of the juveniles screamed, a sound of fear and pain that seemed to transcend species. The parent wheeled without slowing, leaving huge gouges in the ground, and charged toward the noise. Monica strafed the dino's side as it charged past.

Bill took a chance and stood up to get a better look, and immediately felt a wave of relief. The National Guard had arrived. Well, "arrived" didn't mean much when your HQ was at the opposite end of the lawn, but he'd take it. Collins was sticking out of the top hatch of the lead Hummer, yelling orders.

Soldiers and citizens were scattering before the charge as the giant predator roared with rage and pain. As it wheeled again and caught someone in its jaws, Bill had an incongruous thought. "Spielberg will probably sue us," he muttered.

"Even if Spielberg survived Yellowstone, that's not a T-Rex," Monica replied. "Doesn't count."

"Thanks. I feel much better."

The Hummer with the machine gun raced up, and the roof turret rotated. The fifty-cal began its signature rhythmic drumming, and the dino snarled, turned, and charged.

"What the hell is that thing made of?" Monica exclaimed. "It's gotta be half lead bullets by weight by now. What's keeping it going?"

Abruptly there was a *boom* that was completely distinct from any other weapon Bill had ever heard. With a *splat*, the dino's head exploded like a ripe watermelon, and it skidded to a halt on what was left of its face. The juveniles stopped, looked at their parent, and Bill would swear until his dying day, their jaws dropped in surprise.

Then they turned and sprinted for the perimeter fence.

"Shit!" Monica exclaimed, then yelled to the lawn in general, "Count them! We need to know how many there are!"

Bill looked around at the carnage, the chaos, and the blood, his brain totally locked up. Then his thoughts re-engaged. "The gate!" he exclaimed. "We have to close it!" He turned and dashed toward the shed—or what was left of it—pausing only to grab a shotgun that someone had dropped.

"Bill! Do not go in there alone!" Monica yelled from behind him. He heard running feet, then the roar of an engine. A second Hummer skidded to a stop beside him, and Monica held out a hand from the open door. Bill grabbed her hand and hauled himself in. The Hummer took off before he was even seated.

"We have to close it before anything else comes through. We can't allow cross-contamination—"

"Too late, Bill. Those raptors are going to tear right through the Pleistocene population. And if any of them are female, then we've just added a breeding population of carnivorous dinosaurs to Outland." Monica shook her head rather than continue the thought.

They jumped out as their ride pulled up in front of the shed. Bill checked his shotgun, and Monica popped the magazine on her AR-15 and shoved in a new one. A quick pull on the charging handle and she nodded, ready.

They edged into the shed, trying to be cautious without wasting time. Every second was critical, but getting jumped by a lurking raptor would certainly be bad strategy.

Then Monica said, "Oh, mother *fuck!*"

Something had come through the interface at the other end of the shed. It was either a rhinoceros or a stegosaurus. Or something else entirely. Or maybe the love child of a rhino and a stegosaurus. Bill was pretty much past caring at this point.

But it was big. And it seemed to be all armor. There was a crest protecting the neck, and there were horns. Yet it was less roundish than the popular pictures of stegosaurs. This one seemed more brick-shaped, and looked like it would come on like a locomotive.

"We, uh, we should maybe back away," Bill said.

"No shit, Sherlock. Slowly. Don't turn your back. We don't want it to—oh, goddammit."

The rhinosaurus had apparently seen that strategy before and wasn't having any of it. With a huff that didn't sound too far off from a steam engine, it charged. Bill and Monica, abandoning any strategy, turned and ran. As they went through the door, Bill had a fleeting glimpse of someone holding the biggest goddam gun he'd ever seen, propped on the edge of a vehicle, then *boom!*

It was that same unmistakable sound, halfway between a gun and a cannon. Something hit the ground with a *whump* behind him. Bill turned to see the rhinosaurus lying on its side, halfway out of the shed, with its chest blown open. He exchanged a glance with Monica, and they ran back into the shed.

This time they made it all the way back to the gate before encountering anything. Just on the other side stood one of those Andrewsarchus thingies. It was easily the ugliest animal he'd ever seen. It actually looked like someone's idea of a creature-feature special effect.

"What the hell is going on?" he exclaimed. "Is there a queue waiting to come through? Someone selling tickets?"

"They're cooking breakfast in the longhouse, Bill," Monica replied. "The aroma is attracting wildlife."

The creature spotted Bill and growled, then took a step forward. "Oh hell no," Bill said, and shot it in the face. Without waiting to evaluate the results, he pumped and shot again. The habit of loading shotguns with alternating shot and slugs had become standard in Rivendell, and the second discharge tore the top of the creature's head right off. It dropped without a further sound.

Bill stepped up to the gate, glanced around, and spotted the portal box. And the half-dozen or so Andrewsarchuses standing behind it. They spotted him at the same moment, showed their teeth, and advanced. Without hesitation, Bill shot the portal box, and the interface collapsed.

Bill gritted his teeth and threw his shotgun to the ground. "Mother fucking fucker of all fucking fucks with mother of all fucking fucker fucks fucking all the fuckheads with never-ending fucks!" he yelled, stomping around in a circle. "Fucking fucking fuckity fuckity fucking hell and many more *fucks!*"

Monica regarded him with her head cocked and a slight smile, having watched the entire performance. "Not exactly Shakespeare, but I admire your enthusiasm. I do have some notes, though ... "

Bill sighed, and took a few calming breaths. "Truck gate. Gone. And whatever second gate they were using to bootstrap themselves across universes. Plus whatever other equipment and vehicles they had. Gone. Plus whatever supplies they stole."

"We can probably get it back, Bill. We have other gates."

"Well, someone can. I've seen those Andrew things. I'm not volunteering."

She grinned at him. "Well, so far you're ahead one to zip. But yeah, we'll make sure we go in with full kit." She put a hand on his shoulder. "We'll get your babies back."

Bill rolled his eyes, then changed the subject. "Hey, who's been taking down all the monsters, anyway? And what kind of cannon are they using?"

"Dammifino. But whatever it is, I want one."

"950 JDJ," Timminson said, rubbing his shoulder with a wince. "We got it in Omaha. I'm surprised you haven't confiscated it, Monica."

"The day is young," she replied in a slow drawl. Monica ran her hand across the barrel of the gun in a light caress.

"Damn, she never touches me like that," Bill stage-whispered. Then he sighed and turned serious. "Any idea on damage? Deaths?"

Timminson looked around, then yelled "Hardwick!" She double-timed over. "Report?"

"Fifteen confirmed dead so far," Hardwick replied. "Six of them appear to be conspirators, the others were just in the wrong place at the wrong time. Six other conspirators in custody. Two are critical and may not live. Some fence sections were bent in the stampede, but crews have got it more or less back up with some baling-wire assistance. The shed's a mess. We're going through Bill's inventory list to determine what was taken. So far, it's mostly tools and equipment. They were pretty focused. Things you'd need to build a colony, looks like."

"Thank the universe the dinos didn't go at the longhouses, given the cooking aromas," Bill muttered. Then in a louder voice, "Any consensus on escaped raptors?"

"Witnesses are about evenly split on three or four. I don't think we'll be able to nail it down better than that." The soldier paused, looked at Timminson. "Getting rid of the carcasses is going to be a pain. They're probably not edible, or at least not going to be palatable. The lieutenant is suggesting just pulling them outside the fence line with a couple of tractors and letting nature take care of it."

"Thanks, Hardwick. That'll be all," said Timminson. She nodded and trotted off.

Bill sighed and looked at Monica. "Another set of seditionists. Yet more trials. This is getting really fucking old."

Monica grimaced. "If it was up to me, I'd skip the trial entirely. But, ya know, due process and all."

85. FALLOUT

October 26

Richard was watching the crew attempting to straighten the shed walls when a change in background sound alerted him. He turned to find Monica stomping toward him. She had that particular gait that indicated no one under any circumstances should get in her way. Or try to talk to her. Or even twitch. Bea was two steps behind her, looking equally pissed.

Richard sighed. This wouldn't be good, on a day when nothing was good. "Hi, Mon," he said as they pulled up. "Bea. More bad news?"

"Depends on how you look at it, I guess." Monica glowered. "I talked to a couple of the conspirators. They were surprisingly informative. I didn't even have to threaten them. Much."

"And?"

"It will come as a surprise to absolutely no one in this entire dimension that this batch of bozos couldn't possibly have put this op together. Guess who had a major hand in it?"

Richard groaned and rubbed the bridge of his nose. "There is not a single possible answer to that question that isn't bad, bad, bad. Who?"

"Cummins. And a couple of his Ashland cronies."

"Shit." Richard glanced up at the sky, and noted absently that it looked like snow soon. "And if we accuse him, he'll go right into his *You're so mean to me* routine. We have to handle this just right."

"Uh huh. I have an idea that's just right. Want to come?" Monica leered at him, and Richard felt a shudder go through him. Not for the first time, he wondered if Monica was a real-life version of Dexter. She certainly had a not-very-subtle flavor of psycho at times. But then again, six older brothers…

Richard made a *lead on* gesture, and Monica turned on one heel. Bea and several soldiers formed up behind her, and Richard suspected that as usual Monica had carefully planned her "spontaneous" actions. He trailed the group as they made a beeline for the longhouse that had been given to the Ashland refugees.

In less than a minute, they were at their destination. Monica stopped in front of a man who was standing outside the entrance with a rifle, looking suspiciously like a guard, and said, "Where's Cummins?"

"It's *Chief* Cummins," the man retorted, looking belligerent.

"No it's not, motherfucker. And you're pretty mouthy for someone who's outnumbered eight to one. Go get him."

"Why should I, bitch?"

Bea stepped up without warning and smacked the man in the face with the butt of her weapon. He went down with a cry, and she said over her shoulder, "Strap him."

Richard watched as one of the soldiers bent down and put zip ties around the man's wrists and ankles. Other men began pouring out of the longhouse door, shouting angrily and waving weapons. Two shots rang out, spraying dirt and wood splinters at the feet of those in the lead, and the soldiers all brought their weapons to bear. The Ashland crew skidded to a stop, suddenly silent. They looked at Monica, they looked at Bea, and they looked at a half-dozen armor-equipped National Guard with weapons hot, and reality suddenly set in. Any firefight would be extremely one-sided. No one made a move to point a weapon.

Monica spoke. "I don't give even the smallest fraction of a fuck about the deaths of the pieces of shit who tried the takeover, but they caused a lot of damage to our colony and got a lot of people—people I know and am friends with—killed or hurt in the process. Several of the surviving pieces of shit independently implicated your ex-chief Cummins in the fomenting, planning, and recruitment of that whole operation. I am here to arrest him, and I don't care how many of you motherfuckers I have to go through to get him. I will, if necessary, shoot up the place and arrest his corpse. Now, what's it going to be? You have five seconds to decide."

The scene remained frozen for several seconds before the longhouse door opened with a creak. *Have to get that oiled*, Richard's committee mind thought irrelevantly.

Cummins strode out onto the porch, looking calm and smug. He hitched his thumbs in his waistband in an unconscious parody of a certain movie sheriff, then glanced to his right and left, making a show of sizing up his support. "A pretty little speech, missy. Now how about you run along and play with your dolls, and let the men get on with business, hmm?"

"You're under arrest, Mr. Cummins," Monica said in a flat tone. "Take off the weapon and place it on the ground."

"It's *Chief* Cummins, and I don't recognize your authority to arrest—"

Cummins had placed his hand around the butt of his pistol as he spoke. Richard just had time to think *big mistake* before Cummins's head exploded in blood and brains. He went over backward, rigid as a tree that's been felled, and landed with a wet smack.

The Ashland crew stiffened with shock, but had enough sense not to react. Monica stood at battle ready, AR-15 pointed at them. Behind her, seven people stood in identical poses. And behind them, Richard stood, trying to keep his bladder from signaling its displeasure in the most embarrassing way. *Oh my fucking God,* he thought. *It's the fucking OK Corral. I'm in a goddam western.*

"Weapons on the ground. All of you. I won't tell you twice." Monica moved the barrel of the AR-15 fractionally. After a brief hesitation, men began carefully placing weapons down.

Without turning her head, Monica gave orders in a loud voice. "Clear the longhouse. Anyone refuses to move, taze them. Anyone brandishes a weapon, shoot them. Anyone gives you any attitude at all, taze them, strap them, and carry them out like luggage. Don't be gentle. Then search the place. Confiscate all weapons."

There was no further trouble from the Ashland group. Notwithstanding Monica's tough talk, some of the more-senior individuals were assisted out with all due care and provided with chairs and blankets. It took a half hour before one of the soldiers reported all clear.

"Who wants to be spokesman?" Monica said to the group of people milling around on the lawn.

A woman stepped forward. "I'm Dorothy Hammond. My husband was the mayor of Ashland, not that it gives me any particular authority."

"Doesn't matter," Monica replied. "I just need someone with enough brains to understand and explain the situation to … " She motioned with her chin to the group of would-be rebels now surrounded by soldiers.

Hammond nodded. "They all know me. They'll listen."

"Good. So here's the skinny. Cummins was hip-deep in the conspiracy that just resulted in fifteen dead, including nine innocent bystanders. And he didn't work alone. We're still interviewing, but it looks so far like a lot of your people were unhappy with the results of the convention and election, and decided to do something about it." Monica paused. "There will be repercussions. There will be trials. Or there will be one god-almighty gunfight, us versus you, and we've got most of the guns, all the gates, the National Guard, a fifty-mil turret-mounted machine gun, and a portable cannon. You will lose, and badly. Is that clear so far?"

"For the record, most of us do not support armed insurrection," Hammond said. "I'm certain the conspirators are a minority, and I'd wager I could even name those involved, with a fair degree of accuracy."

Monica smiled. "I believe you. And I don't want to punish the innocent with the guilty. But our priority is the safety of Rivendell and its citizenry. If the guilty try to shelter amongst the innocent and use them for cover, then innocent people will die. And if it becomes necessary, we'll ship you all back to Ashland, at gunpoint if need be, and let you fend for yourselves." Monica paused and nodded to Richard.

He jerked, startled. Monica hadn't discussed a script with him, and he realized he'd just been handed the baton. He blinked twice, thinking fast. "But we'd rather do this by the book. That does mean investigations, trials, convictions, and so on. Or as a third alternative, for the disaffected segment of your population I think we may actually have

337

a solution that's a little more palatable than just sending them overside. But we'll need your guarantee that there will be no more trouble. You, the whole group, are effectively on parole now. It's up to you, personally and the group, to make sure you don't give us any reason to unleash the kraken again." Richard inclined his head slightly toward Monica.

Monica glared back at him for a moment, then turned back to Dorothy Hammond. "For now, I'm going to treat you as the Ashland rep. If you all—"

"What about Donald Brady?" Hammond asked. "He *is* a member of the committee, and—"

Richard interrupted her. "And as a member of our government, he'd be in a position of conflict if he also acted as your representative. And anyway—"

"We don't trust him," Monica finished for Richard. "He hasn't actually been named in any of the interrogations— *yet*—but this whole thing's got his reek all over it."

"I understand." Hammond thought for a moment. "I'll have some discussions and get back to you. Can you give me more information about this alternative?"

"Bill Rustad will. He's honestly the only person who really understands what he's talking about." Monica stepped back and turned to her squad. "Everything under control?"

Bea nodded. "Weapons all secured. We've taken names in case we need to kick more ass."

"Good. Let's wrap it up."

Timminson waved to the others. "You heard the kraken. Let's get it done."

Monica glared at Richard. "I'll get you for that."

86. Negotiations

October 27

Richard thumped his mug to get attention. "All right, come to order. Let's get this ball rolling." He waited for silence, looking around the long table. The regular council members sat at one end, while Hammond, Brady, and Ashland ex-councilors Crenshaw and Knowles stood or sat at the other end. They variously looked back at him or let their gaze wander idly around the room. It was significant that Brady had placed himself with the Ashland group rather than with the Rivendell government.

"Bill will fill in the technical details, but here's the high-altitude summary. We've found a version of Earth with a very shallow ecosystem. We call it Forest Fire Earth. We think there was a meteor impact or global volcanic cataclysm that wiped out most of the plants and animals. Something similar to what killed the dinosaurs, but much more recent. Paradoxically, this makes it an ideal venue for an agricultural colony. No big predators, not a lot of competing plant life, most diseases and parasites have probably been wiped out. For those who just don't like what we're doing here in Rivendell, it's an easy alternative."

"Shipping us off to Australia," Brady snarled. "And being sanctimonious about it."

Richard sighed. "Mr. Brady, you keep trying to put us on the defensive with sweeping accusations and, let's be honest here, playing the victim for all you're worth. But I really don't give a damn if you like it or not. Your other alternative is to be returned to Earthside with nothing but the clothes on your back, to fend for yourselves. We've had two attempted coups now from assholes who didn't like the way things are set up, and we're out of patience." He glared directly at Brady for a moment. "We have more than enough evidence that some Ashlanders were involved in this one. If we take it to trial, those found guilty will almost certainly be popped across to Dino Planet with a day pack and a gun. I think we've all seen up close how that works out."

Lieutenant Collins leaned forward and interrupted, a rare event for him. "And at least some Ashlanders—and some of the neo-Nazi types from our own stock—will take us up on this offer voluntarily regardless of your objections, which is going to reduce your voting base for next election if you decide to stay. Assuming, of course, that we don't garner enough evidence to include you personally in the trials. So there's that to look forward to if you insist on staying."

"We'll want to take *all* our citizens from Ashland," Brady said.

Richard took up the thread. "That's a personal choice. No one's going to be forced to stay or go. Except those involved in this latest coup attempt, of course. They will be given a choice of Dino Planet or the new colony. We'll also give the guys from the previous attempted coup the option of joining you—"

"We don't want them."

"I didn't ask, and you don't get a vote. What you do with them afterward is up to you. And maybe it'll help a bit to

340

talk about the new colony as Plymouth Rock instead of Australia."

Brady snorted but didn't respond otherwise.

"And we'll have a gate of our own?" Dorothy Hammond asked, speaking for the first time.

"Oh, hell no," Bill said. "At least not the equipment. We'll set up a persistent interface to Outland. But it'll be barred and guarded on this side, and there will be strict protocols for letting people through."

"So you'll control our food supply," Brady exclaimed. "That doesn't sound totalitarian at all."

"Unbelievable," Richard snarled back at him. "We're bending over backward trying to set you up in reasonable comfort, despite your having tried to overthrow us by force and take everything. And still you're whining and acting hard-done-by. Grow the fuck up, bitch."

Brady glared back but said nothing, as Richard was now obviously angry, leaning forward with his fists on the table.

"You'll be able to take some livestock to get yourselves started," Bill said into the tense silence. "Everyone will get a credit based on their prorated contribution to Rivendell, to purchase from our existing stock."

"And when will this be happening?" Hammond asked.

"As soon as possible without endangering people," Richard replied. "Notwithstanding Mr. Brady's lamentations, we do want this to work. And not just because we get rid of troublesome elements. If you're successful, we could end up with regular trade between colonies. Plus, for a lot of future refugees, it might be preferable to Outland's socialist dystopia." He made air quotes around the last bit.

Brady opened his mouth to respond, but Hammond stopped him dead with a raised hand. Richard tried to avoid looking surprised. A shift had just occurred in the

Ashland power dynamic, with Brady knocked down a notch. Couldn't have happened to a more deserving individual, as far as Richard was concerned.

"We'll discuss this with our group, Mr. Nadeski. Although I imagine it's a foregone conclusion. Unless someone is just plain vindictive, you're giving us what we want: self-determination." She stood and nodded to the table in general, then walked out without looking at Brady or the other ex-councilors. Brady, Crenshaw, and Knowles exchanged startled glances, then hurried to follow her, trailing like ducklings.

"I think Ashland just got a new mayor," Bill commented with a grin.

Richard smiled back. "Gotta be an improvement. Okay, on to the next item."

87. Cleanup

October 31

Snow was falling. It had started the day before, and seemed determined to bury the world. Richard shivered despite the layers of clothing he was wearing. It was expensive stuff, too. He'd never have been able to afford this level of quality in his student days. Still, Nebraska cold had a certain vindictive quality to it, an almost personal level of animosity toward anything living.

And Outland, if anything, was even colder.

"Nope," Bill replied to Richard's muttered comment. "Granted, this is colder than we'd normally get in Lincoln, but with the volcanic ash back Earthside blocking sunlight for the last several months, they're looking at full-on Fimbulwinter there."

"Wasn't that supposed to happen *before* Ragnarok?" Richard growled.

"Picky, picky. But here's the odd thing…" Bill paused to smile. "Forest Fire Earth is *warmer* than what's normal for Nebraska. They haven't even hit freezing yet. You can still walk around there with nothing more than a good hoodie. Maybe we should make the Ashlanders stay here and we'll cross over."

"Sure, that'll work." Richard concentrated on negotiating the steps as they got to the longhouse. The airlock was really paying for itself now, although it had a tendency to accumulate snow and muck. "It would make a nice backup plan, though, in case the winter gets too harsh," he mused. "Maybe let's make sure we put the Ashlanders down a good distance from here. Leave our area free."

Someone had made coffee. Several carafes worth. An extravagance, these days, but perhaps a necessity today. Richard reached for the closest one, but Bill snaked him. "Asshole," Richard muttered as Bill filled his cup.

It took a minute or so to coffee up, then Richard said to the group, "So what's up?"

"We've got the shed mostly repaired," Nick volunteered. "It'll never be as pretty, but it'll keep the weather out."

"Think of it as having character," Erin said. "How many buildings do you know of that have dinosaur scars?"

Richard snorted, then waved at Charlie, who was there to report on progress.

Charlie grunted as he shifted his weight, favoring his bandaged side. "The stuff the seditionists pulled through was scattered around, and there was some damage, but none of it was edible, so I guess the wildlife lost interest. We've had to kill three more dinos and two Andrews while collecting everything. Those critters are dumb, dumb, dumb."

"Or just not used to *not* being the biggest sumbitches in the valley," Bill volunteered. "Habits die hard."

"Well, thank dog for the big gun," Charlie replied. "I might add that Timminson seems to have established *de facto* ownership of the thing. Won't even let Monica try it."

"Really? When's his funeral?" Richard grinned, then turned to Lieutenant Collins. "And the prisoners?"

Collins sighed and put his mug down before replying. "The Ashlanders have agreed to take them in, which means we can't justify pushing them through to Dino Planet. But we've made it clear that if even one of them so much as touches a gun in the meantime, the whole deal is off and we gate them immediately. Personally, I think it's a mistake to give seditionists safe harbor like that, but we're between a rock and a hard place on this one. They'll be taking the first set of revolutionaries as well when they go over, so we'll be able to free up the people currently on guard duty. So that's a plus, anyway."

Richard nodded. "Bill? Gates?"

"All set to go. We've set up a persistent interface between us and Forest Fire Earth, which we're renaming Farm World, by the way. The interface runs through a two-point-one-meter concrete pipe that we found. We've installed a heavy-duty barred security barrier, and booby-trapped it. Try to force your way through and you'll end up in your own pocket universe." He glanced over at Nick before continuing. "We could start construction over there right now, given the climate, but Nick wants to finish all the Outland infrastructure first, with the way the weather is going. But once that's done, we could ship people across and start building the Ashland colony pretty much any time."

Richard looked over at Matt. "And your group?"

"We're resigned to the fact that Lincoln's all but cleaned out. We'll visit Omaha again as soon as weather permits, but longer term I think it's time to try for the West Coast. Bill's got some wild-ass ideas about setting up an ad-hoc internet, too."

Richard rolled his eyes as Bill grinned in triumph.

"Fine." Richard took a moment to drain his cup. "It's going to be a busy year."

ABOUT THE AUTHOR

I am a retired computer programmer, part-time author, occasional napper, lover of coffee, snowboarding, mountain biking, and all things nerdish.

Author Blog:	http://www.dennisetaylor.org
Twitter:	@Dennis_E_Taylor
Facebook:	@DennisETaylor2
Instagram:	dennis_e_taylor

ABOUT THE PUBLISHER

This book is published on behalf of the author by the Ethan Ellenberg Literary Agency.
https://ethanellenberg.com
Email: agent@ethanellenberg.com
Facebook: https://www.facebook.com/EthanEllenberg LiteraryAgency/

Made in the USA
Middletown, DE
29 September 2023

39775478R00205